Gumshoe
on the Run

Rob Leininger

Novels by Rob Leininger

THE GUMSHOE SERIES
Gumshoe *
Gumshoe For Two **
Gumshoe on the Loose
Gumshoe Rock ***
Gumshoe in the Dark ****
Gumshoe Gone
Gumshoe Outlaw
Gumshoe on the Run

* Nominated for a Shamus Award for best PI novel of 2016
** A Finalist for a Best Book Award in 2017
*** A Finalist for a Best Book Award in 2019
**** "Diabolically entertaining"—Publishers Weekly

THRILLERS
Killing Suki Flood [under option for a movie]
Richter Ten
Sunspot
Maxwell's Demon

MYSTERY
January Cold Kill

OTHER
The Tenderfoot [A different kind of western. Brains vs brawn]

Olongapo Liberty [rated R. The way it *really* was to go on liberty in the Navy during the Vietnam War. This one is not for the squeamish. This is the way it was, bad tattoos and all. Read the reviews on Amazon.]

Nicholas Phree and the Emerald of Bool [A children's story written for adults. For ages 10 to 110, but readers older than forty will get more of the humor. This one is laugh-out-loud funny, for the young at heart who remember those good old stories that really took you away.]

For Pat, as always.

(with apologies to folks in Muncie)

Dear Reader,

The Gumshoe novels are humorous, fun, and deadly. They're also rated R (Risqué). Never X and most certainly not XXX or explicitly descriptive, but they *are* risqué. I've found that some readers have no tolerance for bawdy situations. To those readers, I suggest that you sit this one out. Agatha Christie and Earl Derr Biggers [Charlie Chan] mysteries are good, as are the Erle Stanley Gardner and John Marquand novels.

To readers who don't mind a little bawdiness: This is for you. Life is good; life is supposed to be fun.

Gumshoe
on the Run

Chapter One

Ma, Vale, and I were in Waley's Tavern on East Fourth Street in Reno while the Green Room in the Golden Goose Casino was being renovated. Waley's had the advantage of being nondescript, dim, and underutilized by the public. It was a new place for us, but I'd still managed to snag the remote for the TV where News at Eleven on Channel Eight was into its second minute. By now I should've known to hold off on the news and wait until sports and weather was on, but I'm a slow learner.

"Aw, jeez. Turn that crap off," Ma growled.

"Alden Ridel?" I said, gazing at the TV over the bar. "Missing FBI bigwig. Wouldn't think you'd have a problem with that." I like to yank Ma's chain. Ma was Maude Clary, my boss at Clary Investigations where I was still in training that was now into its fifth year.

"Nope. I got a problem with *you*, boyo. How about you turn that shit off before trouble walks in the door."

Too late, but it might've been an unexpected hint of clairvoyance in Ma. I was about to hit the remote when the door to Fourth Street opened and a girl came in. Tall, thin, short dark brown hair, and, near as I could tell in Waley's dim lighting, extremely pretty.

Vale laughed quietly. "Oh, boy. I've heard this is *not* good—girls coming into bars with you here, especially ones that look like models."

"You were that girl last year," I reminded her.

"Uh-huh. And look how that turned out."

"You complaining?"

She looked at me. "Not really. I mean, it was the most bizarre thing I've ever done, but it worked out okay."

"Okay, then." I glanced at the girl again. Easily six feet tall, maybe a hundred eighteen pounds.

"Bony Moronie," Ma muttered. "Skinny as a stick of macaroni."

I stared at her. "Come again?"

"Don't tell me you never heard the song."

"What song?"

"Bony Moronie. By Larry Williams."

"Sounds old and politically incorrect. How old were you when that beaut came out?"

Ma shrugged, then said, "Ten."

"You remember the song and how old you were? *And* the artist? That's a little bit creepy, Ma."

"Unlike *you*, I remember shit. Fourth grade. For half a year I was 'Bony Moronie' to a scrawny little dimwit by the name of Joey Clay. He would sing that idiot song at me and keep out of reach so I wouldn't knock his block off. And not one word about him callin' me Bony Moronie or you won't live to see midnight."

"Testy." I turned toward Vale. "Take heed. That's what nicotine withdrawal will do to you."

She laughed.

The girl handed something to Bill Waley, owner of the bar, gave us a quick glance, then left. No problem, except for a subtle premonition that got me off the barstool and hustling out the door in time to see an antique yellow VW bug with its sewing machine engine still running as the girl hopped in and shut the door. It pulled away from the curb and headed west into the night. Gone.

I went back inside. "All that angst for nothing," I said to Ma as I sat between her and Vale again.

"You better hope," Ma said.

A clip of Ridel about to enter the Hoover Building in D.C.—rated as the ugliest building in the country—was still on TV. Pale, chubby guy in his mid-fifties with beady eyes in a face as round as a pumpkin, not a hint of a smile. Then his sister, Katherine Ridel Wells, chief judge in the Nevada District Court in Reno, came on asking viewers to contact the FBI if they knew where her brother was or had any information about what might have happened to him.

Bill Waley handed me a slip of paper. "Girl who just came in asked me to give this to you."

"Oh, shit, *no*," Ma said. "Burn it. *Now*."

• • •

Alden Ridel, deputy director of the FBI, was missing. One step below FBI director must be like vice president of the United States—an office that FDR's VP, John Nance Garner, once declared, "Isn't worth a bucket of warm spit." That sounded right because not one person in a thousand could have named the FBI's deputy director until he went missing. Ridel had flown into Reno-Tahoe International Airport for a family wedding a week ago, picked up a Jeep Cherokee at Avis to drive to Gardnerville, south of Carson City, and that was the last anyone had seen of him.

Dozens of people went missing every day in the U.S., but I had an inexplicable knack for finding missing people who happened to be in the public eye—very likely a form of karmic punishment for having been an Internal Revenue Service thug for sixteen long years. It started the first day I became a PI (in training) at my nephew's agency. Not four hours into my new career I found the decapitated head of Reno's mayor in the trunk of my ex-wife's Mercedes and things had gone downhill from there.

I fingered the paper Bill Waley gave me. It was folded twice. Set it on fire or read it? Not an easy choice. I like fire, but I also like to read.

Ma glared at me. "If that has anything to do with this Alden Ridel guy, you are *so* fired I'll take back your entire last year's pay, with interest and penalties."

I smiled. She sounded like the IRS. I even detected the little note of glee in her voice we at the IRS were unable to control as interest and penalties were being levied.

"Might want to listen to her, Mort," Vale said.

Maybe I should. Because of what had happened last year in September, Vale—Valentina Marchant—a gorgeous ex-secret-service agent, had been the country's *número uno* pinup girl for the past ten months—if the term "pinup girl" was still in vogue and not so politically incorrect as to get me burned at the stake by folks with no sense of humor or history. But when you're thirty-five and beautiful, 36-25-35, and a second-degree black belt in judo, third degree in Tae Kwon Do, *and* you end up on the internet wearing nothing but sandals and a transparent thong the size of a Costco ID card—you're a pinup girl and there's no use crying about it.

Mortimer Angel was written on the paper in flowery purple ink, so this wasn't a case of mistaken identity. It did, however, bring up the question of how this girl in the yellow sewing machine VW knew I was in Waley's Tavern at this time to receive the paper.

My name is Mortimer Angel. My profession, such as it is, is sleuth-in-training. A gumshoe. Vale joined the team last October. She was in training too, not that she needed the money. Her book, *Outlaw*, was in its fourth printing and her share of the royalties had topped six million bucks. An old guy, Bill Cook, whose jewelry store Vale had robbed topless, wearing the afore-mentioned thong and sandals, had made upward of two million. Luscious virtually naked woman drops by your house one evening with an unloaded BB pistol to rob your store and you end up a millionaire? Your odds of being hit by a rogue asteroid are a whole lot better than that.

"Oh, for hell's sake," Ma said. "Let's get it over with." She grabbed the paper out of my hands and opened it.

Good deal. Whatever happened now was her fault.

I looked over Ma's shoulder. The three-sentence note was laser-printed in arial black type:

Be at VOR Station WS61 at 1600 hours tomorrow. Come alone. No second chance. Ella.

Huh.

Arial type, but Ella had signed it in that same purple ink. Latitude and longitude coordinates of the VOR were given in case I didn't know where to find WS61.

Fact is, I didn't know what a VOR station *was*.

"What the hell's a VOR?" Ma asked.

"One never knows until one asks Mrs. Google," I said. Which I did. Waley's Tavern had Wi-Fi.

"VOR," I read aloud. "VHF Omnidirectional Radio Range. The most common ground-based navigational aid (NAVAID) you'll use."

"*You'll* use?" Ma interrupted. "The *hell* I will."

"It gets worse," I said, continuing: " 'VOR navigation allows your to fly point to point along established airways between VORs.' "

Ma stared at me. "Allows your to fly?"

I shrugged. "I reads 'em like I sees 'em. This might've been written by a high school freshman. Got a picture here too." I held my phone where Ma and Vale could see it. Low square building with a white conical structure on its roof, topped by a cylindrical tube and surrounded by a Cyclone fence to slow vandals down by about thirty seconds.

"Lovely," Vale said. "But not in my backyard."

Mine either.

"The note says 'come alone'," Vale read.

"No problem," I said. "Although Ella looked like a nice kid. If she were coming, she could've brought fried chicken and wine." That got me an elbow in the ribs, left side.

"Don't go," Ma said.

"Hey," I said. "It says 'no second chance,' so I'm not likely to get another invitation."

"As if you want to see a VOR Station."

"As if I don't. I'm up for new experiences."

"Seriously, Mort," Vale said. "This looks like trouble. I mean it's too weird. Why could she possibly want you to go around to some old VOR Station? Don't go."

I folded the note and stuck in a pocket. "I'll give it due consideration."

"Yeah, right." Vale leaned forward to look past me at Ma. "I know him. She was pretty. He's gonna go."

"Pretty or not, she's not gonna be there," I said. "Read the note again, lady. I'm supposed to go alone."

"Do and you're fired, boyo," Ma said. She held up her drink to the bartender. "Yo, Bill, how 'bout another one of these little puppies?"

"Little?" I said. "You're drinking doubles."

"You're fired."

As if.

• • •

It felt strange to be there without Harper. She and I married as planned on the sixteenth of December last year, a date with special significance—exactly one year to the day after Lucy, my wife at the time, put Harper and me together in Rawlins, Wyoming, knowing that she, Lucy, had less than a week to live. Losing Lucy still cut deep, but Harper was my life now, my anchor, and I was hers.

She was an English teacher at Reno High and this was Tuesday, August fifteenth, second day of the new school year. Except for Christmas and Easter vacations, her life wouldn't be her own for the next nine months. People think teachers have it made, getting summers off, but she would put in over 2500 hours in those nine months, five hundred more than nine-to-fivers do in a year. Teaching, I have learned, is not for the weak or the faint of heart.

Late as it was, Ma, Vale, and I were having a business-related meeting in Waley's Tavern, thumbing our noses at the IRS. Larry K. Sanders, 52, ambulance-chasing lawyer, stood accused of murdering his wife. The police had their suspect and weren't looking any further. Sanders' latest girlfriend, Angela, 25, who wouldn't see a dime of Sanders' money unless she married him, was supplying both the motive and alibi for said murder. The case was lucrative, but messy, like cleaning a tub of squid, and we could count on bumping into well-fed, surly detectives of the Washoe County Criminal Investigation Unit.

We called it a night at 11:25, having rung up a useful business expense of $36.50. Harper was asleep when I got home. I got into bed without waking her and lay awake a while, thinking about the VOR, the delivery girl, the note, no second chance, and come alone. I'd Googled it using the coordinates I'd been given, and seen it on Google Earth. It was in the middle of nowhere, eight miles southeast of a ghost town named Colton Spring, about twenty miles east of Lovelock. Lovelock was a small town ninety-three miles northeast of Reno on Interstate Eighty.

Come alone, no second chance?

Only a fool would gallop into that dumbass scenario.

• • •

Well . . . shit.

• • •

To get to Colton Spring I drove through Lovelock and past Lovelock Correctional Center where felons like O.J. go to get corrected, then east through arid mountains and across hard-packed sand flats not unlike the Black Rock Desert where the land speed record of 763 mph was set in 1997, finally ending up in the middle of nothing at all but sand and dust being blasted by August sun in a cloudless sky. It was a hundred two degrees out and not a breath of wind, which made it all the hotter.

As expected, Colton was deserted. I parked behind a disintegrating dry-goods store and checked the time. 3:15. I had no idea what was supposed to happen in the next forty-five minutes, but I was ready for anything.

Or so I thought.

I'd hitched a small trailer behind the Toyota 4Runner Harper and I bought in January and towed a 250cc Vitacci Raven dirt bike to Colton. Harper and I had taken to riding the Raven up into the Sierras, leaving it, and day-hiking ten or fifteen miles in the mountains. I wasn't big on boy toys, especially boats, which soak up money like a sponge, but the dirt bike was useful and it didn't take up space the way monster fifth-wheel mobile mansions do.

I rolled the dirt bike off its trailer and rode it eight miles around a line of hills and across the flats to the VOR station, got there at 3:25. Powered by solar panels, the station was the only manmade object I could see in all that wasteland: a cinderblock lower building with a metal door, a white cone and cylinder affair above made of plastic or some sort of composite material to house antennas.

I had a backpack that held a liter of water, power bars, windbreaker, cell phone, Ka-Bar USMC fighting knife, and a 10mm Glock 20 loaded with 200-grain hard-cast lead bullets. The bullets were meant to deter bears since they weren't uncommon in the Sierras. Hard cast gave the gun more recoil and wore the barrel more, but I could take the pounding and I didn't put much hard cast through the G20 during practice. I hadn't had occasion to shoot a bear yet, which suited me just fine. They have rights too.

I faced west. Behind me, the VOR was gathering dust behind a chain link fence while, presumably, doing its job, not that I saw any planes overhead. I circled the building twice, read a sign informing me that if I damaged the site the fine could be $10,000 and five years in O.J.'s house, which made me wonder about the bullet holes in the sign. Dimwits with guns will shoot at anything so it's a good thing a low percentage of gun owners are dimwits.

I spotted movement at the base of the hills three miles away, beyond which the defunct town of Colton Spring was baking in the heat.

I watched, and the movement slowly became a person on a dirt bike, pedal powered. I had no idea what to expect, so I pulled the Glock out of my backpack and buckled it at my right hip in a black nylon holster.

The rider was making good time over the flats. At a mile away I decided it was a girl, which made me think she would be six feet tall and slender. At half a mile I knew it was the girl who'd delivered the note the previous night, presumably named Ella. She had on runner's nylon shorts and a tank top, dark glasses, and a wide-brim sun hat. A fanny pack was around her waist.

I checked the time: 3:52.

She pulled up, breathing hard but not breathless. She wore no bra under the tank top and had no obvious reason to do so, especially in this heat. She stopped and straddled the bike. Now that she was near, I could see her legs were hard with muscle. Arms, too. Muscle weighs more than fat so I upped my estimate of her weight to one-twenty-four, not a lot for a six-foot girl. She was tan and, up close, still very pretty. No sign of a gun or other weapon on her.

"Ella?" I said. I guessed her age at about twenty-six.

She smiled. "Uh-huh. And you're Mortimer Angel."

"No, I'm not."

She tilted her head. "No?"

"My mother named me Mortimer not long after being in labor for sixteen hours. I came in at eleven pounds plus.

Mortimer is very likely payback. If we're going to be on a first-name basis, call me Mort."

She smiled. "That's a lot of information."

"There's more if you want it. I once spit a watermelon seed fifteen feet into an open Mason jar and won a dollar."

"That's wonderful. Let me guess. You were thirteen at the time."

"Nope. Thirty-eight."

"Why am I not surprised?" She removed the dark glasses and assessed me. Her eyes were a beautiful shade of blue. "My, you're tall," she said. "Six five?"

"Six four. Weight two oh four. Your turn." I wanted to see how she would handle that.

She gave me a narrow look, then said, "Six-one. And, uh, a hundred thirty-two pounds."

The "uh" made me smile. "Nice try. What do you weigh dripping wet?"

She may have snarled, then said, "One *twenty*-two, if you must know. But back to your name. You were on TV a lot last year because of that thing you did with the attorney general. They had you as Mortimer, not Mort."

"That's fake news for you." I looked behind me at the VOR Station. "Okay, here we are. What's your last name? Let's start there."

"Kassel." She spelled it for me.

"Is Ella short for Ellen or Eleanor?"

"Neither one. I'm just Ella."

"Okay, what's the story here, Ella Kassel?"

"What do you mean?"

"Your note said to be here. I'm here. Now what?"

"Now I don't have the foggiest. All I did was deliver the note."

That spun my head around.

"You didn't write it?"

"Sort of, I guess, but not really. It was dictated."

"Dictated?"

"Uh-huh. In a phone call yesterday evening about an hour before I gave the note to that bartender to give to you."

Okay, this had gotten weird. And possibly dangerous.

If she was telling the truth, someone else wanted me out here. But there was nothing here except Ella straddling her bike, the two of us sizing each other up, so what was this? A ploy to get me at ground zero during a nuke test? This was, after all, Nevada.

It would be best if I didn't have thoughts like that but they just whip on through.

"Dictated by whom?" I asked. I said "whom" because Harper teaches English and I'd picked up a bit of stuffy language by osmosis.

Ella shrugged. "I don't know. Just some woman."

A woman? I hadn't expected that, not sure why, other than this felt like the kind of thing a man would run.

"You just did what you were told?" I said.

"Well, I got fifty dollars in a letter that morning with a note telling me I would get a phone call later that day or in the evening and the money was mine if I just did what I was told. When I got the call it didn't seem like anything bad so I did it." She ended that with another shrug, so I backed my estimate of her age down to twenty-two.

"Who sent the letter?"

"I don't know. It didn't have a stamp on it so it didn't go through the regular mail. Someone must've put it in the mail slot at my apartment building early that morning."

Even weirder.

"You do odd things you're told to do. Just like that?"

"I sure as heck wouldn't *hurt* anyone if someone told me to. But all the woman wanted was for me to type that note, print it, and give it to you at that bar. For fifty bucks," she added unnecessarily.

Someone other than Ella knew Ma, Vale, and I were at Waley's, a place we hadn't been to before that evening. I didn't like that one bit. And here *we* were, Ella and I, in the middle of nowhere. I liked that even less.

"Did this unknown female person tell you to put your name on the note?"

"Well, no. I just, you know, did that myself."

Maybe she was eighteen.

"How old are you?" I asked.

She squinted at me. "Asking how much I weigh was bad enough, but you also ask women how old they are?"

"I have an uncontrollable curious streak."

"Twenty-nine. But ask me how old I am after I turn thirty and you could get hurt. So, how old are *you*, Mort?"

Mort. Good deal.

"Fair's fair. I'm forty-six. But let's get back to what might be important right now. You typed that note, which also means you know it said for me to come alone. Yet here you are."

She shrugged, still straddling the bike, possibly for a quick getaway. "I was curious, that's all."

"You didn't think it could be dangerous to do what the note said not to do?"

"Well, no. I mean, *you* came alone and that's what you were supposed to do."

"You've never delivered money to a kidnap drop, have you?"

That stopped her. For a moment anyway. This was not the kind of girl who could be stopped for long.

"*Kidnap* drop?" she said. "Is *that* what this is?"

"I don't have any idea what this is and neither do you, but let's get back to you being here which means I'm not alone as was explicitly requested. Your presence might piss someone off."

"Like who?"

I sighed. "Whoever dictated the note and asked me to come alone." I was getting dizzy, talking in circles.

Actually, when I thought about it, the note didn't tell me to come at all. Me. That was assumed because Ella had asked Bill Waley to give me the note and she'd written my name on its folded front, but my name didn't appear in the note itself. Maybe that was splitting hairs. I was only here out of curiosity, and so, evidently, was Ella. The note also said "no second chance," so this might be nothing at all, or a dumbass practical joke, though I doubted it.

"You didn't hand me the note in the bar. You gave it to the bartender." I thought I'd see what she had to say about that.

"I saw you sitting there with two women. I didn't want

to, you know, have to try to explain the note. Which I really couldn't. And I was in kind of a hurry. I'm a grad student at UNR. Psych major. I'm working on a thesis that needs to be in by the first of January. I was working on it when I got that phone call, developing an idea I didn't want to lose."

Psych major. Perfect. I love those.

She glanced at my hip. "Do you really need that gun?"

"I certainly hope not."

"Me, too. Guns are . . . no one should need a gun."

"Agreed, but it's good to be prepared. I've got water, food, knife, and a first-aid kit in my backpack." And other stuff she didn't need to hear about.

"You could take off that gun."

"It makes you nervous."

"Of course. Guns are dangerous."

Yup, psychology, not ROTC.

"No," I said. "*People* are dangerous, and certain kinds of snakes. But set a gun on a table and watch it for a year, I promise it won't do anything, unlike, say, a king cobra or Ted Bundy. But I hope I don't have to shoot either a snake or a person, and I won't unless one of 'em attacks you or me."

"Attacks *me*?"

"I'd feel protective if someone attacked you, yes. You seem like a very nice person."

"Well, please don't use that gun on anyone. I can take care of myself."

Like talking to a wall, but I wasn't about to change her mind, didn't really have a dog in that fight, so I let it drop.

Finally she swung a leg over the 15-speed bicycle and leaned it against the chain-link around the VOR station. A very long leg since the shorts were extremely short. Which made sense, considering both her tan and the temperature. I was in blue jeans and a short-sleeve shirt, ball cap, Keen boots, and a layer of dust due to the ride across the flat on the dirt bike.

"Not going to take off the gun, are you?" she said.

"Nope."

"Fine. Whatever." She turned away, looked all around, checked a Fitbit on her wrist. "It's almost four. It doesn't look like anything's gonna happen out here."

"Got any fried chicken with you, Ella? Wine?"

A faint droning sound came from the south. I turned, saw a single-engine plane three or four thousand feet up, wingtips swaying. Good deal, at least someone was getting some use out of this VOR, unlike us.

"No," she said." A Clif Bar and some water. How about you?"

"Three or four power bars. We could have a picnic."

She smiled. "A Clif bar picnic. Classy." She stared at the VOR. "What's this thing used for, anyway?"

I told her what I'd learned last night.

She rolled her eyes. "Be here at four. Crazy. Well, it's four now and this place looks like a big nothing."

The droning sound was louder, coming from almost directly overhead. I looked up. In another few seconds the plane was going to pass right over the top of the station. Great navigation.

A dark speck fell from the plane, gaining speed.

Huh.

"What's *that*?" Ella said, looking up.

"Dunno. Could be a skydiver."

Which figured, actually. Nothing else was going to get here anytime close to four o'clock.

We watched it fall, craning our necks, looking almost straight up.

"Aw, shit," I said after ten or twelve seconds. "No."

I watched a few seconds longer, then realized it was coming fast and was going to hit us, or come damn close. I took Ella's arm and got her fifteen feet away by the time the body slammed into the earth face down with a horrid thud and rebounded almost as high as my waist in a cloud of dust before thumping back down and lying still.

Dead still.

Chapter Two

Ella screamed.

I didn't because my gravitas is right where I want it, but I stared at the thing on the ground, dumfounded. I had never seen a body bounce like that. Actually, I'd never seen a body fall from a plane before. The shock wave had come up through the earth into my feet.

Ella backed away from the body in horror.

Finally I thought to look up. The plane had turned and was headed east toward the mountains, losing altitude, hugging the terrain. I backed away from the deflated body and turned around just as Ella got her arms around me in a trembling hug and bawled an inch from my ear.

Tall girl, and loud. And strong. Not an ounce of excess meat on her, but what she had was all muscle and she had a damn good grip on me.

Holding her, I shuffled around until I faced the body again—a man, bald, in a gray suit. He'd been wearing shoes but the impact had blown them off his feet, not something Ella should see. Nor would she like it that the guy's hands were tied behind his back, or that his skull had split open and a bit of brain matter was on the ground.

"T-t-that was *h-horrible*," she wailed.

But, well-timed. The guy had come down at 4:01, one minute late. Amtrak doesn't run on schedule like that.

I have learned to keep certain thoughts to myself.

I looked east. The plane was headed south, flying low, not easy to see against the brown hills. *Keeping off federal aviation radar*, I thought. I didn't say that aloud either. I doubted that this was Ella's kind of thing, but for me it was par for the course. Different, but definitely par.

I had started my new career at my nephew's detective agency as a gumshoe (in training) at the age of forty-one after those sixteen years with the IRS. Three months after I found the head of Reno's missing mayor I opened a FedEx package and found the severed right hand of U.S. Senator Harry Reinhart—his vote-getting appendage in a bid for his party's presidential nomination. Not quite a year after that I found a missing foul-mouthed gangsta rapper with bullet wounds in his head and chest, strung up in the cobwebby rafters of an old residential garage. My life as a private eye had proceeded along those lines ever since.

But now what? Ella was still clinging to me and the deceased was sprawled in the sun on hard-packed dirt and, because of my DNA, over which I had no control, I had a growing awareness of nipple bumps pressing against my chest. Not so much the expected pneumatic pad of breasts, however, because they were A-cup in size, and I know this because I'm a pig, and male, and unrepentant.

"Ella," I said quietly.

She shivered, still clinging to me.

"Ella." I thought if I said her name often enough she would eventually respond. Which she did.

"Ella."

Her head pulled away an inch. "What?" Still in my ear, and I could tell she was still in a state of shock. Hopefully not medical shock, but I was ready to elevate her feet if it came to that.

"Are you okay?" I asked.

No answer. Her arms tightened around me so I held her and kept trying to comfort her. Probably not quite like hugging a stick of macaroni, but what did I know?

I watched as the plane disappeared south.

We stayed like that for another minute, Ella shivering in my arms. Finally her grip loosened and she backed away just far enough to look at my face.

"I'm sorry," she said in a teary voice. "I've never seen anything so awful in my life."

I continued to hug her, waiting for her to get hold of herself.

"Is he . . . ?" Ella said.

She didn't finish, but I guessed she meant dead. Very, I thought, but all I said was, "Yes."

Her body shook. "I . . . I'm sorry. That was dumb. Of course he is. It's just . . . I've never seen *anything* like that before."

Could a person slip into shock in a temperature of a hundred degrees while standing up and being held after witnessing something like this? I didn't know, but rather than elevate her feet I felt it would help if she got moving.

"How about we walk around the station here, Ella?"

"O-Okay."

I put an arm around her waist, used my body to shield her from the sight of the corpse, and guided her around the VOR, a distance of maybe eighty yards, then I said, "Sorry about this, but I need to look at the, uh, this guy."

She shuddered against me, took a deep breath as we rounded the Cyclone fence and returned to the west side of the VOR where the body had come down. "I'm, I guess I'm sort of okay. I don't want to look at it, though."

"No reason you should." I hesitated, then said, "How about you keep an eye out toward that ghost town, Colton Spring?" Which was behind a low line of hills to the west.

"Okay." Then she gave me a look. "Why?"

"No reason. Just something to do. Let me know if you see anything."

"Like what?" She was sounding a little more with it.

"Like . . . anything." Like any indication that someone out there knew this was going to happen and knew I was here. That a body falling from a plane wasn't all there was to this—whatever *this* was. And, possibly, knew I wasn't here alone as requested in the note.

"Okay. But shouldn't we report this?"

"We will. Do you have a cell phone with you?"

"Yes."

"Try to get a signal. I'll check the . . . this guy."

She dug a cell phone out of her fanny pack and faced west. I approached the body and crouched beside it. The guy had come down face first, but the bounce had flipped him over and he was staring up at the sky, or would be if his face wasn't strangely flat, skull broken, and if his eyes didn't look like peeled hard-boiled eggs.

Well, jeez, Mort. Eggs?

Maybe not eggs, but checking for a pulse wasn't in the cards. This guy was *dead*.

I took a breath, feeling a bit woozy myself, then looked the body over without touching it. Guy in his mid to late fifties, hard to tell his height while he was lying down and I wasn't about to stand him up. Pudgy white male, soft, with an office pallor, maybe two hundred thirty pounds. Not much else to see without touching him, which I didn't want to do. But he was wearing a nice suit. I could bring myself to touch the suit, where it wasn't glistening with blood. A fair amount of blood, as if seams had ruptured on impact. Not the suit's seams, but *his*.

Jeez, again, Mort.

Pretty good aim on the drop. Or pure luck. I didn't think the guy in the plane had come across a WWII-era Norden Bombsight at a garage sale and hooked it up.

"I can't get a signal out here," Ella called to me.

"Figures," I called back. "We'll have to wait till we get to Lovelock." I thought we'd head that way pretty soon. No reason to hang around here. Chest compressions looked like a waste of time.

I pressed on pockets, disturbing the crime scene—probably a misdemeanor, not that I hadn't done worse in the past five years—surprised when I felt something like a wallet in the inside pocket of his coat. If it really was this guy's wallet, I wanted to see what was in it. What I really wanted was a name.

I got a thin nitrile glove out of my backpack, put it on, then unbuttoned the coat, eased the left side off the corpse and slid the wallet out. Ick. Opened the wallet, saw green bills stuffed in the money fold in back, several credit cards in their slots, a Virginia driver's license for an Alden Lund Ridel. And I'd seen his face on TV just last night.

The missing deputy director of the FBI.

Well . . . *shit*.

Ma was gonna fire me for sure this time; I was gonna be jobless and end up in a trailer park in Muncie, Indiana.

• • •

I had a cell phone in my backpack. I got it and took a few pictures of the late Alden Ridel from different angles. I checked for a signal but, like Ella, I got no bars.

"I think I see something," Ella called to me. "It looks like someone's out there."

Great.

I stood up and went to her side. "Where?"

She pointed. "Sort of low down in the hills we came around from that ghost town." She glanced at me. "I saw your car there, and the tracks your motorcycle made."

"Dirt bike," I said. About six steps down from a Honda Gold Wing. I squinted at the hills three miles away, too far to pick out anything but movement. "I don't see anything."

"It was just . . . maybe like someone walking. Not now, but I saw something a minute ago."

A puff of whitish smoke low in the hills caught my eye. I stared at it for six or eight seconds, then a *thunk* came from the VOR station, as if someone had hit its cylinder or cone exterior with a ball peen hammer. Five seconds after that a deep booming sound rolled in from the west where I'd seen the burst of smoke.

Aw, shit, no. This wasn't over yet.

I grabbed Ella by an arm and hauled her around to the far side of the VOR.

"What?" she said. "Where're we going?"

I peered beyond a corner of the building at the hills. "Someone's shooting at us."

Her mouth dropped open. "That, that's . . . *crazy*."

Uh-huh. From three miles? Not even Bob Lee Swagger could make that shot. A fourteen-hundred-yard shot was world-class. This guy was trying to hit us at five *thousand* yards? Not gonna happen.

Except for something called luck.

Pretty good shooting just to hit the VOR Station. But he wouldn't know he'd hit it. He wouldn't hear the bullet strike the building and even with a hundred-power spotter scope, if such a thing existed, he would never see where the bullet had hit, so he was shooting blind.

Another puff of smoke erupted.

I waited, counting it off, gave up after fifteen seconds

when the sound of the shot reached us. I had no idea where the round hit. The sniper probably didn't either. The problem was getting the elevation right. Three miles? Say the bullet was a fast one, leaving the barrel at 3000 feet per second. It would slow on the way. Lucky to arrive at 1800 feet per second. Call it an average of 2400 fps, so it was in flight for . . . I tried to get the numbers sorted out in my head, which wasn't easy because this was physics, not IRS stuff which I did in my sleep. Bullet in flight for, call it seven seconds. About half the time going up, half the time coming down which meant three and a half seconds of drop, so . . . I tried to remember the formula I'd learned at the gun range, then decided I was completely lost, so I gave up and guessed that this guy was aiming four or five hundred feet over our heads, maybe more. I doubted the sniper was using math either because I didn't think that would work, so this was just shoot and pray. But he'd hit the VOR, so that would cost him ten thousand bucks and five years in prison. If.

Another puff. I counted it off. At six or seven seconds a burst of dirt lifted off the flat two hundred yards short of the VOR and twenty feet off line.

The sniper might see that. If so, he would be raising the elevation a hair. But he couldn't see us so what was the point?

Oh, yeah. Zeroing in on the VOR building to try to get the range in the ballpark.

"Why is he doing this?" Ella said in a jittery voice.

"Dunno. But he doesn't have a hope in hell of hitting us."

I didn't bother to mention that luck thing.

"Well, what're we gonna *do*?"

"Wait it out?"

Maybe I shouldn't have made it a question, because she said, "Wait it out? Are you *serious*?"

"He could fire a thousand rounds and not come close to hitting us back here."

"Yeah, but he's between us and your truck and my car at that ghost town. How long will we have to freaking wait it out?"

Good point. Excellent, actually.

"And what if he's still there when night comes?" she asked.

Another great point. Making the Mortimer look like a slacker in the brain department, so . . . fuckarama.

"We could run for the hills behind us," I said. "I've got that dirt bike."

"Which is on the other side of this VOR thing, so he would see you and maybe shoot at you."

"Sounds like he's firing a bolt action. He might get off one or two shots, but I'd be out of sight pretty quick."

"He might get lucky."

Well, shit. She figured out the luck thing.

Another puff of smoke. A while later a round hit fifty or so yards behind us. Getting better. I didn't like that.

Even so, at three miles it would take a lot of luck to get a hit, and on the bike we could put more distance between us and him. The elevation problem would be compounded to impossibility every second. He would have to be lottery-lucky to actually hit us.

Worth the risk, but I still thought waiting him out might be the way to go.

At which time, a dusty red pickup truck rounded the hills on the flat and headed our way. Fast.

Well, that sucks.

Got a sniper who might only be trying to pin us down and an accomplice coming to finish the job. Maybe. But I wasn't about to wait around on a maybe and then take a bullet or try to fight this guy off with a Glock.

"Someone's coming," Ella said, voice pitched high.

"I know. I see him."

"Well, what're we gonna *do*?" She looked at me. "You have a gun. Can you shoot him? Whoever's in the truck?"

"I thought guns were dangerous."

"Shut *up*. That . . . that was before *this*."

I had to smile. *Had* to.

"To answer your question, no, I can't shoot him."

"Why not?"

A handgun is all but worthless after fifty yards. Even thirty isn't good. Whoever's in the truck could stop two hundred yards out with a rifle and pick us off."

"Well, then, *what're we gonna do?*"

"Right now, run. Stay put, Ella."

I ran to the front of the VOR, shoved the Raven off its stand and hopped on. As I started the engine a rock thirty feet away splintered and the ricochet slammed into the VOR's cinderblock wall with a nasty *thwack*.

Had to be a lucky shot. I didn't want to see if he could do that again.

I glanced toward the west. The truck was about two miles out, headed our way at a good clip. A line of folded hills to the east were three or four miles away. The Raven might do seventy, but maybe a little less than that carrying three hundred twenty pounds. The truck would be faster.

Time to go. *Now.*

I slid the Raven around the VOR, rear wheel spitting dirt and dust as I rounded corners. "Put this on." I tossed her my backpack.

Ella donned the pack then leaped on the seat behind me and wrapped her arms around my middle. I took off fast, headed east, whipping up through the gears, topped out at sixty-eight, didn't see anything in the side mirror, but an explosion of dirt lifted a hundred feet ahead of us and only six yards to my left. Last gasp from the sniper. We blew on by the fresh gouge in the dirt about one second later.

"You okay back there?" I shouted over the engine noise.

"Just *go.*"

Good enough. I would know if she fell off. Probably.

• • •

This was karma. This was what I got for having stayed with the IRS a year or so after I discovered I had a soul. Decapitated heads, severed hands, a stinky decaying "gangsta" rapper in the rafters of a hot garage, Lucy and I buried alive in a Cadillac. On and on and on it went.

If the IRS wants to hire you, *don't.*

• • •

I headed for the nearest hills at the edge of the flat. We were a mile and a quarter from the VOR when I saw the truck in the mirror, just passing the station. The sniper was out of play, so I put him out of my mind, but that truck could be doing ninety. It was shaping up to be a tight race.

We hit hardpan and the Raven inched up to seventy for a couple of miles, then the incline of the playa slowed us as we neared the hills.

The truck was half a mile back.

Then a quarter.

We reached the hills where low rounded ridges sent fingers of dirt and rock tapering out into the flats until they were nothing. I took the Raven into the mouth of a gully between two low ridges, hoping the truck would follow.

Which it did.

A hundred yards into the gulch I sent the bike upslope to the north, bouncing up dirt and rocks at an angle. If the truck tried to follow, it would more than likely overturn.

The driver didn't try. Too bad.

I glanced in the mirror as I neared the top of the ridge and saw him pile out of the truck with a rifle. He snapped off two shots at us, didn't get a hit, then we were over the ridge and gone.

"What the *hell*?" Ella shouted, almost in my ear.

My thoughts exactly.

Except. I wanted some sort of retribution, so I stopped the bike out of sight, killed the engine, and got off.

"What're you doing?" Ella asked.

"Payback. Stay put."

I duck-walked over the ridge just far enough to see the truck. Long shot, probably close to two hundred yards, but I pulled the Glock and aimed a few feet high. The guy was just getting back in his truck. I fired three rounds, and damn if the third one didn't go through his windshield. The guy scrambled out the driver's side door like he was on fire and took refuge behind his truck. He was too far away for me to get a good look at him, but he looked like a big guy, heavyset, wearing jeans and a gray T-shirt.

I jogged back to Ella.

"Did you get him?" she asked.

"No, but I got his truck and I think he's gonna have to change his undies."

She gave me a faint smile. "Undies, Mort?"

"One never knows."

We got back on the Raven and took off. We gained elevation on the far side of the ridge for a while. I stayed there to keep out of sight of this new shooter, who would no doubt be pissed about his windshield. After half a mile I went back over the top far enough to peer down into the gully. I stopped. The truck was back out on the flat headed north, not very fast, paralleling the range as if searching for a track that would take him up into the hills. Farther west by the VOR station another pickup truck was headed our way, blue with boards enclosing its back bed, barreling northeast across the flats, raising a cloud of gray-brown dust. Best guess, that was the sniper.

But what the *hell*?

We had the advantage on the dirt bike up in the hills, but the trucks could have dirt bikes lying out of sight in their beds. I gunned the Raven's engine and took off at an angle across the slopes, trying to keep out of sight as I took us higher into the Stillwater Range, down the north side of one ridge, across a shallow valley and up and over another ridge, gaining elevation, feeling more and more lost.

Never try to figure out how the day will go when you get out of bed. You will be wrong ninety-nine times out of a hundred. Or more.

Chapter Three

So—a slender, pretty girl, arms around my waist on a dirt bike as we raced up into the hills, traversed gullies and ridges, crossed dirt tracks made by four-wheelers—which I didn't like one bit because it meant the trucks could get up here—and watched as the gas gauge crept toward E.

What's the plan, Mort?

Don't get dead. That was pretty much it.

Synopsis? You're sent to an identifiable place in the middle of Nowhere, Nevada, supposed to come alone, end up with a girl who disliked guns until she didn't, then the second in command of the FBI lands facedown fifteen feet away from a height of, say, three thousand feet, hands tied behind his back, then a sniper without a hope and a prayer opens up on you and the girl, and someone in a truck with a rifle chases you, and another truck joins the chase.

Which probably wasn't over yet and could get worse. A plane and two trucks? How about a helicopter? Three or more guys killing an FBI deputy director oughta be able to come up with a helicopter. If not, someone might call that plane back to help find us up in these hills.

As I pounded the Raven over rocks and rills I would have to keep a lookout for any or all of that.

But why? And why *me,* since I was supposed to have been alone at the VOR station?

No answer as to why, but that "why me?" part was also par for the course. I'd been in the national spotlight several times in the past, none as glaring as last year's spotlight with Vale, who had been ninety-nine point seven percent naked with me driving her all over Montana as "the naked bandit" fake-robbed several stores and businesses. Kind of a long, bizarre story there.

Maybe I was convenient, or only meant to enhance the story, not that being chucked without a chute from a plane needed much in the way of enhancement. But perhaps my involvement would shine a more newsworthy spotlight on Alden Ridel who was, after all, nothing but a lowly deputy director, a guy whose name, a week ago, would be known to less than a tenth of a percent of the population.

So why the sniper? Why the trucks?

Whoever they were, they'd gotten Ridel. Kidnapped him, killed him, mission accomplished. But it seemed like they were after me, too, me personally, so the job wasn't over. None of that made the slightest bit of sense.

In the meantime, Ella and I were on the run, headed for the hills.

Dry, empty hills.

With not quite half a tank of gas left and no way to circle back around to our cars.

· · ·

We were at six thousand feet in the Stillwater Range when the sun was just a spark in a notch of the hills to the west. Shadows in the ravines made it difficult to pick out the best route, as if there was such a thing. I'd found a dirt trail that went south. Not the best way for us to go if those trucks were out here, but it was faster than bucking over the hills and would take us closer to Highway 50 and the town of Fallon, still over forty miles away. The gas gauge was on E. That sucked, but at least we were still going.

Earlier, we'd spotted dust raised by a vehicle before its driver could see us, and I'd taken the Raven upslope and dumped it behind an outcrop of rock forty feet off the trail. A brick-red truck had cruised by at maybe fifteen miles an hour with a bullet hole in its windshield on the passenger side. That was an hour and a half ago.

"Look," Ella said in my ear, pointing a finger over my shoulder. "There's a light."

I slowed the bike, looked off to the left and saw a tiny bright orange flare in the hills. Then it was gone. But in the seconds I'd looked I realized it was a reflection of that last speck of sunlight as the sun went behind hills in the west. The reflection might have come off a mirror or a window four or five miles away, not much higher than we were, but across a good-sized valley then up a ridge.

Right then the bike hiccupped, burped a few times, then died. It coasted to a stop, having used up the last drop of fuel and every last whiff of fumes.

"Well, shit," I said, even though I'd been expecting it.

We straddled the bike. The valley between us and that scintilla of light was dark with shadow. The reflection was gone. I tried to pinpoint where we'd last seen it.

Ella still hugged me. "Now what?" she asked. I felt her shiver, probably not with cold. Yet.

"Now we hoof it."

"I figured *that*. But . . . where to?"

"That light you saw. It might've been a reflection off a window of some kind. Glass, anyway."

"You don't know?"

"How would I?"

She sighed. "Sorry. I'm just . . . I don't know. We're so far away from anything out here."

"At least it was southeast, which is the way we want to go."

"We do?"

"If we keep going that way we'll eventually cut across Highway Fifty. That would get us to Fallon."

"Well, okay. But what about that reflection?"

"Could be a trailer, or a cabin, maybe an old junker car that still has glass in its windows. Some sort of shelter, if we're lucky. It'll get cold up here and we're not dressed for it." You especially, I didn't say.

She shivered again.

We got off the bike. The temperature was in the low seventies, but it would probably drop into the fifties later. I pushed the bike a hundred yards along the trail then down to a stand of scrubby pinion pines that might conceal it.

I looked across the valley. Might as well keep heading that way, across and up the side of the ridge, hopefully find whatever had reflected that bit of sunlight. I told Ella the plan then said, "Think you can walk that far?"

She laughed.

What I'd asked didn't strike me as all that funny, but her laugh was musical and sounded genuine. I wondered if she'd sung in a choir.

"I run ultras," she said. "Mostly fifty milers, but last year I did the Western States One Hundred—Squaw Valley to Auburn. I made it in twenty-one hours, nine minutes."

Well, shit. I couldn't walk or even crawl a hundred miles, much less run it.

"Which," she added, "isn't even close to the women's record for that race. Ragna Debats ran it in under eighteen hours at age forty-two."

"Then you've still got years left to beat her. Anyway, today you can carry me up to that next ridge."

Another melodic laugh, quickly subdued. "How about you?" she asked.

"How about me what?"

"It's probably a lot farther to that light than it looked. It could be seven miles or more. Can you walk that far?"

"Harper and I jog ten miles a few times a week, hike as much as fifteen. I'll make it."

"Who or what is Harper? Your dog?"

"My wife."

"Oop, sorry. It's just that that's an unusual name."

On the Raven, we hadn't been able to chat. Too loud and too busy watching for trucks, planes, helicopters, dirt bikes, more guys with rifles.

"Anyway, you're married," she said.

"Lucky guess."

She slapped my arm, not hard. "Smartass."

"You're the first person who's ever called me that."

She smiled. "I bet. So, you're married. That's not a big surprise. You, uh, you . . ." She didn't finish. She turned away and stared across the valley we were about to cross.

"I'm what?" I asked.

She pursed her lips, then said, "Kind of a catch. It's no wonder some woman snatched you up."

Huh. No way was I going to comment on that.

"I bet she's pretty," Ella said quietly.

"She is. She also teaches high school English and pole

vaults over thirteen feet."

"Really? She pole vaults?"

"Thirteen feet ten inches when she was nineteen years old. She got a college scholarship. How about we get goin' here?'

"Good idea." She hesitated, then said, "Fourteen feet, almost. That's . . . amazing."

"She vaults, you run. You two would get along great." I estimated the direction we had to take. A quarter moon was up. I could guide off that when it got dark. For a while anyway. In a few hours it too would slide behind the hills.

"This way, kiddo," I said.

She smiled. "Kiddo? Really?"

"I've got a little gray in my hair, you don't, so kiddo it is whenever the urge strikes me."

"Something else might strike you if you call me that again, Bub."

"Feisty. And 'Bub.' I like that. Sounds nineteen forties. C'mon."

I set off downhill and she followed.

• • •

Walking cross country, also known as bushwhacking, is always somewhat harder than it appears from a distance when the terrain looks smooth and ravines and washes are inconsequential features across rocky earth. Ella managed the hike better than me, but my sense of direction was better. Down to the bottom of the valley, switchbacking up the next ridge, we came to another small valley we hadn't known was there, hidden as it was behind that first ridge. By then the world was dark, stars out, the only light was a ghostly wash cast by that quarter moon headed for the western horizon. It would soon set, but by then I had the North Star in sight, which helped to keep me oriented.

"You're a grad student?" I asked. I've heard it said that human voices keep predators away, like mountain lions. Hoped so, anyway.

"Uh-huh. In psychology. Working on a Ph.D."

"Got that. What's the thesis about?"

"You might like it."

Doubtful. "What's the, uh . . . the title?"

"I haven't nailed it down yet, but the current working title is "Psychology of teens who participated in the 2020 Portland riots. A Critical Survey."

"Sounds political."

"I'm keeping all suggestion of politics out of it. It's just who participated and why they thought it was okay, which wasn't easy for me because it's hard to defend burning and looting. I did a lot of research up there last year. Really, the thesis itself is actually kinda boring. I'd much rather hear about you and the woman you drove around Montana last year while she had to rob places pretty much naked."

I stopped walking. "Really? You want to hear about that?"

"It's interesting . . . um, psychologically."

"Only psychologically?"

She was quiet for a moment. "Okay, I admit I'm more than a little intrigued. I mean, I followed the story on the news while it was happening. The woman had a fabulous figure." She hesitated, then said, "I imagine there's some inside stuff that, you know, didn't get reported?"

Could be. Like Vale, topless, having to shave off all her pubic hair in the passenger seat beside me as I was driving. Something like that.

Which wild horses couldn't drag out of me.

I started walking again. "You didn't read her book?" I said. "*Outlaw*? It's all in there." Nope, not all.

"I did and it was fascinating, but I doubt that 'it's all in there,' as you say. You and she had to spend a few nights in a couple of motor homes and that wacko guy made both of you go inside completely naked."

"Wacko. Excellent. The hardest part of psychology is getting the professional jargon down. All the rest is easy."

She laughed. "Don't sidetrack the conversation."

"We were tired. We slept."

"Naked. In a tiny little motor home."

"Yes."

Silence, then her voice came out of the darkness. "Is that *all*, Mort?"

No.

"Yes," I lied.

"Uh-huh." Her voice was saturated with disbelief.

I didn't respond, hoping she would drop it. Which, to my surprise, she did. We hiked in silence for quite a while. Finally she said, "What did your wife think about all that?"

"Harper and I were engaged at the time—but married in spirit. She worried about the wacko, but she thought the rest of it was amusing."

Ella stopped walking. "Amusing? That's all? No way."

"Way."

"That . . . isn't possible."

"When we get back to Reno I'll introduce you. You can get it straight from her."

"Seriously? I mean, that'd be interesting."

"Psych major research?"

"Sort of. But, no, not really."

"Let's keep goin', girl."

"Girl. I like that."

It's been my experience that most women do. I can do psychology too, no Ph.D. required.

• • •

We kept going, stumbling along in the dark. She wanted to talk so I heard about a boyfriend she'd dumped two years ago, a brother in the Marines, a sister with three kids, and her thesis advisor had hit on her one too many times and she'd had to shut that down. She told me she'd been in a high school play, *Cats*. She had a fairly big part in it, not the lead, but she sang one song solo. I told her about Valentina and more of what we'd had to do last September, and about a girl, Winter, running a sword through my chest and out my back, and my escape from a burning cabin in the forest west of Reno, and Dani at twenty-five below zero high on a mountain in Wyoming one night, and how we survived by sharing a sleeping bag without clothes, crammed in like sardines.

Ella stopped walking. We were having trouble keeping up a steady pace. "You and a woman you'd only known for one day in a sleeping bag without clothes? Really?"

"No choice. There wasn't one cubic inch of extra room

in the bag. We did it to survive. Did I mention that it was twenty-five below the morning we woke up?"

"Yes, but, wow. Naked for fifteen hours with a woman like that? That must've been, um . . . kinda stimulating."

"C'mon, girl. Keep it moving here."

"Okay, but tell me more about this Dani person. It would be like, you know, research."

Uh-huh.

Chapter Four

At 10:25 that night we came upon a weathered cabin at the end of an almost-indiscernible dirt track. I would like to claim it was due to my skillful navigation, but in fact it was pure blind luck on my part that got us somewhere in the vicinity of the cabin, and Ella's sharp eyes that spotted the faint imprint of tire tracks in the dirt. We followed it north three hundred yards before reaching the cabin.

The front door—the only door—was padlocked with a rusty old Korean-War-era Master Lock, visible when I hit it with the light of my cell phone. I knocked, we shouted, but got no sign of life. By then the temperature was into the mid-fifties up there at seven thousand feet. Probably a nice view to the west in daylight, but right then it felt like we were in a vast expanse of black nothingness.

"Now what?" Ella said. She wore my windbreaker, but her legs were bare up to the last two inches of her thighs. I had on jeans and a short-sleeve cotton shirt. We were both chilled, but the situation wasn't dangerous. Yet.

"Now we break in," I responded.

"Really?"

"Survival takes precedence over any sort of misplaced

reluctance to do what has to be done. Anyway, the place looks abandoned."

"Except for that lock."

"Which might've been there for twenty years. We need shelter."

"So how do we get in?"

"Leverage. Or I might try to kick the door in. Worst case, I'll break a window, but we'll get in."

I hunted around with the light, finally found a rusty piece of rebar two feet long. I stuck it between the hasp and the door and gave it a hearty yank. Screws squealed out of old wood and the lock swung loose.

"Me first," I said. "Unless you want to take the lead to check the place out for rattlesnakes."

"Shit, no."

I smiled, pulled my Glock and pushed the door open, shined the light inside. No rattlers, but I saw a table, chair, a single bed, small wood stove, sink, two-burner propane cook stove, a red throw rug on the wood floor, bookshelves loaded with paperback books. At best, the cabin had two hundred square feet of living space.

"What's in there?" Ella asked from behind me.

"Have a look. It's safe."

She came in, hit the light on her cell phone. "Someone lives here," she said in a hushed voice.

"Looks like it. If not, they didn't clear out more than a month or two ago."

"Not even. Look." She pointed to a Fallon newspaper with a date under the masthead from five days ago.

"Well, damn," I said, not sure what to think about that. I didn't want to run down our cell phones' batteries so I looked for a light switch, found one on the wall right by the door. I turned it on and a ten-watt bulb came on in the ceiling. I followed the wiring and located a couple of car batteries tucked into a corner.

I checked for cell service while Ella nosed around. No bars, no signal, so I wasn't going to be able to tell Harper what had happened or that I wouldn't be home for a day or two. She wasn't a worrier, but I didn't like this anyway.

Ella checked books on the bookshelf, took one out and

looked at its cover, then turned and faced me. "A woman lives here, Mort. Not a man."

"Think so?"

"I *know* so. This place is spotless, and she's got a complete collection of Amanda Lake mysteries. My mom reads these. I've read a few of them over the years when I was visiting her. They're fun. Not great literature, but fun."

"Pretty rustic place here for a woman," I said sexistly, proud that I might've just invented a new word.

"Women can do rustic, for heaven's sake."

She turned on a spigot at the sink and cold water came out in a thin stream under very little pressure. She turned it off, faced the room and gave the place a long look. "Now what?"

"Not sure yet."

"Got a bed here with a comforter and a blanket." She lifted them and checked the sheets, even crouched down and gave them a sniff.

Right then Spade and Hammer appeared up near the ceiling in a dark corner, giggling and poking each other in the ribs. Good thing I was the only one who could see or hear those two clowns. They only showed up when I was in a situation that had the potential to get rather risqué. They had become something of an early-warning system.

"For sure a woman," she said, standing up. "They even smell fresh, which is kinda weird since from the outside this cabin could almost be the Unabomber's. Or something like that." She gave me an apologetic look. "We read about him in abnormal psych in my junior year. I wrote a paper." She looked down at the bed. "This bed's a single, but . . ." She gave me a bland look, giving me a chance to comment and make a terrific fool of myself. Women do that because it often works.

"Uh-huh." I didn't fall for it. I opened cabinets and found cups, dishes, pans. A kitchen drawer held flatware, inexpensive, but clean. I poked around, ignoring Ella who was sitting on the bed. I tasted water from the tap at the sink. No smell, fresh. Ella and I were a bit dehydrated from our hike so we drank a pint or so each. I kept checking the place out. Under the bed I discovered an antique army cot.

Last time I'd seen one of those was at a great uncle's house when I was no more than five or six years old. Even then it was a curiosity, a relic.

But here it might be a solution to a problem. Spade and Hammer narrowed their eyes at me. The jerks.

I unfolded it. Three wooden legs spread and tightened a canvas bed. I let out an inaudible sigh of relief. Various circumstances had forced me to share beds with quite a few women I'd known less than twenty-four hours, one of whom was Harper. Several years ago she and I arrived cold and soaking wet at a roadside house at midnight and a nice elderly lady had taken every last bit of our clothing and stuffed it into a dryer. Under the mistaken impression that we were married (Harper did the talking and referred to me as her husband even though we'd met only three hours ago), the woman offered us the one and only bed available in the house in a spare bedroom. That was a hell of a night.

But now I looked down at salvation in the form of a WWII army cot. I could've kissed the thing. And high on a shelf on a back wall of the room I spotted a sleeping bag amid cardboard boxes. Even better. I took it down and rolled it out on the cot.

Spade and Hammer blew raspberries at me and faded into vapor. Gone.

Ella stared at what I'd done but didn't comment on it. "Wish I could brush my teeth," she said.

"Me too. I mean mine, in case that wasn't clear."

Ella smiled, then rolled her eyes.

She found toothpaste and a toothbrush in a drawer in what served as a kitchen. She held up a tube of Crest. "Got this. No way I'm gonna use this lady's toothbrush, though."

Nor I, but we rubbed toothpaste over our teeth with fingers, swished and rinsed.

Better than nothing.

Not much left to do but sleep. I looked at the cot. "I'll take this. You take the bed."

"Really? That looks . . . very uncomfortable."

She was undoubtedly right. "I'll be fine," I said.

"You sure?"

"Yup," I lied.

Seconds of silence dragged out. I'd heard silences like that in the past and learned it was best to wait them out.

Finally she said, "Great," then took off her shoes.

I looked at the cot, hoping it would hold my weight. It was short, so I was going to slop over. This wasn't going to be like a night in a Hampton suite.

"I'm glad this bed is so clean," Ella said.

I recognize invitations when I hear them.

"That's good," I replied.

More silence. Then she said, "Would it be okay with you if I take off my top? I don't normally sleep . . . um, so dressed up like this."

"Your bed, your rules. And I'm all the way over here." Seven feet away.

"Could you turn out the light?" she said.

"In a moment."

I unzipped the sleeping bed, checked for mouse poop, spiders, anything moving, then hit the light switch. I got on the cot carefully. If the thing broke, that would be trouble. I would play hell trying to replace an eighty-year-old cot. I had a vision of spending a month or two on eBay.

I heard rustling sounds in the dark as she pulled the tank top over her head. I got my boots off.

Then: "Mort?"

"Yeah?"

For a moment she didn't say anything, then, "Nothing. I just, you know, hope you really are okay over there."

"I am. Thanks for asking. Good night, Ella." I settled into the sleeping bag, fully dressed except for boots.

"Night," she answered.

Which probably would have ended all the chatter and its subtext, but right then headlights threw a shifting glare through two windows, one on either side of the door.

Aw, shit, no.

"Omigod," Ella yelped.

"Stay put," I said. I got the Glock out of its holster on the floor beside me. I held it in one hand and peeked out a window in stocking feet.

All I saw were blinding lights headed our way, but the sound of a truck's engine was unmistakable.

"Company," I said. What I didn't tell her was it could be a red truck with a bullet hole in the windshield.

"Probably the woman who lives here. Maybe I should get up and get dressed."

"I'll handle it. Stay put."

Which she didn't. She came up beside me and peered out the window as the truck stopped thirty feet away, and the lights went out. But before they did, I saw that she also had her shorts off and her panties were about half thong and sage green. And, of course, she was topless.

"Back to bed," I said. "Scoot."

"It's probably the owner so don't shoot her."

"I'll make every effort not to, now go." By then I'd figured the red truck guy would've given up when the sun went down. So, yeah, this would be the cabin's owner.

I heard Ella get back in the bed.

A truck door slammed and a flashlight came on, the light bobbing as the person holding it came closer. Then it stopped and a gruff voice said, "I'll be a dirty sonofabitch."

A man's voice, not a woman's.

Great.

The door was flung open. The guy yelled then shined his light in my eyes, blinding me.

"Who in blue blazes are you?" he demanded.

"The name's Mort," I said quickly. "We were lost in the hills, finally came across your place. Sorry about the lock." I'd thought about giving a fake name, then realized I couldn't. Alden Ridel was extremely high-level FBI. The FBI would be all over his death. Ella and I had run into the hills, but our cars were at that ghost town, Colton Spring. In a day or two, maybe less, federal agents would get here. This guy would be able to describe us, so I didn't want the FBI to think Ella and I were trying to hide, even if we were going to do just that, something I'd been mulling over as we'd hiked up to the cabin.

"We?" he said.

"He means me," Ella piped up. Good girl.

The guy shined his light on her. She was sitting up in bed with the blanket pulled up to her chin. Well, maybe a little lower since I saw tanned shoulders and collarbones.

Now that I wasn't being blinded, I could see the shotgun he was holding, aimed about at my socks.

"Easy with that scattergun, partner," I said.

He reached around the door frame and hit the light switch. From the doorway he looked at me, at Ella, back to me, then back to Ella, which is where his eyes stayed for the next ten seconds, then they finally drifted back to me.

"Lost, you say?" He turned off his flashlight.

"That's right. Dirt bike ran out of gas. It got dark. We finally came across this place. I'm sorry we had to break in. I'll pay for any damage."

"Yes, you will. Mind putting down that gun you're holding?"

I backed up and set it on the table. "We good?"

The guy smiled. He looked to be in his early seventies, five foot six, lean but with a little gut, blue eyes, white hair, four-inch gray-white beard, bushy moustache. "Guess so." He cracked the shotgun and held the breech out for me to have a look. "Unloaded," he said. "Last time I fired this damn thing it like to dislocate my shoulder. That was eight years ago. Now it's just for show, but you'd be surprised how good that works."

No I wouldn't.

He leaned the shotgun against a wall and shut the door. A faint odor of bourbon rode his breath as he took a few steps into the room and gave Ella and me another long look.

"It's been years since I had company up here," he said. "Same deal. This guy's truck had a flat, no spare, he was thinking he'd have to walk out, thirty-three miles if he happened to go the right direction, which wasn't likely. My name's Pete Glenn. What'd you say your name is, son?"

"Mort. Mort Angel." And I was glad we were company and not intruders.

"Angel. That's an interesting one." He looked at Ella. "What's yours, miss?"

"Um, Ella Kassel."

"That's a pretty one," Pete said.

"Thanks."

"How long have you lived up here?" I asked him.

"Forty years. Almost half my life." He gave me a look. "I'm eighty-two. Don't look it, though, do I?"

"Nope. Not a day over fifty."

He cackled at that, then looked around the cabin, twisted his lips in thought as he stared at the cot and the sleeping bag.

Then Ella said, "Oh!"

Pete and I looked at her. "Oh?" I said.

She had a paperback in one hand. "Pete *Glenn*. These Amanda Lake books were written by Glenda Petersen."

"Uh, well, yes," Pete said, sounding slightly abashed.

"You're her. I mean she."

He looked down at his feet. "Guilty as charged."

"Omigod. I've read four or five of these."

He smiled. "Hope you liked 'em."

"I did. My mother has all, all . . . how many are there now?"

"Thirty-one. I'm writing number thirty-two."

"That sounds about right. One entire shelf of Mom's bookshelf is filled with them."

"Well, bless her for keeping me in cornflakes up here. I'm not one of the big names, but at least I have fun doin' it."

He took in the room again, then said, "It's late and I sure ain't driving back to Fallon and back up here again tonight, nosiree, so here we are and here we're gonna stay, so"—he gave the sleeping arrangements a long look—"you, Mort, are gonna have to bed down with Ella here—not sure why you weren't already, just sayin'—and I'll take the cot, which won't be my first time. I'm dog tired, so any more talking'll have to wait till morning, if that suits you. *And* you," he said, nodding politely to Ella.

"It's okay," she said, looking at me, not him.

"Right now I've gotta apologize in advance," Pete said, "but I'm going to have to ask both of you for a pretty darn big favor here."

"Name it and it's done," I said. This was his house. We were guests, uninvited ones, too. Whatever he wanted, we would have to do.

He looked at my jeans. "I would be mighty grateful if

you would do me the kindness of not wearing those clothes in my bed. I put clean sheets on it just this morning."

"We'll be fine," Ella said, still looking at me.

Pete smiled, then said, "I sure hate to have to tell you there's more, but I'm kind of a picky son of a gun. I never go to bed without washing up some, so I'd appreciate it if you two would do the same."

"How?" Ella asked. "You don't have a shower here."

"I scrub with a warm washcloth before I settle in. You can do the same. Do a good job and I've found sheets'll last two weeks that way."

"What a wonderful idea," Ella said. "It was hot today, and after the motorcycle ran out of gas we must've hiked six or seven miles."

"Well, good," Pete said. "I'll heat up some water."

He stuck a pan under the tap and let water flow for a few seconds, then set the pan on the propane stove. "Don't take but half a minute to get it hot," he said. "Only takes a couple ounces of water." While the water was heating he got clean washcloths out of a cupboard.

He dipped a washcloth in hot water, left it in the pan for Ella. "Mort and I'll go outside while you wash up."

I put my boots on without tying the laces and we went out and stood in the night, facing away from the cabin.

"That's an almighty pretty gal in there," Pete said. He kept his voice down and kept the statement neutral.

"Yes, she is."

"She your girlfriend or something?"

"No. A friend, but not what you'd call a girlfriend."

"You had that cot all ready to go. This isn't going to be awkward, is it? For either of you, I mean. Having to share a bed? 'Specially without all those clothes."

Yup.

"Nope," I said. "I'm good."

"You better be, since you either sleep in that bed or in the truck sitting up, which would make for a rotten damn night. If I were fifty years younger we could flip a coin to see who gets the bed and the girl, but as it is, awkward would be a king-sized euphemism if I won the toss, so buck up and take it, son." He laughed quietly in the night.

I smiled. "I've had practice with situations like this."

"Do tell."

I didn't get a chance because Ella called from inside, so we went back in.

Pete heated more water. "Your turn." He handed me the pan with a washcloth in it, then went outside.

I turned off the light, stripped and scrubbed. I put the skivvies back on and left the pan and cloth by the sink on the countertop then climbed into bed.

Sort of.

It was a single and I'm no midget. Good thing she was Bony Moronie.

Good thing I didn't say that out loud.

Ella called for Pete to come inside. Which he did. He turned on the overhead light.

"Y'all okay over there?" he asked without looking our way.

"We're good," Ella said.

"Sweet dreams, kids."

He heated more water, then turned off the light and we heard him washing, then getting into the sleeping bag.

I was on my left side, facing Ella. She was on her side facing me. Our heads were inches apart on a single pillow.

"This's kinda cozy," she whispered.

"Isn't it, though?"

"Except I'm about to fall out on my side over here."

"Same here, cupcake."

"There's still a little space between us." Her voice had an uncertain note to it.

There might've been an inch. "Want to close the gap?" I asked.

"I guess. Anything would help."

I pulled her closer until our chests touched. "Are you okay like this?"

"It's . . . whew."

I smiled.

"I guess I'm okay," she said. Then she giggled quietly. "This would make it into my diary, you know. If I had one."

I couldn't figure out what to say to that.

"Here like this with the famous Mortimer Angel," she

added in a breathy whisper.

"Uh-huh." Infamous, not famous, but it wasn't worth wasting words over the difference so I didn't correct her.

Pete started snoring. Not softly, either. Bourbon has a way of shutting things down.

We didn't say anything for half a minute, then she put an arm around me tentatively. "Is this okay? I don't know what to do with my left arm."

"Ella?"

"What?"

"I could go sleep in the truck."

"Oh! *No*. I didn't mean *anything* like that." Her arm tightened on me. "I'm okay like this. Really. I'm just being, I don't know, silly, I guess. Holding you like this is . . . well, it's kind of strange, but it's also kind of nice."

"Yes, it is."

I felt her soften, tension leaving her body. She eased a bit closer until our bellies touched. I didn't say anything, but I put a hand on the small of her back and tucked her in more firmly. My fingertips touched the elastic band of her panties so I pulled back an inch.

She took a deep breath. "Okay. That's good." For a few seconds she was quiet, then she whispered, "I guess this is sort of like what you said about you and that lady, Dani, in a sleeping bag in Wyoming."

"It's . . . similar."

"I know it's not the same. What I mean is, "My figure isn't anything like hers. Not even close."

I might've given her more information than necessary as we'd hiked uphill in starlight to the cabin. I probably shouldn't have mentioned Dani's G-cup breasts, but in fact that was part and parcel of that crazy story. It even added a touch of humor, since trying to get an arm out the top of the sleeping bag required the kind of arduous maneuvering past her boobs that had defeated Rommel in the desert.

Her face was pale in the darkness. "Don't sell yourself short, Ella," I whispered. "You're a very sexy girl."

She shivered. "I still feel like I'm right on the edge of this bed. Could I sort of lay a little bit on top of you, or you on me? If that wouldn't be, you know, too much."

I didn't think that would be out of line considering how out of line we were already. Harper would laugh about this, *and* the chaperone on the cot. What she *wouldn't* laugh about were bullets that had been fired at us or the trucks chasing us or Deputy Director Alden Ridel of the FBI flat on his back in the desert after landing face first at a hundred twenty-odd miles an hour, missing us by about the length of a Chevy Volt. None of that would get so much as a hint of a smile out of her.

So I pulled Ella up higher on my left side, got an arm under her and held her against me. I gave it a little more thought, then lifted her left leg over mine. "Okay?" I asked.

"Yes." She kissed my cheek. "You're a nice guy. And warm. I'm better than okay. What I mean is, this is quite pleasant—and sort of wow, but that's nice too."

I held her a little tighter. I figured that would speak more eloquently than words.

Which, maybe it did.

She kissed me. "This is nice. Now maybe I can get to sleep. Not, you know, right away, but after a while."

A while turned out to be twenty minutes.

It took me longer than that with her in my arms, but I finally made it. And, yeah, it was warm and pleasant and I got another merit badge for my Boy Scout uniform.

Chapter Five

"I'll drive you two into Fallon later," Pete said the next morning, after we'd had an early breakfast. "But not until you've worked off your hotel bill here."

I smiled at that. "Give me a hammer and I'll go pound something." In fact, I didn't want to hang around too long.

Ridel had probably been found by now. If so, agents could already be scouring the hills. The Raven would have left a track across the flats even a fibbie could follow. The hills would slow them down and we'd walked for miles, but the feds would get here eventually.

"I might use that line in a novel, son."

We were outside. Ella was looking off to the west. She wore one of Pete's sweatpants and my windbreaker. Not exactly Fifth Avenue, but she looked radiant. She smiled at Pete and said, "Give him that hammer. I'd like to see him pound away on something."

I shot her a warning look. She laughed quietly and faced the view again. I guessed she was feeling okay about last night.

Pete grinned at me, didn't say anything.

"What needs doing?" I asked. "I'm ready."

"Got a hundred gallons of water in a tank in back of the truck that has to be transferred. That's eight hundred pounds. And I've got a pile of wood to cut and split."

"I can't lift eight hundred pounds, but I can cut wood. Split it, too."

He smiled. "Might transfer the H2O with a hose and a Honda generator running a pump, but I'll let you haul a couple of heavy five-gallon gas cans out of the truck."

Which I did.

He had the water thing all worked out. He fired up the Honda and plugged in an electric pump which sucked the water out of a big plastic container in the bed of his pickup and sent it to a holding tank behind the cabin. The whole thing took less than five minutes and all I did was watch. Pretty easy way to work off a hotel bill.

But he had a dozen logs ten inches in diameter, eight feet long each, in the back of his truck, so I was given a job that mattered. He backed the truck around the cabin and stopped near a flat area covered with wood chips thrown from a chainsaw, then killed the engine.

"Guy in Fallon loads the logs for me," he said. "Up here, I drop the tailgate and pull them out, roll them around a bit so I can cut 'em into sixteen-inch rounds then split 'em and stack 'em." He indicated a lean-to about half filled with wedges of firewood.

He said, "If you drag 'em off the truck and lay 'em out, I'll cut 'em up, but I'd sure be happy to have you set 'em on that stump over there and split 'em with a five-pound maul. That's real work."

"Be happy to." And I was. The logs weighed a hundred thirty pounds each. I pulled them off one by one, hoisted them onto a shoulder and dropped them near a four-by-four he was using to lift one end of a log to make it easier to cut with an old Stihl chainsaw.

"I'll cut them if you want me to," I offered.

"Cutting's the fun part. Splitting's the bitch." He glanced at Ella who was watching all this. "Sorry about the language, hon."

"You should hear *me* sometime," she said. "I'd turn your ears as red as Rudolph's nose."

He grinned. "Doubt it, since I lugged a machine gun the size of a bazooka around Vietnam. Heard about every swear word ever spoken, but I don't put any of that in my books. Amanda Lake mysteries are pretty clean. 'Hell and damn' are about as raw it gets. Could be why they don't sell millions, but I write what I like to read."

He handed me a pair of ear protectors and put on a pair for himself. "I'll cut and kick the rounds over to you. You split and toss the splits over by the lean-to."

I gave him a thumbs-up. He glanced at Ella. "This'll be pretty loud. You might want to go inside and read a book. Amanda Lake number seventeen is my favorite, if that matters."

She left, and Pete fired up the Stihl. We got into a routine, cutting, splitting, tossing, then stacking the splits in the lean-to. With the two of us going at it, it took about an hour and a half.

"Damn, that was easy," he said. "Normally that'd take me three full days." He put the scabbard on the chainsaw and set the saw in a small shed that held gas, oil, and a bunch of tools. We went into the cabin and washed up. "I'll drive you down to Fallon now. And don't think it'll be a wasted trip for me, either. I'll pick up another load of logs before coming back. You and Ella oughta come back and stay the night again. With your help I'd about get the wood situation under control for the entire winter."

"We could do that," Ella said, giving me a pointed look and a smile.

"Wish we could," I said to Pete. "But something came up yesterday that needs looking into, so we'll have to beg off." I hadn't mentioned bullets or men in trucks chasing us. Things were quiet up here. I didn't want that to change for Pete.

"Sorry to hear it," he said. "It's been nice, having folks to talk to. But you're welcome any time."

I folded the cot and we set the cabin back to rights. By then it was after nine and I was antsy to call Harper and let her know where I was and that I was all right. I didn't like being out of contact this long.

* * *

The trip down off the mountain took longer than I'd thought it would. Bumpy rocky trail cut by gouges six or eight inches deep, switchbacks galore.

"Wish I could get this doggone two-track graded," he said. "But I imagine it'll hold up another couple of years."

Before going down, the trail went up and over a ridge to the southeast. Then down the east slope of the Stillwater Range to the flatlands below. We tracked along the base of the range for a mile or so, then went out east on the flat to a dirt road numbered 121.

"Dixie Valley Road," Pete informed us. Ella and I were on the front bench seat, Ella in the middle. It was eighty-five degrees out. Ella's legs were long, lean, bare, and tan. She looked good in butterscotch running shorts, a tank top and sun hat. Too good. People would remember her.

Road 121 reached Highway Fifty at a point west of a nothing little place called Middlegate. Pete turned right onto Fifty then drove us the forty miles to Fallon. Highway Fifty cut right through the middle of town. During the long ride in I'd thought about all the things that had happened yesterday and decided I wanted to make damn certain it didn't roll over Pete. I was glad we'd given him our real names. He would be able to tell the feds he'd dropped us off in Fallon. They would track us that far. From there, Ella and I would simply vanish. I hoped.

Three blocks from the Fallon Nugget, the only casino worthy of the name in the town of nine thousand people, I pointed to a side street. "Turn down that way, Pete."

He slowed the truck but didn't stop. "Not much down there. Nugget's just ahead. Got good food there if you need a mite more."

"I know. Not right away, though."

He shrugged and turned left. Two blocks south of the highway he dropped us off at a cross street. I reached across Ella and gave him three twenties for gas as I stuck a pair of hundred dollar bills half out of sight into the seat cushions.

As Ella and I scooted out the passenger side door, Pete said, "I got things to do here in town. You didn't have to pay for gas, Mort."

"Yes, I did." I looked at him through the open door. "It's also for a new lock and hasp for your door, which you'll have to repair. Don't argue. You've been a lifesaver, my friend."

Ella went around the truck to the driver's side window and stuck her head in, kissed his cheek. "Thank you."

He didn't say, "Aw shucks," but it was in his eyes. What he did say was, "Remember, you two're welcome up at my place anytime. Be happy to have the company."

"I'd like that," Ella said. "It's peaceful up there. Maybe I can talk Mort into going up there again."

Pete smiled. "You two take care now." He looked at me. "Take the road less traveled, son." He held my eye for several seconds then turned right at the intersection and rumbled off toward the west.

The road less traveled. I'd been doing that the past five years and had the scars to prove it. Now I was on that road, again—gumshoe on the run.

"What'll we do now?" Ella asked, looking around.

"This," I said as I opened my backpack. I pulled out a pair of nonprescription glasses with thick black frames, a dirty-blond wig that looked as if it had been in a hurricane, a fake moustache, a ball cap, and a blue T-shirt with *Reno*

Aces on the front and number 15 on the back in yellow.

"What on earth is all that?" Ella asked.

"We're going dark." I put on the glasses, wig, and moustache, and handed her the shirt. "Here, put this on."

She held it up and laughed. "You're kidding, right? This's like twelve sizes too big."

"Uh-huh. Put it on anyway."

She stared at me. "You're not kidding."

"Put the shirt on, kiddo. This isn't over yet. Some unknown person had you write that note and deliver it to me. You and I are in someone's sights. We don't know who or why, but the missing deputy director of the FBI landed almost at our feet right on time from a small plane, which is pure trouble and means we can't walk around as if it isn't. Something's going on. Ridel might've gotten tangled up in something personal, unrelated to his job, but here's a little factoid I got from Ma that she got yesterday morning from ex-U.S.-Attorney-General Susan Kenny who still has contacts in D.C.—Ridel was not well-liked at the FBI. He wasn't thought to be a team player. As such, he might be a target for a few unindicted upper-echelon criminals at the FBI even though he's upper echelon himself, or was, so it's possible someone or several someones high up in the FBI had him kidnapped and booted out of that plane. We need to disappear until this gets sorted out. For now, that means being in disguise, so get that shirt on."

A scared look filled her eyes. She hadn't thought about any of that. She wasn't used to intrigue the way I was. She pulled the shirt on over her head. It bagged on her, hiding her slender figure and tank top as I'd hoped it would. She was tall enough that the bottom two inches of her shorts were still visible, which kept her from looking as if she might not be wearing anything underneath the shirt.

"This thing is beyond huge," she said.

"Exactly what we want."

She looked at me. "And you look . . . weird."

"Don't tell my mom."

She rolled her eyes. "Okay, you *are* weird. But what're we supposed to do now?"

"Get off the street and get reinforcements on the way."

I removed her sun hat and replaced it with a ball cap.

She took the cap off to look at it. "Coors? Really? I'm advertising beer?" When I didn't answer, she shrugged and put the cap back on. "Reinforcements?"

"You wanted to meet Vale? I'll call her soon as I can. If I get her working on this, you'll get your chance."

"Vale's the woman you, uh, drove around Montana last year, right? In the book she was Valentina."

"Same person."

"Cool. I'd love to talk with her."

"But first we've got to get off the street. C'mon." I took her hand and headed west on East Center Street toward a commercial district of small shops. She took a quick hop to catch up then matched me stride for stride.

A block ahead I saw a sign for La Fiesta—food, a place to sit and stay off the street, regroup. But on the way, other side of the street, I saw a sign that read Hair & Nails, so I jaywalked us on over and we went inside, and, yes, as I'd hoped, they also sold wigs.

Before a salesgirl could even ask what we wanted, I'd taken a curly blond wig off a Styrofoam head and handed it to Ella. "Put this on." It was several shades of light blond.

"I'm not really the blonde type," she said.

"You are now. Put it on."

She took off the ball cap, put on the wig and looked at me. Loose curls hung four inches below her shoulders. It turned her into an entirely different person. She checked herself in a mirror and groaned.

"She loves it," I said to the twenty-something salesgirl who was rolling her eyes at this whirlwind performance. "How much is it?"

"Thirty-seven ninety-nine."

I dug two twenties out of a pocket and gave it to her. "Keep the change." Ella and I got out of there. The entire thing took less than a minute. We continued walking west.

"That was awfully fast," she said, getting the ball cap settled on over the wig.

"As I'd hoped."

I took us into a men's clothing store and bought a pinch-front cowboy hat in black for eighteen bucks. We were out of there in record time too.

"You've done this kind of thing before," Ella said.

"Yup."

"More than once. Kind of a lot more, looks like."

"Yup."

"That's . . . weird."

"You're starting to echo, sunshine. And, look, there's a La Fiesta. Let's get off this street and get something to eat."

We climbed a half-flight of stairs and went into a fairly new-looking brick building with a neon *OPEN* sign in the window. I got us settled in a booth with a view of the street outside. The time was 10:40. Other than two women in a dim corner thirty feet away and us, the place was empty.

"This's sort of cool," Ella said, "but also sort of scary, all this . . . this subterfuge."

"Scary'll keep you on your toes and your eyes open." I kept the cowboy hat on and gave her a menu I'd snagged on the way past a deserted hostess station. "I know I'm having enchiladas. See what you want."

She set the menu aside. "Enchiladas sounds good. I'm still hungry from our hike yesterday."

A waitress strolled over and we ordered drinks and food. She left, and Ella and I were alone.

She looked around. "Can I take this wig off now?"

"Nope."

She sighed. "Well, shoot, okay, here we are, but where do we go from here?"

"Hold that thought," I said. I pulled out a burner and punched in numbers for Vale's regular cell.

"What?" she answered, which was one of the ways we answered incoming burner calls and unknown numbers on our personal cell phones.

"Call back on two," I said, then hung up.

Ella stared at me. "Two?"

I held up my burner. "This. She'll know."

Ella glanced around the room then back at me. "Was that Valentina?" she asked quietly.

"Yes, but she prefers Vale." My burner rang. "Are you alone?" I asked.

"I'm in the office with Ma. Do you know you're all over

TV here in Reno and maybe all over the country?"

"Uh, no. I've sort of been off grid."

"Well, you are. The FBI was here in the office earlier this morning wanting to know where you are. They left a while ago. We're supposed to contact them if you show up. You're wanted for questioning. Ma's about fit to be tied."

"There's valium in my desk—left side drawer. Let her know."

"I'll put her on. You tell her."

"Maybe not," I said. "I need help. Now."

"What you *need* is a lobotomy."

"Not helpful. Okay, listen up. I'm with Ella in the La Fiesta in Fallon."

"Ella. Is that the girl who brought that note to the bar two nights ago?"

"The same."

"She's also wanted for questioning."

"Figures. She left her car close to mine at a ghost town called Colton Spring, twenty miles east of Lovelock."

"Well, that explains that."

"What explains what?"

"Your 4Runner was torched out there, not all that far from that VOR station. It's a lump of charred metal. And a VW bug registered to an Ella Kassel was also set on fire."

Well, shit. I'd liked that SUV. It wasn't a year old. I would tell Ella about her VW when the time was right. Finding those vehicles would put us at the top of the FBI's to-do list, but with Ridel dead I'd figured that out already, hence the disguises. Somewhat more aggravating was that I'd have to deal with State Farm sometime in the future, and buy a new set of wheels.

"Can't worry about that now," I said to Vale. "I need you to focus. Get forty thousand dollars out of the gun safe in my house—no, better make it fifty—and my go-bag. It has disguise stuff in it. You'll find it in a closet by the front door. Black nylon bag with blue piping. There's a folded wheelchair there, too. Bring it. And get some eyeshadow and lipstick for Ella, something suitable for a blonde. Not sure if we'll need that but I want to be prepared. You still have the combo for the safe?"

"I've had it since that Amberton thing in March."

"Good." A gun safe worth thirteen thousand dollars was a gift from Lucy's father three years ago. "Do you have a gray wig? Not too gray. Something nice that would make a twenty-nine-year-old girl look closer to mid-forties from a distance of, say, twelve feet or more—if that's possible."

Ella gave me a questioning look.

"Yes. Ma gave me one to follow a guy around Sparks earlier this year."

"Bring it. And some low-key makeup that'll work well with the wig. You got a quick look at Ella. She's six-one and not much more than a hundred twenty pounds. She'll need jeans that fit and a short-sleeve shirt. I don't want us to try to find that around here. Bring it and the gray wig and all the rest of it to La Fiesta soon as you can. Wear a disguise. I'll want you to drive Ella and me back to Reno. We've got to get out of here on the sly. It might not be long before Fallon becomes a hot zone."

"Which means you're avoiding the FBI."

"Lucky guess."

"Yeah, right. And you're doing this with Ella? What I mean is, you intend to keep her with you, is that right?"

"Not sure yet, but I want to be prepared. How much of this cluster-fudge has been made public on TV so far?"

"I've heard that Director Ridel was found dead in the desert out by Lovelock. Your pictures, yours and Ella's, are being broadcast just about hourly as persons of interest."

"Great. Have they said how Ridel died?"

"No. And please tell me you didn't shoot him."

"I had nothing to do with his death." Probably.

"That's good. Uh, hold on, here's Ma. She wants a word with you."

I closed my eyes, mentally battening down the hatches.

"Mort! What the *hell*!"

"Howdy, Ma," I said cheerfully. I winked at Ella.

"You're fired! *Fired*!"

"Vale tell you about the valium in my desk?"

"You couldn't find someone that no one's ever heard of, could you? You had to find the *freakin' deputy director of the FBI!*"

"Ella was there, so this time it was a tie. I'm upgrading my game, sharing the glory."

Silence. Then, "Oh for fuck's sake. Here's Vale again. I need a drink."

"You're inside the La Fiesta?" Vale asked.

"Yup. In a booth. We're keeping a low profile, about to have enchiladas."

She sighed. "I'll hurry, but it'll take a while to round up all this stuff. It could be two hours before I get there. Will you be okay until then?"

"Probably. My daughter and I are just having an early lunch, and I don't hear sirens."

Ella stared at me. Vale laughed. "Anything else before I get going here?"

"Yeah. Watch your back. I mean it. In fact, don't come in your car. Rent one, and not in your name."

"It's that serious?"

"Don't know, but it could be. Be damn sure no one is on your tail before you rent it. Watch out for a red pickup tailing you, or possibly a fed or two. You'll recognize FBI by the corncob walk if they're on foot. And pull the battery from your cell phone before you leave the office."

Another heavy sigh. "I don't know how you get into stuff like this, Mort."

"It's a knack. Thing is, I don't know a damn thing this time so I'm having to play this one very close."

"It's not like you and I haven't been there."

A red pickup with a bullet hole in the passenger side windshield rumbled by on the street. I craned my neck and caught the first two letters of its license as it went by: HK.

"Vale," I said. "Get Ma to find out anything she can about a red F-350 pickup truck with a bullet hole in the windshield." I gave her the first two letters of its plate.

"A bullet hole?"

"That's right.

"Did you put it there?"

"I might have."

"She'll be thrilled to hear that."

"I like to keep her busy and out of trouble. Tell her to

find that truck without leaving digital fingerprints. Make sure she understands that. Get going on the care package. We're okay right now, but things have a way of changing without notice."

"On it." She ended the call.

"She's bringing you fifty thousand dollars?" Ella said.

"Mad money."

She laughed softly. "Who has fifty thousand dollars in a safe in their house?"

"Bill Gates would laugh at fifty grand." I didn't tell her the safe held a quarter million, earning no interest and not insured by the FDIC.

"And how does a person rent a car not in their name?"

"I could tell you, but then I'd have to kill you."

She made a face. "I've never found that very funny."

"Okay, then how about this: I could tell you, but then I'd have to undress you."

She tilted her head and smiled. "That's . . . better. And *very* interesting. But you didn't answer the question."

"Hold that thought." I checked the time. 10:56. Good timing. I wanted to call Harper. She should be between classes right then. I called her on the burner.

"Mort!" she answered. "Where on earth *are* you? Are you okay? And why're you calling on a burner?"

"Got yours with you?"

"It's in my purse. Want me to call you back?"

"Yes."

"Okay. Bye."

Thirty seconds later my burner chimed.

"Where are you?" Harper asked.

"Fallon."

"That's . . . strange. What's in Fallon?"

"La Fiesta and a plate of enchiladas."

Ella gave me a half smile.

"Enchiladas? Are you *sure* you're okay?"

"Yup, I'm fine, and I've got a bunch of cool stuff to tell you, but it's a longish story, so most of it will have to wait. You've got a class about to start, don't you?"

"English Four—that's seniors. In a few minutes I'll be handing out thirty-five paperbacks. Othello."

"Cool. Sexual jealousy and crazy Iago. They'll like that. Great way to start the new school year, babe."

"You sound okay, big guy. You are, aren't you?"

"I am, but you remember the girl who brought that note to the bar day before yesterday?" I smiled at Ella.

"Uh-huh. Bony Moroni. Vale told me."

Boy, was I glad I didn't have the phone on speaker.

"Her name is Ella," I said. "She's with me right now, but like I said, it's a long story. It probably won't surprise you to hear that she and I had to share a little single bed in a cabin high in the mountains last night. A bigger surprise would be the eighty-year-old guy who was snoring on an army cot eight feet away who didn't want Ella and me to wear clothes in his bed."

Ella stared at me, open mouthed.

"An army cot?" Harper said. "They still make those?"

Trust Harper to zero in on that and not on the girl. She was one in a million.

"Dunno. This one might've still been in service during the Korean War. But like I said, all that will have to wait. Anyway, Ella and I are in Fallon and we've got this kind of complicated thing going on—"

"What kind of thing?"

"You haven't heard?"

"Only that you weren't home last night and you didn't call to let me know where you were. I get isolated here at school. What's going on?"

"I haven't the faintest idea, and I probably won't know more anytime soon, but—"

"Hold on, Mort. Barbara just came in and . . . wait a minute . . . she, she says you're on TV. Not *you*, but your name."

"I know. I just got that from Vale."

"She says you're *wanted*, Mort. Something about the missing FBI director guy being killed and they found your 4Runner somewhere in the desert not far from where they found him and it had been set on fire."

"It's a real long story, hon."

"Sounds like it. Barbara said the FBI wants you for questioning. And a girl, which I guess must be Ella."

"It is. *She* is."

"The *FBI*," Harper said again, with emphasis in case I hadn't caught that part.

"Got it. The fibbies and I haven't been on the best of terms the past few years, to say the least."

"So, well . . . what're you gonna *do*, Mort?"

"Thinkin' about it. But I need wheels so I think I'll buy a truck—not in my name. I might also get a small travel trailer, but I'm not sure about that yet. I'll let you know."

Silence. Then: "Wow. I can't keep up."

"This FBI thing is bogus, hon. But it's complicated. I'll fill you in on where I'm at with this when we've got more time. Right now we're at the La Fiesta in Fallon and Vale is headed our way with disguise stuff and money."

"But you *really* are all right, right?"

"I am, hon. But this is a strange one." I couldn't tell her how strange. It wasn't a good time to get into details about long-range sniper fire or unknown guys in trucks chasing us. "Call me when school gets out and you're alone and have time to talk."

"Okay, but be careful, Mort. And, uh, this classroom's starting to fill up. I have to go. Say hi to Ella for me. Bye. I love you."

"Love you too." I ended the call and looked at Ella. "Harper says hi."

"You told her you and I shared a little bed last night without clothes? *Really*?"

"I don't keep anything from her. Not Dani—that's the woman in the sleeping bag—and not Valentina last year."

"That's amazing. She was okay with it . . . I mean them? And with us, last night?"

"Yes." I hesitated, then said, "I've been lucky that way. It started with Jeri, my fiancée five years ago. She's the first one to tell me she doesn't own me, that she doesn't *want* to own me, that she will *never* own me. Those are almost her exact words. I realized then that I didn't own Jeri and didn't want to. People don't own people. Lucy was the same way, and so is Harper. Harper doesn't have a jealous bone in her body. She trusts that nothing will ever come between us, nothing at all. And she's right."

"That's . . . wow. And pretty nice, I have to say. I've never been in a relationship anything like that."

"Not many people have."

She sighed, took a sip of water. "What did you mean when you said you'd buy a truck, but not in your name?"

"I could tell you, but then I'd have to undre—"

Right then the enchiladas arrived, piping hot. We dug in and all further talk was left for later.

• • •

We were still there at noon. The waitress came over and cleared our plates. "Can I get you anything else?"

"Coffee," I said. I looked at Ella. "Tea?"

"No, thanks."

"Coffee and a phone book, hon," I said to the waitress. I called her hon because she was about my daughter's age.

"Local phone book or Reno?" she asked. "Or both?"

"Just Reno, if you have one."

She did. She brought it over with my coffee, then left. Ella leaned closer. "Who're you calling?"

"No one. Watch and learn." I shoved the Reno book to her. "Open it, run a finger down the page and tell me the first man's name you come to. First name, not last."

"Really?"

"Yes, really."

She rolled her eyes, opened the book, let her finger go down the page, then said, "Arnold."

"Okay, good. Now turn a few more pages and find me a last name."

More eye rolling. Then: "Mercer."

"Arnold Mercer. Works for me." I took the book from her and set it where the waitress could get it.

Ella stared at me. "What did I—we—just do?"

Chapter Six

Vale pushed through the door at 1:06. I waved her over. She wore glasses with gray lenses and blue frames, a red wig, floppy hat, and was dressed in slacks and a cream shirt that did little to hide a terrific figure. She handed me my go-bag as she slid into the booth beside me. Ella and I had ordered diet Pepsis and a basket of tortilla chips to keep management from running us off for hogging a booth long after we'd finished eating.

"Vale, Ella—Ella, Vale," I said, then snagged a chip from the mostly-empty basket and munched on it.

Vale laughed at me. She held a hand across the table to Ella and they shook the way women do—which is to say, without the manly testosterone crunch to establish which one would be the alpha dude.

"Nice to meet you, Ella," Vale said.

"Me too. Really." Ella hesitated, then leaned forward. "I read your book. It was . . . I mean, what you had to do to save that woman's life was amazing." Her face turned a shade darker under her tan.

"Amazing isn't the first thing people say to me when they tell me they read the book. Gross, erotic, and freaky are the top three, or their equivalents. I've also heard envy, but not often. But it was what it was. With Sue's mother's life at stake, Mort and I didn't have a choice. But," she said with a faint smile, "it worked out okay in the end."

"Good," I said. "Got that out of the way. We need to get going here. You have something for Ella?" I asked Vale.

She handed Ella a plastic shopping bag. Ella pulled out jeans and a shirt. And a gray wig.

"Put the clothes on now," I told her, "but not the wig. I don't want anyone in here to be able to tell anyone your hair color changed or that you looked older. You can put it on after we get outside."

As she scooted out of the booth I said quietly, "Hurry back. You need to hear whatever Vale has to say." Ella nodded and headed for the ladies' room. I watched her go for a moment.

"Those are some *awfully* long legs," Vale said. "And very shapely. They'll attract attention."

"Which is why I had you get her jeans. She can't walk around in those running shorts. She would be recognizable anywhere west of the Mississippi."

Vale laughed, then looked around and said, "What the hell's going on, Mort?"

"No idea, but Ridel was tossed from a plane. I bet that hasn't made the news yet."

Her eyes widened. "A plane?"

"From about three thousand feet. He landed less than twenty feet from us. Right on time, too." I gave her a quick synopsis of events.

"That's frightening. You heard what Sue said about Ridel not being onboard with all the crap the FBI has been pulling lately?"

"Yes."

"Their upper management might've gotten rid of him using you as a . . . a convenient way to muddy the waters since you're famous for finding missing people."

"I've thought of that."

"Which doesn't actually explain why the FBI would be *shooting* at you."

"Thought of that, too. This's a strange one."

"I hope it's not as strange as what Sue and I did with you last year."

Susan Kenny was the former United States attorney general, now a US attorney in Reno, District of Nevada, a position she'd held earlier in her career. She, Ma, Vale, Harper, and I still got together for dinner at least once a month. Sue and Vale saved Sue's mother from a psychotic stalker last year who thought he was forcing Sue to jump through his lunatic's hoops, when in fact Vale had taken Sue's place and robbed several places wearing only a filmy thong and sandals.

The story had made national and international news. A ghost writer named Emily Mathis had interviewed all of us who'd been involved. She'd written the definitive story, with Valentina Marchant named as the author. As a result, Vale ended up very rich, so what had felt like a dark cloud had that silver lining everyone talks about when things appear to be going to hell in a garbage bag.

Ella came back in jeans and a shirt. "They fit," she said as she slid back into the booth opposite us.

"Nicely, too," I said, making her smile. I handed her a makeup bag. "For when you're wearing the gray wig, but doll up now before we get out of here."

Her lips twisted in a smile. "Doll up. Right."

She found a reddish-brown lipstick in the bag. "This's okay. *And* this." She took out a little palette of eyeshadow in half a dozen shades of brown.

"Good work," I said to Vale. "Any more news we need to know about?"

"You and Ella were mentioned on KKOH just before I got here. Nothing I hadn't heard already, but you're still wanted for questioning. I haven't been near a TV since you called so I don't know what they're saying now."

"No one followed you here?"

"Not that I saw. The FBI's pretty good at that, but here we are and a SWAT team hasn't stormed the place. Yet," she added.

Ella's eyes widened, lipstick poised in one hand.

"Ignore that last," I said to her. "We're only wanted for questioning. They don't turn SWAT teams loose for that." I turned back to Vale. "Got the wheelchair in the car?"

"Yes. Ma said you use it to disguise your height."

"Uh-huh. If anyone asks, I say I got in a motorcycle accident. I also tell 'em the physical therapy sucks but the therapist is pretty. Puts 'em off their guard."

Vale shook her head and smiled. "I got Ma working on that pickup with the bullet hole. She said a bad word when I told her what you wanted. Anyway, I'm ready to drive you to Reno. That basket of chips is about done." She looked at Ella. "Almost ready, Ella?"

"Thirty seconds." She was brushing on eyeshadow.

"How about you?" Vale asked me.

"Yup. Like I said, Fallon's likely to be a hot zone in the not-too-distant future. Let's do it like this—you leave, go south two blocks, turn left and go down a ways, wait a few minutes then come back west. We'll be walking west on that street. You stop just ahead of us. We'll get in fast and you take off."

"That's . . . interesting."

"The waitress here can describe us. That's actually okay, but I don't want anyone to see the license plate when we get in the car. No one should know you were in Fallon. Ella and I will walk out of here and simply disappear."

"Got it." She slid out of the booth. Before she left, she looked at Ella and said, "You're in good hands with Mort. I should know. And *you*," she said, giving me a severe look. "Keep reciting that Boy Scout oath to yourself, mister."

"Hey!"

She laughed and went out the door.

• • •

Sonofabitch.

Ella smiled as she put the makeup kit away. "You were a Boy Scout with her, too, huh?"

I looked at her with one eye. "*Too?*"

"Well, you were with me last night, considering how little we were wearing. I didn't get roughed up at *all.*"

"Are you going to eat those last few chips?"

She shook her head. "No. I'm full."

I left two twenties and a ten on the table. "Then let's get out of here, doll."

"*Doll?*" She thought about that as she scooted out of the booth. "Okay, I like that."

She put an arm through mine as we left.

• • •

We walked two blocks south and turned right. By then she had on the gray wig and dark glasses and had aged fifteen years—from a distance. The Coors cap enhanced the look. We made it a block and a half before Vale stopped twenty feet ahead of us and we got in, fast, me in front, Ella in back. Vale hit the gas and we got out of there.

Other than being tall and slender, Ella didn't look a lot like the Ella Kassel whose picture was being plastered all over TV. Even older, she was still pretty and might turn a few heads. Not much could be done about that except to hide part of her face behind the bill of the ball cap or her wide-brim sun hat. And speaking of turning heads—in an unkempt dirty blond wig and a black cowboy hat and black suspenders, I wouldn't.

"Lookin' good," I told her. She'd aged considerably in the past five minutes, not something women generally see as a positive.

She hitched forward and got a look at herself in the rearview mirror. "Oh, jeez. Except for the hat, I look like my mother the day I graduated from high school."

On the way to Reno, Vale and I came up with several "what if" conjectures, trying to make sense of everything that had happened, but we didn't get far. We tripped over contradictions at every turn. In back, Ella was silent. When I looked back once, her eyes were closed but I knew she was listening to every word.

We rolled into Reno at two o'clock. I told Vale to take us to Kietzke Lane, home to car dealerships and fast food joints. I dug out a fake beard from my go-bag and put it on. It was an inch long, brown with gray in it. I also put on a fake gray-brown moustache.

I pointed to a Chevy dealership. "Pull over to the curb there. Don't go into the parking lot."

Vale glided to a stop outside the Chevy place and Ella and I got out. I unfolded the wheelchair and sat on it, put the go-bag on my lap and Ella's fanny pack on top of that. Vale kept my backpack, minus several items. She wished us luck and took off, then Ella, wearing a big floppy sun hat, pushed me onto the sales lot.

Blue, yellow, and red triangular flags hung from a line strung between lampposts. Helium-filled balloons tethered to the aerials of trucks and cars swayed in the hot air. The temperature was up over a hundred. In my getup I looked like a rancher or farmer. Maybe.

"Over that way," I said to Ella, pointing toward used trucks parked to one side—all kinds, not just Chevys, taken in trade. As she started to push me that way I said, "You need a name, a first name, not your own. What is it?"

She thought for a moment. "How about Amber?"

"Okay, Amber. Whatever I say to a salesperson here, do not contradict me or try to correct me. Oh, and you're my wife. Keep that in mind."

"We're married? Cool."

Made me smile.

I had her stop by an F-250 pickup that looked six or eight years old. Beside it was an older F-150 with half-bald tires and rust damage on its front bumper. I looked that one over to give a salesman time to hot-foot it over to us. When he was ten feet away I kicked the F-150's right front tire while sitting in the wheelchair.

The guy grinned at that, and I said, "Why the hell do people kick tires?" A tag on his shirt said *PHIL*. He had lank red hair and freckles, no coat or tie in the afternoon heat.

"Beats me. It doesn't tell 'em anything."

"Unless the tire falls off."

"Never seen that happen." He glanced at Ella, looked at me, then returned his gaze to Ella. Couldn't fault him for that even if she towered over him by six inches. She still wore dark glasses and the sun hat cast a shadow over her face, further hiding details.

"I'm Arnold, Phil. Wife here is Amber. This thing run okay?"

His eyes returned to me since I was the one doing the talking. "It's good."

Not really an answer, but about what I'd expected.

"Would you tell me if it wasn't?" I asked him.

He laughed, which didn't sound convincing. He was pudgy and looked hungry for a sale in the way salesmen do when they're trying not to look hungry for a sale.

"Enough dickering," I spun the wheelchair around and faced the F-250, then I circled it once with Phil tailing me. I stopped, facing the hood of the truck. It was a crew cab with $16,495 on the windshield, but no year. "What year's this one?"

"It's a 2014."

"Price is a bit high for a '14."

He gave me a quick evaluative look. "I can let it go for sixteen, even."

"Fifteen-five, cash. And a chrome triple-ball mount on the hitch," I said. The hitch had been empty.

"You say cash?"

"Yup. Right here, right now. That's not an offer yet, by the way, but we might get there."

"A chrome triple ball," he repeated. "I can do that." I assumed the fifteen-five was going to fly.

I stood up slowly, didn't try to rise to full height, and popped the hood, had a look inside. Not bad. The engine looked as if it had been steam cleaned. I checked the oil. New and full. Good enough.

"And a new battery," I said. Punch marks on its tag were four years old.

"And a new battery," he agreed, but without a lot of enthusiasm. I'd got him down a thousand and was nickel and diming him, chipping away at his commission, if they worked that way.

"Not sure about this yet," I said. "Depends on its mileage and other things I ain't seen yet. Got the keys?"

He hustled to a sales shack and hustled back, gave me the keys. I levered myself into the cab, keeping weight off my left leg, and turned the ignition, saw 88,513 miles on it. I turned the key farther and the engine caught. Idle was good so I revved it a bit. It sounded okay. I glanced at the gas gauge. Half full.

"For fifteen five I'd want to drive out of here with a full tank, Phil. This rig hasn't gone all the way around the track and up the backstretch, has it?"

"No, sir. It's been checked on Car Facts. If it'd gone all the way around once we wouldn't keep it on the lot."

"How about I take it up the street and back?" I said. It was a demand not a question. "She'll stay here with you." I caught Ella's eye and she gave me a slight nod, then rolled her eyes with a little head tilt toward Phil who'd given her a quick appreciative look.

"Are you okay to drive?" he asked me, glancing at the

wheelchair. "I mean, it's not that I—"

"Bunged up my left knee a while back," I said, cutting him off. "I can stand, walk some, don't need my left leg to drive an automatic."

Phil eased out of the way. "Be my guest."

The engine was still running. I closed the door, put it in gear and turned right off the lot, went five blocks down Kietzke, gunned the engine, hit the brakes, came back one street over. It would do.

"I'll take it," I told Phil as I got out and settled into the wheelchair again. "With that ball mount and battery if you can get it done in less than half an hour."

"I can. Service department has all that in stock."

"And a full tank."

"That too. You got that fifteen-five?"

I showed him the cash, which gave his eyes sunburn. "Okay, then," he said. "Let's get the paperwork done while I have that triple-ball and battery installed. And a fill up."

•   •   •

Phil handed us off to a paper pusher higher up the food chain, Don Manning, who wore a tie and had slicked-back hair. The paperwork took only twenty minutes. Cash is still king, and it's quick. The sales slip along with paperwork for the Department of Motor Vehicles was made out to Arnold M. Mercer. The address I gave him was for Velma Knapp's house on Bell street. Velma and I had shared a backyard fence a few years ago when I had a house the next street over on Ralston. She turned ninety in May, still spry and delighted to be included in what she called "slippery doings." I had a standing invitation to use her address for anything "fun and interesting."

I stayed seated in the wheelchair. I wanted it to make an impression. I wanted Don to see me as anyone but Mortimer Angel. Ella didn't say anything. She got up and strolled around the showroom while Don and I took care of business.

By 2:50 we were cruising south in a brand new used truck. I turned left and headed south on South Virginia Street where it and Kietzke intersected.

"You're Arnold Mercer?" Ella said, squinting at me.

"Yup. We might talk about that later."

She was silent for a moment. "Might?"

"We need to have a serious talk first, miss."

"Uh-oh."

"Right now, you know as much about what's going on as I do, which is to say, next to nothing. Fact is, you might know more because you got that phone call and typed and delivered the note, but we'll call it dead even." I gave her a quick look.

"Oka-a-y," she said. "I get that, but what's this serious talk business?"

"You have to decide what you want to do about all of this. We've been shot at and chased. You're wanted for questioning by the FBI, so there's that. And here's a tidbit I haven't told you yet—your VW was torched. Burned to a crisp out there at that ghost town, Colton Spring, as was my SUV, which is why the FBI wants to chat with us. VIN numbers and plates will still be readable. They know we were out there and who we are."

"Someone burned up my bug?" Her eyes were huge.

"To a crisp, which put you on the FBI's radar. Deputy director falls out of the sky, the feds will be eager to quiz anyone and everyone in the immediate vicinity about it—especially you and me since something *else* happened out there and our cars took the brunt of it—not that we know anything useful—but what I see as the real problem for us is that sniper and the trucks. Someone is after us, or at least they had been set up to get me. *Alone*, I might add. They couldn't have known you would show up. But you're in this deeper now, more than just writing and delivering that note. We don't know how or why they chose you, but I doubt it was purely at random. How much farther you've put yourself into this by showing up at the VOR station, we have no way of knowing."

"All of which means what?"

I changed lanes to get around a slow-moving Buick. "You have choices. I was just laying out the parameters of the problem. You need to get out of range of these guys."

"So do you. And I don't have any idea how to do that

since we don't know who they are."

"*That's* the problem. That red pickup passed by La Fiesta when we were there. It had tinted side windows so I didn't see who was driving. People are trying to find us and we don't know why. So . . . do you have family that could take you in, preferably far away, not in northern Nevada? Parents, siblings, possibly a friend?"

"I thought I was going to stay with you until we know more about this."

"Parents?" I persisted. "Friends? Anyone?"

She pursed her lips. "My mom lives in Gardnerville."

Fifty miles south of Reno.

"Not nearly far enough. Other family? You mentioned a sister and a brother yesterday."

"Vic is a Marine. He's in South Korea. My sister, Terry, is also in Gardnerville. She lives half a mile from Mom and has a husband and three kids."

Same thing, not far enough. And forget the husband—the kids alone made that a non-starter.

"I already thought about all of that," Ella said. "Not in any depth because I wouldn't expose my family to anything like this. *Or* my friends, most of whom live close by."

"Understandable. You didn't mention your father."

"He died in a boating accident about four years ago. Mom hasn't remarried."

"I'm sorry to hear it. Okay, second option is you take a trip or a cruise until this is over, say to the Caribbean. Or Maui. Maui's nice."

"Yeah, right. Like I have the money to do that."

"I don't want this to sound weird, but I would pay for it. I know Harper would be fine with that. I want you out of this."

"Speaking of weird, Mort, I don't want to go to Maui, or the Caribbean, or Paris or London. I don't want to . . . to like go anywhere. But there *is* one more option."

"What's that?" As if I didn't know.

"I stay with you and we figure this out. Together."

I heard faint karmic laughter somewhere in the ether because she had nixed her two best options and I was out of bullets.

"Nope," I said. "Bad idea."

"Why? You could protect me. You've got a gun."

I tried not to smile. Or laugh. "You trust guns now?"

"Not really, but I trust you. And you've got your boss, Ma. And Vale, and, I don't know. Resources. Also, I heard that woman's voice on the phone. I would recognize it if I heard it again."

"Was that on your cell phone or a house phone?"

"Cell. I don't have a house phone."

"Which means someone has your number." I looked at her. "I don't like that, but it could be useful if the woman calls again." In fact, it might be useful now. I would have to get Ma working on that. So far we had no word yet from her about the bullet-enhanced red pickup and its partial plate. Ma loves it when I ask her to work miracles.

"See? There you go," Ella said. "You need me. Also, if I go off by myself and these guys find me, I wouldn't have any idea what to do."

Well, shit. That was true, though I doubted it was worth putting her at risk by staying with me. But she'd said it with enough conviction to put Adam Schiff behind bars for life, so it wasn't likely I'd get her on a plane to Maui.

"Still no," I said, giving it one last try.

"Still *yes*. Unless I'm actually a problem for you with your wife and you're trying to get rid of me without saying so. Is that it?"

I reached out and took her hand. "No. Not at all. You *really* need to have a talk with Harper."

"Well, then. You're stuck with me."

"Nope."

"Yep." Ella's eyes bored into mine like trenching tools. I didn't know she had that in her. Psych majors might be dangerous. Then she switched gears and gave me a sunny smile. "You look good in that beard. It suits you."

"Thanks. The sonofabitchin' thing is hot, though."

She laughed.

Apparently we were done with the no-yes routine so it looked as if I had a girl in tow for a while.

I pulled into the parking lot of a feed store that sold ranch supplies. I turned off the engine, fired up my burner and dialed Ma, put the phone on speaker. Traffic on 395 whisked by not thirty yards to the east of us.

Ma picked up, so I said, "Hiya, Ma."

"You're a shithead."

Ella lifted her eyebrows and gave me an uneasy look.

"Yes, I am, Ma. You nailed it."

"The FBI was in my office wanting to know where you are."

"So I heard. Am I fired?" I winked at Ella.

"What do you think? Of *course* you are. I've had my everlovin' *fill* of this shit, boyo. They've probably got eyes on my office, waiting for you to walk in the door. We'll probably have to go code red on new burners soon, like in the next flippin' hour."

"Probably right, Ma, which sounds like I'm not fired yet, but hold that thought. I've got another task for you." I glanced at Ella. "What's your cell number?"

She gave it to me and I repeated it to Ma.

"What'll I do with that?" Ma asked.

I told her about the older woman who'd dictated the note to Ella and started this train wreck. She would know who killed Ridel and why. If Ma's hacker could backtrace the call we might get this resolved in the next day or two and we could have the sniper cooling his heels in a cell on Parr Boulevard and the FBI could go back to D.C. and we could all get drinks. Whoever the woman was, she was in this thing up to her neck. I wanted a name, location, her weight, birth sign, color of her hair . . .

"Mort?" Ma said.

"What?"

"Quit talkin'. When did this call come in?"

I looked at Ella. She leaned closer to the phone and said, "About an hour before I took the note to that bar."

"Is this Ella?" Ma asked.

"Um, yes."

"You have a nice voice. I'm sorry you got tangled up with Mort."

"Hey!" I fake-yelped, giving Ella a crooked grin.

"Not talkin' to you, Mort. How did the woman sound, Ella?"

"Well, older, like in her sixties. I thought she might be a smoker. Her voice was sort of gruff. Not a man's voice, but not very feminine either."

"Are you sure it was a woman?"

"Pretty sure, yeah."

"Did you hear anything in the background?"

"Not . . . really. I mean, I didn't notice anything."

"Okay, then. Mort?"

"I'm here."

"I'll get back to you. Be nice to her, boyo, or this time you're fired for sure." She ended the call and I took us back onto South Virginia, still headed south.

Ella gave me a look. "She would fire you?"

"She's a kidder. I get fired at least six times a year. It's a thing with us. So, back to you and me. Staying with me is a bad idea." Thought I'd give it one last try.

"You should shut up . . . *Arnold*."

I stared at her. *Shut up*? "You and Harper would get along great."

"I still want to know who Arnold Mercer is supposed to be, since he's not you."

"He's my doppelganger."

"Yeah, everyone's got one of those."

"Uh-huh. Yours is Amber." I turned off the four-lane into the parking lot of J&L Trailers in a truck with dealer plates taped to its back window, good for thirty days.

•   •   •

J and L Trailer and RV Sales was on a hardpacked dirt lot surrounded by unhappy-looking elms with leaves made dusty from passing vehicles. Reno had half a dozen places that sold RVs. J&L was on the low end of the bunch.

Ella and I got out and I settled into the wheelchair. I looked around. Sixty or eighty trailers and RVs of various sizes and vintages were parked cheek by jowl on both sides of the lot paralleling Virginia Street, leaving barely enough room for a sales shack on the west side.

Ella started to wheel me into the lot. "You're really gonna buy a trailer, Mort?" she said quietly.

"The name's Arnold, sweetheart, and, yes, I've decided

to buy a trailer."

"Why?"

"To stay off grid." I didn't have a chance to explain in detail because Phil's sales-clone came over at a good clip. He was pudgier than Phil, three inches taller, but he had the same hopeful expression on his face.

"Don't forget you're my wife," I said to Ella.

She leaned down and kissed me. "I'm Amber Mercer. How could I forget a thing like that?"

I smiled, then the salesman arrived. "How're you folks doin'? I'm Brad. Be glad to show you around."

"I'm Arnold. Call me Arnie. This's Amber. Phil at the Chevy dealership sent us over, said you'd give us a fifty-percent discount on anything on the lot."

Brad chuckled. "That Phil."

As if Brad had any idea who Phil was.

I said, "We're looking for a decent kick-around travel trailer. New or newish. I don't want to buy someone else's problem."

"Right this way, folks." He led us over to a thirty-two-foot Jayco trailer. New, but not what I was looking for.

"Much too big," I said. "I don't want a McMansion on wheels. Let's see something closer to half that size."

His face fell, but it only lasted a millisecond before the smile was back in place. He backed away from the trailer to peer down the row. "Got a real nice one right over here." He led the way. "Only a year old, clean as a whistle."

It was a Forest River R-POD, 20 feet long. The tires looked almost new.

"That's more like it," I said. "Let's have a look inside."

"You okay to . . . to get out of that chair?"

I stood up, hunched over. "I can walk some. Enough. But I'm done with motorcycles."

He gave an uncertain chuckle at that as he opened the door. The windows were open but it was still an oven in there. Nevada in August. But the interior was clean and the layout was about what I was looking for. Shower, toilet, sink in the bathroom, kitchen with sink, stove, microwave, small dining area, a bed at the far end. Even a TV, which might be useful for keeping one step ahead of the FBI.

"Know how many miles are on this rig?" I asked Brad.

"That I do, Arnie. It's got a hubodometer, installed by the dealer in Grand Rapids. A couple in their forties sold it to us. Real nice folks. The hubodometer is on their sales slip. I'll go have a look." He went outside, came back after a minute and said, "seven thousand one-forty-four."

I sat at the dinette while "Amber" opened and closed drawers. "Not much wear on this little beauty," Brad said, as if I couldn't figure that out for myself.

Salesmen all sound the same. I couldn't do his job.

"It's got air-conditioning and heat," Brad said. "We checked it out before taking it in trade. It hasn't been on the lot two weeks yet."

"What do you think?" I asked my brand-new wife.

She looked inside the refrigerator, ran fingertips over kitchen fixtures, had a peek in the bathroom, then sat on a raised queen-sized bed in front with storage under the bed and smiled at me. "I like it. Can we afford it, honey?"

"Can we?" I asked Brad, giving Ella a look.

He took a notebook out of a pocket, flipped through a few pages, and said, "This little beauty's a hell of a deal. Only $27,650."

"What kind of a warranty comes with it?"

"Eighteen months parts and labor, if you don't drive it off a cliff." He laughed. Salesman humor is like IRS humor. It doesn't grow on you.

"Make it twenty-six even. Cash."

His lips puckered and his eyes pinballed for a second. "You say cash?"

"Right now. With a full propane tank and fresh water, I'll hook it up and drive it off the lot."

"Don't think I can go lower than twenty-seven, Arnie."

"Twenty-six. Last offer."

He thought about that, then gave a little sigh, which was pure theater. "You drive a hard bargain, but you got yourself a deal."

Hard bargain, right. I could've had it for twenty-five, but only after a round-robin of tortured bargaining for the next half hour. So it cost a grand to save some haggling, but when Lucy died two years ago, she left me with fifteen million dollars. Harper and I talked it over and we gave ten million away to no-kill animal shelters and charities that use the money wisely, all in the name of Lucy Angel, which had a nice ring to it. We kept five million for contingencies. If you can't have a good life with five million, you're doing something wrong. Billionaires buy islands and Gulfstreams and twelve-bedroom mansions in half a dozen states and countries, but they're no happier than the rest of us, only richer. It must suck to be tripping over bodyguards 24/7.

I turned north off the lot with a cozy R-POD behind us at 3:45. A dealer plate was taped to its back window that matched the one on the truck. I still had $8,500 in cash on hand from the $50,000, and another $3,000 I'd retrieved from my backpack before Vale took it.

Ella turned toward me. "So we're off grid now ... Arnie?" The trailer was also sold to Arnold Mercer. When this was over, Arnold could sell it to Mortimer Angel, resell it, or donate it to someone who really needed it. I thought the latter was the most probable of the three, but if Harper wanted it, we would keep it.

"Yup. Call me Mort, unless we get pulled over. Off grid in this case means we're mobile and we don't have to get motel rooms which tend to require IDs. It'll be easier to keep out of sight this way."

"You said motel rooms. That's plural."

"It is indeed."

She smiled. "But we've only got one trailer."

"It's hard to pull two of these behind one truck, and what's your point, lady?"

"It was just an observation. Anyway, you're driving. Where to now?"

"Walmart. Let's replace the bedding back there, and stock up on food and other stuff. One-stop shopping."

I found us a Walmart and parked well away from the building. We went into the trailer to make a list of what we needed. My burner rang while we were still checking out the digs. It was Harper so I put the phone on speaker. "Are you alone?" I asked her.

"Yes, sort of. I'm at Meadowood Mall. No one's close by. Two FBI guys were waiting outside the house when I got home from school. So nice of them not to drag me out of the classroom in handcuffs. They wanted to know where you are. I told them I didn't know. They didn't like that, especially since I didn't go into a screaming panic when they told me your 4Runner had been burned in the desert. I told them I already knew that. We kind of went around and around for a while—I won't bore you with the details— but it could've given one of them time to plant a bug in the house, which is why I'm calling from the mall. Anyway, that was my day. How'd yours go, big guy?"

"Not bad." I sat at the dinette. "My wife and I bought a truck and a travel trailer this afternoon."

Ella stared at me in shock and Harper laughed. "You and Ella got hitched, huh?"

"No, but the trailer did."

That stopped all conversation for five seconds. Finally Harper sighed and said, "She's there, isn't she?"

"Yes."

"Put her on. And if the phone's on speaker, take it off. This's just between us womenfolk."

I'd listened to similar one-sided conversations before. I killed the speaker and handed the phone to Ella. Her side of the conversation went like this:

"Yes." pause "It was his idea." longer pause "Amber." pause "Thanks." pause "Mercer." She looked at me. "Uh-huh. It's small but actually pretty nice inside." Very long pause during which Ella looked at me a few times. "Wow. I mean, I don't get it, not really, but okay . . . if you say so."

Hearing that, I poked a cheek out with my tongue and lifted a bit of curtain to look outside. Walmart parking lot, beautiful. No SWAT team converging on us from the north at least. I wasn't sure about any other direction.

Finally Ella handed the phone back to me. "Nice chat, hon?" I said to Harper.

"Very nice. Now I'd like to hear why you had to do all that. I mean, I caught your act on TV—FBI Director Ridel dead—"

"Deputy director, sweetheart. He wasn't the top guy."

"My mistake. Ridel's a nobody. I don't even know why they give a hoot."

I smiled. "Did they say in the news how he died?"

"No, but on TV the FBI is like an ant hill that's been kicked. How *did* he die? And I'd like to know why someone would set fire to our car, dear heart."

"So would I." To end the Q & A, I told her everything— Ella going to the VOR, Ridel's body barely missing us as it slammed down, sniper bullets, trucks chasing us, our escape into the hills on the Raven, another guy shooting at us, the bullet hole I put in the windshield of the red truck, running out of gas and hiking in the dark, the cabin, the cot, Pete, washcloths, the single bed situation in which Ella and I ended up all but undressed—got a little squeak of shock from Ella—splitting wood that morning, the drive to Fallon, enchiladas, the red pickup in Fallon with its bullet hole, Vale, Arnold Mercer and the new old truck and the almost-new trailer. Whew.

Harper sighed. "That sounds just like you, Mort."

"Does, doesn't it?

"So what're you gonna do now? I mean, you've got a truck and trailer. Where to?"

"Lovelock."

Five seconds of silence. Then: "That's where that Ridel guy came down."

"Not exactly. He landed twenty miles east of Lovelock. As the crow flies."

"It still sounds dangerous, Mort. Going back there."

"I'll try to minimize that, but we—Ella and I—wouldn't learn much in Muncie, Indiana, so we'll try Lovelock first."

Ella gave me a strange look, then rolled her eyes.

"Muncie," Harper said. "You should go there, give the place a good going-over." She sighed. "You make jokes, but I know you're gonna go to Lovelock, so how about Vale goes up there, too? Not to be seen with you, but to snoop around in places you probably can't and maybe to sort of watch your back, yours and Ella's."

"Not a bad idea, hon. Can you call her, get her going on that? We need to get a move on here."

"Okay. Where're you gonna stay in Lovelock?"

"Don't know yet, but the summer season's winding down so there should be an RV park with vacancies."

"Let me know when you find a place."

"Okay, but the main reason I wanted to call you is, we don't know what's going on or why these guys are still after us now that Ridel's out of the picture, so I want you to stay with Ma until this gets resolved."

"Stay with, as in live with?"

"That's right."

"Isn't that a little extreme?"

I closed my eyes. "I lost Jeri, then I lost Lucy. I am *not* going to lose you, sweetheart. I want you safe and as far away from this as possible."

Silence. Then, "How about I don't lose *you*?"

"I'll be careful. You'll be okay at school, but stick with Ma the rest of the time, not at our house. That'll also keep the FBI out of your hair. Keep your eyes open *and* have a gun with you at all times when you're not at school."

Harper had a compact 9mm Glock 19 and a concealed carry permit. It didn't allow her to carry on school grounds or in federal buildings, but she could go armed pretty much everywhere else.

She let out an unhappy sigh. "Okay," she said. "I'll stay with Ma. What're you doing now?"

"About to shop at Walmart. Gotta stock the trailer."

"Okay. I'll call Vale. Be safe Mort. And keep Ella safe too."

She ended the call.

"She's incredible," Ella said. "I about *died* when you told her we were almost naked in bed last night. I don't know *anyone* who would accept that, but on the phone just now she said that whatever happens, not to worry about it. She even mentioned Vale last year and Dani two years ago and how they had no effect at all on your marriage."

I smiled. "Jealousy isn't Harper's thing."

"Yeah, I *guess*. It's still hard to believe." Ella gave me a tentative look, then said, "Harper also . . ."

Uh-oh. "What?"

"Well, she mentioned a woman named Andie you met while hiking in Arizona a year and a half ago."

"Uh-huh." I waited for the rest of it.

"She said you and Andie, well, you know, it wasn't *sex*,

really, but . . ." She let the comment hang.

"I remember."

She smiled. "I'd be very surprised if you didn't. I got the impression Harper told me about you and Andie as a way of telling me she *really* isn't the jealous type."

"She's not."

"Anyway, she said Andie was a very lucky lady to have run into you out there in the wilds. But what I find even more fascinating is that you told Harper what happened. You certainly didn't *have* to."

"I don't keep anything from Harper. You two need to meet, face to face. Then you'll understand her."

"I'd like that. She must be really something. But let's get back to what she said about it being hazardous for us to go to Lovelock, so close to where Mr. Ridel was killed."

"We'll try to limit that. Are you sure you want to get in the middle of this?"

"No, but *yes*. Stop asking me that. I'm already in."

"Okay, then. Let's shop."

• • •

We left the store at 5:20 with two shopping carts full of bedding, paper towels, plates, pots and pans, flatware, shampoo, body wash, food, skinny jeans and other clothing for Amber Mercer. She pushed me around the store in the wheelchair for much of it, but to hurry things along we split up for a while. Due to a bit of slippery misdirection at the checkout, she wasn't aware that I'd bought her a bra and a couple of T-shirts.

We were still in the trailer at Walmart after stashing stuff in cabinets and cupboards when Ella said, "Lovelock still sounds risky."

"It could be," I said as I pulled curtains tight across the windows to keep prying eyes out. "Which is why we'll be wearing disguises and why you are going to wear this." I pulled the bra out of a bag and tossed it to her.

Her eyes got wide. "This's *huge*. Your eyes must be seriously out of whack. I'm not . . . not that . . ."

"I know. And whoever is running this Ridel operation is likely to know what you look like, so when they see a six-foot somewhat top-heavy woman in her forties, it's much less likely that they'll see young, slender Ella Kassel."

"Top-heavy. That's great." She looked down at herself. "I couldn't possibly fit this bra under this shirt Vale got for me."

"Then it's a good thing I also bought these." I pulled out two men's large T-shirts and tossed them to her.

She held up one with *Arizona Cardinals* printed in red across the front. "You gotta be kidding."

"Would I? Put it on. And the bra."

She dangled the bra from a finger. "I couldn't, uh, fill this even a little bit. It won't look right at all."

"Stuff it with Kleenex?"

She puffed out a cheek. "Well, *that's* embarrassing. Especially after seeing Vale earlier today. She could wear this thing, no Kleenex needed."

"Get going. I'll turn my back."

I heard a box of tissues being opened, then rustling, more sounds I wasn't able to interpret, then low musical laughter. "You couldn't buy a *C*-cup, could you? You had to buy a D."

"Nope. Yup."

"I would need a *pillow* to fill this thing." More tissue got pulled out of the box. "This's . . . kinda nutty," she said. Finally: "You can turn around now. And if you laugh, I'll punch you right in the chops, mister."

"Wow, that'd hurt."

I turned. She was . . . statuesque. Or something. She would turn heads, but no one but her own mother would see Ella Kassel in that gray wig and subdued makeup in a rather full Diamondbacks shirt. Not the FBI, and especially not the guys who'd chased us. Which gave me a thought that hadn't occurred to me until then. Ella was told to deliver the note to Waley's Tavern soon after she got the call, so it was probable that someone watched her go into Waley's to make certain the note got delivered. If so, the observer would know she was . . . and right then another song popped into my head: *Long Tall Sally*. Little Richard, 1956. Heard it while I was on stakeout a few years ago.

"Rockin' song," I said out loud.

"Huh?"

"Nothing. You look, well . . . different."

"I'm sure. This feels *so* dumb. I can't look down and see my feet without bending over."

I gave her a little hug. "It's just cosmetic, it doesn't mean a thing except we're safer this way."

She looked into my eyes, then took a deep breath, let it out. "Okay, I guess. How about I take this bra off now and only wear it when we're, you know, in public?"

"Okay by me."

She didn't tell me to turn around. She reached back under the shirt, unhitched the bra, then did that Houdini-escape routine women do to remove a bra without taking the shirt off. The last move in that forty-eight-step puzzle is to haul the bra out a sleeve, but this time it came out with a snowdrift of tissue that fluttered and plopped to the floor.

"Well, shoot," she said. "*That's* awkward."

We were gathering up Kleenex when Harper called. "I talked to Vale," she said. "She'll be leaving Reno after a while. She said she'll stay away from you and keep her eyes open, but she'll be around if you need her."

"Thanks. And thanks for telling Ella about Andie."

Harper laughed. "You're welcome. You *are* gonna be in disguise in Lovelock, aren't you? I mean a really *good* one. Half the people in northern Nevada would recognize you now that your picture's all over the place again."

"I've got the gray-white Van Dyke you bought me last year, and the matching moustache, suspenders, a weight pack, outback trading hat, the works."

"I like the Van Dyke. It looks good on you. What about Ella? Her face has been on TV, too."

"She'll be in a gray wig, subdued makeup, black-frame glasses inside, dark glasses outside, and a ball cap. She looks in her forties if you don't get too close to her. Oh, and I bought her a bra."

"Really? I wouldn't trust you to do that."

Ella leaned closer to the phone. "You shouldn't. You should see what he bought me. It's freaking huge."

"You bought her a G-cup, big guy?"

"It's only a D, darlin'," I said.

She laughed quietly. "Only a D? I'm shocked."

Ella smiled and looked away.

"Yup," I said. "We better get goin', babe. It's almost a hundred miles to Lovelock and I want to scope the place out pretty good before it gets dark."

"Okay, go. Have fun, Mort." She ended the call.

Ella looked at me. "Have fun?"

I opened the door to leave. "A generic expression she uses a lot. Okay, toots, let's get this show on the road."

"*Toots*?"

"Bring the bra. You'll have to have it on by the time we get to Lovelock. Bring all that Kleenex too."

"Toots? Really? You called me *Toots*?"

"A term used by only the very best PIs. Bring the bra, precious."

She rolled her eyes, then smiled. "You want me to put it on in the truck with you right there beside me?"

"That's nothing. You should hear what Vale had to do while I was driving. That didn't make it into her book."

"Really? What did she do?"

"Maybe later. Anyway, your other option is to put the bra on now and leave it on."

"*That's* not happening. It's not very comfortable."

"Leave the shirt on and put the bra on by reversing the steps you used just now to take it off. Easy peasy."

"I've never seen anyone do that. Ever. I don't think I could, or if it's even possible."

"Try. Practice on the way to Lovelock, kiddo. Get good at it and you could be on *America's Got Talent*."

"Okay, *now* I understand."

"What?"

"Why your boss fires you. I just don't know why she hires you back."

Chapter Seven

We were on I-80 twenty miles north of Fernley in hot dry country, forty miles from Lovelock. I wore a Van Dyke beard and moustache, an outback hat, glasses with heavy black frames. This would be my public persona the entire time we were in Lovelock. Ella was putting polish on her fingernails in a sedate shade of rose. She had the window down an inch on her side to draw out the fumes.

She held up a hand and checked her nails. "My mom would wear this."

"Good. I wouldn't want anyone to think I'm a cradle robber."

She snorted. "Cradle robber."

"I can't look younger so you have to look older. This is not rocket science."

"I'll say." She started in on her other hand. "You're good at this. You've used other aliases, haven't you?"

"Occasionally. When I've been in sticky situations."

She thought about that for a while, then shrugged. "I guess unknown guys chasing us and shooting qualifies as a sticky situation."

"Yep." I thought for a moment. "I blame karma."

She stopped and stared at me. "Karma?"

"I think being on the run and in danger is payback for having been in the IRS for sixteen years. But this particular karma comes with an entertaining upside."

"Yeah? What's that?"

"I get tangled up with extremely good-looking girls."

She smiled. "Tangled?"

"Arms, legs. Also, a dearth of clothing seems to be part of it. Like last night."

"That part's okay, is it?"

"Yup. No complaints."

"Uh-huh. I'll bet." She inspected a hand. "I've always used clear polish. This rose is okay, but it isn't me."

"Which is what we want."

She propped a foot on the seat and started in on her toenails. "Amber Mercer," she said, brushing polish on a nail. "That's okay. Amber Angel would be good too."

Women lay traps. I kept my mouth shut.

•   •   •

Lovelock is a small town on I-80 with a population of just over eighteen hundred. Years ago, when I was still in grade school, the interstate went right through the middle of town, which slowed traffic to twenty-five miles an hour. Good for business, but not for folks in a rush to get back to Muncie, so now the interstate bypasses it and you can blow right on by unless you need gas or a Big Mac. There used to be a Chevron station with a sign out front that read *Two Stiffs Selling Gas*. No more. I liked it, but it must not have been PC. Not all change is good.

Six miles from Lovelock, Ella said, "Eyes front," then took off her shirt, no bra, and leaned forward a bit to put on the Kleenex-enhanced bra—which I thought would be useful if either of us had to blow a nose. As she was doing that, someone mentioned the fact that her breasts and my chest had been in quite close contact in Pete's cabin, so a visual of said breasts wouldn't necessarily be out of line. Not sure who said that, but I still have a bruise on my ribs where an elbow came whipping out of nowhere.

I get that a lot, not sure why.

I'll have to ask Harper.

We got off I-80 onto State Highway 396, which was also Cornell Avenue through Lovelock. At the north end of town it became Airport Road, which made finding the Lazy L RV Park somewhat harder than it should've been. We had a choice of the Lazy L, Candy Beach Campground, or park at a curb on a side street and hope the police didn't hassle us, but Candy Beach didn't sound like my kind of place, so the Lazy L it was.

I pulled into the RV park. It had hookups for thirty-six

trailers or RVs but only nine were in the place when we got there. I chose a quiet spot away from the others, unhitched the truck and stabilized the trailer on leveling jacks. As I did that, the RV park's owner, Ralph Poda, hooked us up to the utilities. Fifty-five bucks a night.

Ralph gave Ella a final appreciative look, then said, "If y'all need anything just call or ring the bell at the office. You got my number." He headed back to a double-wide trailer that served as the office. The time was 7:35. We had a good hour of daylight left.

Ella and I went into the trailer just as my burner rang. Harper, as I'd expected.

"What's up, babe?" I knocked the air-conditioning fan down to its lowest setting to dull the roar. Good unit. The inside temperature was already down fifteen degrees from its initial ninety-four.

"Vale had more to do than she thought. She left Reno twenty minutes ago. She's in a Sedona Kia van from Hertz. Dark blue. Are you in Lovelock now? You should be."

"Yep. We're at the Lazy L RV Park. Google it."

"I will. Vale managed to reserve a room at the Sage Inn and Casino using her Laura Valle ID. It's the best place in Lovelock. She said she got the last available room."

"I'm not surprised. By now, Lovelock probably has five times as many FBI agents as the investigation warrants. The rest will stare at the sky where Ridel came down and take selfies with the VOR in the background. But it's past quitting time now, so the bar will be packed with them."

"So keep away from it. Are you and Ella all settled in there at the Lazy L?"

"Yup. It's dusty here, got scraggly elms, still hot, but we've got air, hot water on demand, and a refrigerator making ice cubes as we speak."

"Cool. I've got my own bedroom at Ma's house on the third floor with two dormers that look out on Arlington Avenue. Did you know the kitchen has three refrigerators, one for each lady living here?"

"No, but I'm not surprised." For years, Ma had shared a big three-story Victorian house with two other women: a widowed older sister, Agnes Villars, and Colleen Pesarik, a political science professor at the university.

"I really miss you," Harper said, "But I'll be okay here. Anyway, what's the plan? Or do you have one?"

"Nothing yet. Just nose around and get used to the town, see if I can find out what the locals are saying about Ridel falling from a plane, or if they even know. I'll try to find out what the feds are doing, get an idea of how the investigation is going. We'll also keep an eye out for a red truck with a bullet hole in its windshield. And I might send you a picture of Ella. She's wearing that bra under what has become a pretty damn tight T-shirt, and—*ouch!*"

Harper laughed. "Give her the phone, Mort."

I did, then went outside to check the hubodometer, see if it appeared to be working. It read 7,262. I did the math and decided it was right on target. I circled the trailer to give the girls more time, which tends to calm the water. I checked power and water hookups and the leveling jacks, took a brief tour of the RV park, then went back inside.

"He's here now," Ella said. She handed me the phone.

I held it to my ear and said, "Yup."

"She sounds nice, Mort. But I don't like you being up there so close to where that Fibbie director guy died."

"I'll be careful."

"You better. If you go out, wear your belly fat thingie."

"Ugh."

"Do it or I'll come up there and whack you one."

"Yeah, okay. I'll send a picture."

"Do that. And put on the Van Dyke."

"Got it on now. Even you wouldn't recognize me."

"Hah."

We ended the call.

Ella stood up and gave me both side views of herself. "Does this, I mean *these*, even look real? It doesn't feel like it." She had on a Walmart T-shirt, new, pink, with a cat on the front. It was stretched tight. In the spirit of being less recognizable she'd bought one a size larger than she would have before this circus got going, but one size wasn't quite enough. I probably should've told her about the bra before she bought more shirts.

"Real enough. Probably feels worse than it looks."

"Great." She didn't sound great.

"You oughta see what I'm going to wear. Then you can quit complaining."

"Oh? What?"

I sorted through the disguise kit Vale brought to La Fiesta and pulled out an inflatable plastic tire-like thing. I blew it up to about three-quarters full then stepped into it and pulled it up to my waist, adjusted it while Ella stared at me with a growing smile of comprehension, then I put on a short-sleeve white shirt and buttoned it up the front. The result was that I now weighed nearly 300 pounds with a good-sized jelly roll around my middle.

I heard a melodic giggle. Not mine.

I jammed the outback hat on over a longish gray-white wig, put on the black-frame glasses, then turned and faced Ella. "How's this?"

"Really? I have to be seen with you looking like that?"

"What? You're *still* complaining."

"Not really. Not with you in that girl's inner tube."

"Girl's?"

"It's *pink*, Mort. With yellow polka dots."

"I hadn't noticed. It doesn't show through the shirt, does it? That'd ruin the effect."

"No."

"So what's the problem?"

"No problem, other than you being colorblind. Harper lets you wear that thing?"

"She bought it for me."

Ella laughed. "Anyway, if you like it, I totally love it. I want a picture of you in it."

"Harper gets one. You don't."

"Hah."

I topped her gray wig with the Coors ball cap and took her picture then she took one of me. I sent them to Harper. Then Arnold and Amber Mercer, a couple in their forties and fifties, got out of there, but not before Amber sent the picture of me to her own cell phone.

I have doubts about this digital age.

•   •   •

The sun was behind the western hills but it was still light out so I drove around, kept an eye out for that bullet-hole truck, came across the Blackrock Grill so we went in and had a decent meal as the light outside faded to black. Back in the truck I came across a Safeway so we went in and bought perishable food for the fridge. I spotted a stand of canes by the customer service area and ended up with a heavy black gnarled cane with an L-shaped head.

"Oh, jeez. I'm married to an old guy who uses a cane?" Ella said.

"Not old, sweetheart, just older. But you're a treasure for sticking with me. You can carry the heavy stuff back to the truck."

"Sweetheart, my ass."

Nope. Didn't touch that one. Nice cane, though. Thing was solid hickory. I wished it concealed a three-foot sword, but when I asked at the service counter the girl there said, straight-faced, that they wouldn't get another shipment of those in until next week.

Strange kid.

•   •   •

We loaded the refrigerator with milk, eggs, bacon, cheese, yogurt, salad fixings, cottage cheese, beer, other stuff, then got back in the F-250 and headed south in the dark, drove past four motels, six bars with neon glowing in the windows, all the typical places one finds in small, fairly isolated towns. The nearest Costco was almost a hundred miles away.

The Sage Inn and Casino was the biggest motel in town, two stories, brightly lit with floodlights. A video sign out front showed rolling dice that came up winner seven, a spinning roulette wheel, and a video poker slot machine that stopped on four kings.

I pulled into the parking lot. It was full of black Crown Vics and Suburbans that looked and smelled federal, two forensic vans, vehicles that might hold a SWAT team—God only knows why since Ridel was dead—and a white stretch limo with Nevada plates. I wondered who rated the limo.

I cruised the lot slowly. A three-ring circus had come

to Lovelock. It didn't take long to find Vale's Kia Sedona parked in the midst of it all.

"Vale's here," I said to Ella.

"We're not gonna go in there, are we?"

"Don't know yet." I pulled out my burner and called Vale, put the phone on speaker.

"This is Laura," she answered cautiously, using the name on her current fake ID. I figured she would be in a platinum-blond wig, Skeleteen hippie glasses with gold wire rims and round, rose-tinted lenses, full makeup, hoop earrings, and possibly some sort of a funky hat. She would look good, but not like Valentina Marchant.

"It's Arnold." She would know my voice.

"Always nice to hear from you, Arnold, but I'm kinda busy right now."

"Where are you? Can't talk, can you?"

"In the bar at the Sage, and not really."

"Hearing anything?"

"Not much. Yet."

"We're at the Lazy L RV Park in a white twenty-foot R-POD trailer with blue striping, pretty much off by itself."

"Got it. Nice talkin' to you. Bye."

I folded the burner, stuck it in a pocket.

"Wow," Ella said. "That was . . . kinda cool. I bet some guy is buying her drinks."

"Hopefully a fed with a tongue going loose."

She looked out at the night for a moment, not really seeing it, then she turned toward me. "You know, two days ago I was just a grad student, then I got that phone call and suddenly I'm mixed up in . . . I don't know what, exactly."

"Neither do I, kiddo."

"Do you ever call your wife kiddo?"

"Sometimes. Does the word bother you?"

"Well, not really. It just seems like right now, doing what we're doing, I'm more than just a kiddo."

"Toots is better?"

She smiled. "Actually, I like that one. It fits the way we look. Sort of rustic noir."

"My kind of broad."

She let out a peal of laughter.

• • •

Later, while we were cruising the town, I pulled into the Super 10 motel and came across a battle-scarred blue Ford F450 stake truck with a back bed enclosed by old wooden side boards.

Huh.

It looked like the second truck that chased us across the flats and up into the Stillwater Range. I'd seen the red truck up there, hunting us, but not this one. I wondered if it had really been after us, or if the guy was just blowing across the hardpan thinking he was Craig Breedlove in the Spirit of America at Bonneville?

But this truck being here was too big a coincidence to ignore, so I stopped, opened the door, got one foot outside.

"What're you doing?" Ella asked nervously.

"Getting the license and VIN of the blue truck here." I explained why, got a piece of paper and a stub of pencil that had come with the truck, no charge, then said, "Keep an eye out, toots. Yell if you see someone headed our way."

She laughed, but it sounded forced. She wasn't used to sneaking around like this. Psychologists sneak, but they do it differently, crawling around inside people's heads.

I shined my cell phone's flashlight on the VIN through the windshield and on the rear plate, wrote the numbers down, then got back in the truck and took off.

"Now what?" Ella asked.

"Now, Ma." I parked on the street and called Maude. She was at home, not in the office, but she had ways of getting information twenty-four-seven, even on the road. I put the phone on speaker to keep Ella in the loop so she wouldn't forget what we were doing. Anytime she wanted to bail out, I would put her on a cruise ship to Pago Pago.

"What?" Ma answered.

"Got a plate and VIN for you. Need a name."

"Read 'em off."

I did, then said. "Anything yet on that truck with the bullet hole?"

"You'd know if I did, boyo." She disconnected.

"Boyo?" Ella said.

"It's like toots but not as cool. 'Toots' is the bomb."

She rolled her eyes. "What will you do if you get the guy's name?"

"Keep it in mind. Wing it as needed."

"Yeah, that sounds professional."

"It really does, doesn't it?"

Got another eye roll.

I went through the Super 10 lot again to see if I had missed the red truck. I saw more federal government cars that would belong to low men on the totem pole who didn't rate rooms at the Sage, but no red truck. I took us around to all the other motels one more time: Surestay, Royal Inn, Cadillac Inn, found a few more Crown Vics but still no red truck. I'd seen it in Fallon, but not here. Were these guys federal, or locals hired by feds? Or neither? No idea, but they'd fired bullets at us. That meant something.

I was cruising a back street when my burner rang. It was Ma again.

"Yup," I answered, pulling to a curb.

"Guy who owns the truck you just asked me about is Vince Dolak. Five-ten, hundred sixty-five pounds, got an address in Reno so he's a homegrown shithead. He had a couple of DUIs three and four years ago, and an arrest for a bar fight, no charges filed, that's all. I'll send you a DMV photo. Not thinking about going after this guy, are you?"

"No idea. At least not yet. But he sounds like the kind of guy who would be in on this, and his truck matches one that might've chased us into the hills not long after Ridel almost landed on us. He could be the guy who was firing at us from three miles out, but we've got no proof of that. He could also just be someone out running his truck through the desert at the wrong time, wrong place. He might not be involved at all."

"Watch out for this dimwit anyway. I'll let Vale know. Where's the truck at?"

"Super 10 motel. I might try to get a room number. I wouldn't tell Vale, though. I don't want her to try to get a look at this cretin."

"Watch yourself, okay?"

"Got me a black belt, Ma. And a gun."

"Either of which could cause you to do something for

which I wouldn't post bail. I wouldn't trust either one."

Then she was gone.

"You have a black belt?" Ella said.

"Judo. Workin' on my second degree. Which means I know just enough to get myself in trouble."

In fact, it was somewhat better than that. My teacher, a black guy, ninth-degree black belt named Rufus Booth, had taught me a number of useful "back-alley" moves not allowed in competition that would end a confrontation and ensure that it wouldn't flare up again anytime soon. I had used one of those moves against a lowlife named Ramon Surry several years ago when he tried to stick a knife in me. He ended up in a cast that enclosed his entire right shoulder and arm. But he didn't take the hint so eventually I had to kill him with a big-ass rock.

Rufus wasn't impressed by my knife-countering move against with Surry—except, in fact, he was, but he didn't want to come out and say it. His mantra is, "Avoid trouble; run if you can." That didn't have a lot to say about trouble hunting you and what to do if it caught up, but there was another obscure saying by Edward Noyes Westcott that went like this: "Do unto the other feller the way he'd like to do unto you, an' do it fust."

Not sure about that "fust," but I got the gist.

I glanced at the digital clock on the dashboard. 9:55. What to do? I had Vince Dolak's name but not his room number. I might be able to ask at the desk and get it, but that could alert him to the fact that someone was looking for him.

Probably not worth the risk. And what would I do with his room number anyway? Kick the door in at three in the morning and try to drag him out into the night?

Nope. He might not be involved in this at all. I could just see myself hauling an innocent guy out of his room in the wee hours and end up facing an assault charge.

It might be time to call it a night and find some booze. I might also be able to get some investigative mileage out of that. Vince's truck was at the Super 10, so he would be asleep or on foot. On foot, he might've walked to a bar for a couple of beers. I cruised the immediate neighborhood and found the bar nearest the motel: Whiskey River Saloon.

Go in and have a look around? Thanks to Ma, Vince's picture was on my cell phone. I might get a look at him.

I parked a block from the bar, around a corner. I took another look at Ella, decided no one would recognize her in that getup. I doubted that anyone would recognize me.

She gave me a wary look. "What're you thinking?"

"Vince might be in there. How's 'bout a drink, sugar."

"You thinkin' of getting me drunk, mister?"

"That's not what I said."

Her voice got serious. "Is it safe?"

"I think so. Enough, anyway. The thing is, life is full of risk. We could leave, go back to Reno, but that'd be a risk too. Best bet is to hop a cruise ship to Fiji, hope this thing dies down and doesn't reignite when we get back."

"You and me? To Fiji? Okay."

"*All* of us. Harper, Ma, Vale, you, me."

"That would be the smart thing to do, wouldn't it?"

"Yup. Get out of Dodge."

She gave me a long look then shook her head. "Smart, but you aren't gonna do that, are you?"

"Every time guys shoot at me I get this testosterone problem."

"Which *I'm* not going to fix, and that sounded like a no, so I guess we're going in."

"*I* am, anyway." Thought I'd see how that went over.

"Yeah, like I'll sit out here in the truck while you have a beer and play Mike Freakin' Hammer in the bar. Anyway, you won't stand out as much if I go in with you."

I stared at her. Mike Hammer? No. She didn't really conjure up Hammer, did she? That was *my* thing, not that I had any control over it.

"What?" Ella asked when I didn't respond.

"Nothing." I opened the door and looked back at her. "C'mon. I'll buy you two or three double bourbons."

"Really? You think getting me drunk will work?"

"Work how?"

She smiled, didn't answer. But we were circling this bear, poking it with a mighty short stick.

• • •

The bar was dim inside, lit mostly by beer signs and the lighting in the well behind the bar, but a few overhead lights set on dim made it possible to navigate without bumping into things. *The Whiskey Ain't Workin'* by Travis Tritt was playing over speakers in the ceiling. My Van Dyke and long gray hair was perfect in there.

"Honky-tonk angel," I said to Ella, bumping her with a hip. She bumped me back. My cane thumped on the floor as we made our way through the saloon. Two couples were at tables, half a dozen men scattered around.

Vince Dolak was on a stool at the bar beside either a federal agent or a lost history professor—the wrinkled suit and loose tie around his neck belonged to one or the other.

I wondered if the FBI even knew that others had been out at the VOR with me and Ella. Maybe. At some point the tire tracks of the red or blue trucks might've crossed over the tracks my dirt bike had made. The FBI wouldn't miss that. It would tell a story, incomplete and ambiguous, but a story all the same. The FBI might be looking for the person or persons who had made those tracks. If so, the guy beside this agent was very likely someone the FBI was looking for, which might be why Vince was sitting there talking with him. The FBI guy would certainly be looking for Ella and me, which meant he was now surrounded by people he was trying to find. How cool was that? Less cool, however, was that Vince Dolak might also be looking for Ella and me. In fact, he worried me more than the FBI.

Our disguises had better hold up.

Vince was as Ma described him, and he looked more or less like his DMV picture: shaggy black hair almost to his shoulders, a four-day beard, small eyes that tracked me in the mirror as we passed behind him. Maybe not me. He might have been tracking Ella, the way she was filling out her T-shirt with enough Kleenex to last half a year. If so, he wouldn't be seeing Ella Kassel.

I sat at a barstool, leaving an empty stool between me and Vince, put Ella on my other side out of his reach but not out of his sight in the mirror. I ordered a Bud Light for myself and a gin and tonic with extra lime for Ella, and we tried to hear what Dolak and the fed were saying. Tritt was still up in the rafters making it hard to hear anything, but during a ten-second lull between Travis and Kenny Rogers I got this:

Vince: ". . . wouldn't be easy."

Fed: "Not that hard. The guy was loaded with GHB."

Vince: "What the hell's that?"

Fed: "It's a date—" then Kenny drowned him out with *The Gambler*.

GHB. Date rape or "club" drug. I connected the dots. Ridel had been dumped from the plane at three thousand feet, alive but unconscious, which figured. Even with his hands tied, Ridel might've been a handful if he were still kicking. If the plane had autopilot, the pilot might be able to handle a conscious Ridel by himself. If not, two people would've been needed. But having been given GHB, Ridel never knew what hit him—which, upon landing, was the Nevada desert.

I oughta slap myself.

Ella and I sat there for another twenty minutes, didn't catch anything useful, and I started to get nervous, giving Dolak too long a look at us, mostly at Ella.

I left a five and a ten on the bar, grabbed my cane, and we strolled out the door. Ella shivered in the cool night air and hauled my arm around her waist as we walked back to the truck.

What to do about Vince, if anything? I gave it some thought, decided any sort of direct confrontation was out of the question. I had no proof he was hunting Ella and me. What would I do with him if I caught him and hogtied him? Beat a confession out of him, find out why I'd been sent to the VOR station, then have him report back to the person who had set this up? That would cause nothing but trouble—I could go fishing for trout and catch an alligator. But it might be worth tracking this guy, so I took us back to the trailer, got a GPS tracker from my go-bag, drove us to the Super 10 and installed the tracker out of sight under the rear bumper of Vince's stake truck.

When I got back in the truck Ella said, "This's sort of creepy, Mort."

"Yup."

"Is *that* all you have to say?"

"I could write an entire book of creepy and dangerous and read it back to you. But we are in this and we don't know why we're in it, so we have to do what we have to do. But I'll put you on a cruise ship any time you want. All you have to do is say the word, toots."

"No. I don't want that." She sighed. "Anyway, if we're done with all of this for the night, how about we go back to the trailer so I can take a shower and, I don't know, veg out for a while? I feel grungy, and you split and stacked all that wood so you're a little bit funky."

"A little funk bothers you? I'm sorry I married you."

She smiled. "Yeah, me too. I didn't even get a ring."

Chapter Eight

Best thing I bought at the Safeway earlier that evening was a paperback by John Lescroart: *The Missing Piece*. I sat at the dinette while Ella got wet in the shower and sang "I'm gonna wash that man right outta my hair," seven feet away. Nice voice, interesting song. We had both removed disguise paraphernalia and looked like ourselves again.

I got to page ten by the time she came out wrapped in a towel and . . . and that was all. Did I mention that she was six-one? The towels we bought at Walmart were four feet in one dimension and two in the other. She'd wrapped it around herself in a kind of spiral since nothing else had any hope of covering all the bases. I blame her for that. She should've looked for beach towels but hadn't thought that far ahead. Maybe. It was possible she'd thought very far ahead, which didn't bother me one bit, but I was glad I'd pulled the curtains across the windows.

"Wow," I said. "Look at you."

"What *about* me? After everything Harper told me, and after sleeping together the way we did in that little bed in the cabin, we're going to be shy and weird around each other in this trailer? Seriously?"

"I guess not. Especially not weird since I don't know how to do that. And, hey, what'd you pick up to read at the Safeway? The novel I got is pretty good."

"Terrific segue." She held up *The Inmate* by Freida McFadden and said, "I got a psychological thriller, and in case you didn't know, you're still stinky. The water's hot. How about you get wet and clean?"

Which I did. Not much room in there and I had to crouch to fit under the shower head, but the water was hot like she'd said and there was plenty of it, so I burned some propane heating it and got clean. I put on briefs, wrapped the last towel around myself, and came out.

Ella was sitting at the dinette. She whistled ironically and stuck her nose back in her book. She looked very good, spiral-wrapped in a towel. I could yank one end of it and spin her like a top.

A travel alarm on a countertop read 11:08. I stifled a yawn and gave the bed a glance. Which didn't get past her.

"Which side do you want?" she asked, standing up and setting her book on the table.

"The one closest to the door and my gun. I don't want to have to shoot past you if someone barges in on us. They teach that at the better home-defense classes."

"You're going to keep your gun by the bed? Really?"

"We don't know what's goin' on, cupcake."

She was silent for a moment. "I guess it's not a bad idea, considering. Just don't shoot me if I get out of bed in the middle of the night."

"I almost never do that."

• • •

She got beneath the sheets, appeared to struggle for a moment, then produced the towel she'd been wearing and held it out to me. "Could you put this someplace where it'll dry?"

Right then, Spade and Hammer appeared up by the ceiling above the bed, grinning, snorting, winking at me.

"Mort?" Ella said, still holding the towel.

"Yeah, okay." I took it from her, draped it over the back of a dinette chair. I stood there trying to guess what she'd been wearing under the towel, panties or nothing at all, but it came out fifty-fifty.

I was about to flip a coin when she said, "You coming to bed?"

I rolled my eyes at myself. "Yup."

I turned out all the lights but one, dimmed the last one down to a twilight glow, then said the hell with it and slung my towel over the back of the other dinette chair to dry, then slipped beneath the covers.

We settled in without touching, didn't say anything for a while. I listened to the distant sound of traffic, of which there wasn't much this late at night. A loud engine wound up and faded into the distance. A dog barked. I heard faint music from somewhere. Ella moved closer, put an arm on my chest and pressed herself lightly against me.

"I hope this is okay," she said.

As an answer, I put an arm around her and pulled her in closer. This was like a slow dance.

I felt her body relax.

We stayed like that for half a minute, then she stirred. "Um, this is very nice, but I'd really like to say something, Mort. If that's okay."

"Fire away."

"But I don't know if I should."

"It's just us chickens in here, sunshine."

"It's, well, I don't like sleeping in clothes of any kind. I did last night, but . . ."

"But you don't usually," I said.

"No."

I slid a finger under a silky band of elastic at her waist which answered that question, pulled her panties down an inch, and left things like that. "I'll leave the rest up to you, lady."

She hesitated, then removed her panties and set them aside somewhere in the dark. She slipped a finger under the waistband of my Jockeys, eased them down an inch as I had done with hers. "If you want," she said.

So the slow dance continued and I got comfortable.

"Thank you," Ella said softly. "I wanted it to be like this that first night. Not to do anything more than this, but after what we'd been though . . . just to, well, be closer to you. Underwear felt artificial and sort of inhibited, as if we didn't trust each other or ourselves. Anyway, it just didn't feel right. And, of course, Pete was right there."

She looked at my face in the gloom. "You're okay with this, aren't you?"

"My neanderthal DNA is a lot more than okay, lady."

She smiled. "In that case, could you hold me like you did last night? If it wouldn't cause a problem."

"What kind of a problem?" I'm a shithead.

"Like—if it ended up giving me too much information. I mean, now that there's nothing between us."

"Would it matter . . . if?"

"Not to me."

So I pulled her partway on top of me. She snuggled in, got comfortable, put one leg over mine and an arm all the way across my chest.

"This's nice," she breathed in my ear.

We stayed like that for a while, but it had been a long day and we'd been up a long time. Her arm went slack and her breathing slowed and she fell asleep. I held her loosely, one hand on the small of her back, and smiled in the dark. She was a terrific girl.

Minutes later I was asleep.

• • •

I cracked an eyelid in the morning and saw the alarm clock. 5:15. Gray light was just starting to show beyond the curtains. I was on my left side and Ella was spooning me, breath warm against my neck, one arm around my waist, not unlike the way she had held onto me on the dirt bike. With everything that had happened the other day, I hadn't given the bike much thought. It was still up in the hills. It would've been a priority to retrieve it if my 4Runner hadn't been set on fire, but the feds had my name now so the bike could wait. No telling how many agents might still be combing the hills for clues, bodies, witnesses. I was on the run and so was Ella. Last place I would go right then was back into those hills. I could turn us into the FBI and end the running, but I wouldn't do that until I was certain the FBI itself wasn't responsible for Ridel's death.

I fell back asleep, warm and comfortable with Ella's breasts and belly pressing against my back.

• • •

I was whipping up scrambled eggs and bacon when a gentle tapping sounded at the door. I pulled a curtain back an inch and peeked out. Vale was there in a wig, makeup, and a retro wide-brim Panama hat. The time was 8:10 a.m.

I ushered her inside. Ella and I were fully dressed but not wearing wigs or other disguise elements.

"Not interrupting anything, am I?" Vale asked with a subtle gleam in her eye.

"Breakfast," I said. "If you want bacon and eggs it's eight ninety-five and tax. Pull up a seat. My name is Arnie and I'll be your waiter."

Vale looked at Ella. "You survived two days with this guy?"

"It feels like more."

"Keep it up, you two." Well, shit. I said it then parsed it in an entirely different way. I glanced at Vale. "Don't say it."

"Say what?" she said with sweet innocence.

"Nothing." I was about to say *What's up* then decided against that too. English is a minefield, nothing but double entendres.

Instead, I said, "Anything happen last night—?"

"You tell me, big guy," Vale said, still chipping away at me and Ella.

"—at the *Sage Inn,*" I went on, somewhat louder than before, pushing through the interruption. "It sounded like you were plying some guy with drinks while pretending to like him as you pumped him for information."

More flowery innocence. "You think I would do that?"

I looked at Ella. "You're a sweet kid. Do not pick up on this. I don't want you corrupted."

Ella shot a glance at the bed, which hadn't been made yet. "Yeah, I already got that."

Well, shit. I was outnumbered and outmaneuvered. "Is it just me or is there an estrogen fog in here screwing up communication?"

"It's just you," Vale said.

I gave her a pointed look. "Do you or do you not want bacon and eggs?"

"Do not. I've already eaten, thank you."

"Just as well." I slid eggs and bacon onto a plate and held it out to Ella. "Your four eggs and four strips of bacon, ma'am. And English muffin with butter and marmalade."

Vale lifted an eyebrow, so I said, "She runs ultras. Marathons aren't enough." I cracked four eggs into the pan and scrambled them with cheese while three more strips of bacon sizzled in a second pan. "You're here for a reason," I said to Vale. "What'd you find out?"

She took off the hat and wig and shook out her hair. "Director Ridel was drugged. He was unconscious when he was shoved out of the plane, but not dead."

"Knew that already. GHB."

She tilted her head. "Good work. I guess you two have been busy."

I gave her a look, alert for another double entendre. "What else you got?"

"The plane was a Cessna 177 Cardinal, built in 1975."

"Wow. How much booze did it take to get that?"

"You mean how much did *Alan* have? All I had was a martini. One."

"Yeah, good ol' Al. Guy never could hold his liquor."

She smiled. "A few. He was quite attentive. The FAA had the Cessna on radar over the VOR but it dropped off after turning and heading south. FBI agents asked around and a Nevada highway patrolman remembered seeing a single-engine high-wing plane flying low over I-80 south of the 95 junction that afternoon, headed west. Not much out that way, but there's half a dozen private dirt airstrips on ranches near Pyramid Lake and Highway 447 between Nixon and Gerlach. They searched and found the Cessna on an abandoned strip behind low hills, not visible from the highway, used to belong to a rancher, Jack somebody, who died twenty years ago. The strip was dry desert, not in great shape but still useable."

"You must've gotten Al pretty drunk to get all that." I slid the eggs and bacon onto a plate and dug in standing up, plate in one hand, fork in the other.

"There's more. The plane was stolen that afternoon from Reno-Stead Airport north of Reno. A flight plan was filed for Fallon Municipal. The plane took off at 3:32 p.m. The pilot knew exactly what to say and how to say it. Tail number, call sign, the works. Even used the real owner's name since Stead's a small airport."

"Maybe the real owner shoved Ridel out of the plane."

"The FBI thought of that. The owner was in Houston at the time. The Houston in Texas. There are others."

"With a rock-solid alibi like that, I'd take a closer look at him."

"You would. The FBI isn't."

I smiled. "Ouch."

"Not *him*, anyway. They're looking at anyone else who might have had access to the plane's keys. Needless to say, the plane never made it to Fallon. Forensics has been all over it. As of last night they hadn't come up with anything useful except evidence that it was definitely the plane used to dump Ridel."

"Not sure where that leaves us, but good work on Al."

"Thanks. One last thing: the VOR station quit working at 4:09 that afternoon. Two techs were sent out from Reno to fix it. They're the ones who found Ridel. They called it in. They opened the station and found broken electronics inside, like a computer or radio or something. That's when they found a bullet hole in the station. The feds have that, but Al said they don't know what it means. All they have is that Mortimer Angel's truck was found eight miles away with flames still gutting it. Ella's VW, too."

Perfect. I might be linked to a bullet that took out the VOR at the time Deputy Director Ridel of the FBI landed on the desert with a load of GHB on board. Ma was gonna be *so* damn pissed this time.

"So, what're you two doing today?" Vale asked, giving me a raised eyebrow.

"Not sure." I told her about last night's blue truck that might or might not be involved somehow. "I'll check on it, see if it's still at the Super 10 motel, but other than that we're pretty much stalled here. I might have to pull a gun on Vince, the blue-truck guy, and see what he has to say."

"I wouldn't. Ma said she wouldn't post bail." Vale looked around. "You've got a nice little trailer here. It looks comfortable." She included Ella in the comment.

"It is. Was," Ella said, then amended that back to, "is." Her face turned a shade darker under its tan.

Vale smiled, then stood up. "Being with Mort is like being in a word blender, Ella. Don't let it get to you." She opened the door and looked back at me. "Keep in touch, cowboy."

"You too, sweetie pie."

Vale laughed and went out.

• • •

"Sweetie pie?" Ella said.

"That was either irony or sarcasm. I can never keep those two straight." I sat where Vale had been sitting and took a bite of eggs.

"You said we're stalled. And you're not actually gonna pull a gun on that guy in the truck, so what's next?"

"Dunno. I'll think of something. Unless you do first."

"Me?"

"You wanted in on this. You're in."

"I could make the bed. How about that?"

"Always useful. Fluff the pillows too, toots. A woman's work is never done."

"You could get hurt, saying stuff like that."

"Okay, leave the pillows. *I'll* fluff them."

We were spinning our wheels. We now had a bit more information but it didn't seem pertinent to our situation. Ridel was tossed from a Cessna 177, a plane with a high wing. That made sense. He might bounce off a low wing and knock the tail off. I'd use a plane with a high wing too. In any case, I had no way to follow up on any of what Vale told us without bumping into a bunch of federal agents.

I yawned, felt my jaw creak.

Ella noticed the yawn and smiled. "You want to go back to bed for a while before it gets made?"

"You're a rather tempting wench, which makes that an appealing thought, but . . . no." I stood up. "Our job isn't quite the same as the FBI's. The desired result, I mean."

"It's not? And I sorta like 'wench'—*and* tempting."

"I'll try to use wench more often. And, no, the FBI is after the person or persons who kidnapped, drugged, and dumped Ridel, which isn't us, but we want to find out why those same people involved us and are still coming after us, or appear to be."

"Well, that's kinda sorta the same, isn't it?"

"I suppose it is. Actually, we have more information than the FBI or the Secret Service or whoever is running this show. The FBI only knows Ridel was dumped from a plane, unconscious at the time, but *we* know you got that phone call, wrote a note and delivered it to Waley's Tavern—the FBI doesn't. We know I was told to be at that VOR station at the exact time Ridel came down, so we know this whole thing was prearranged, well-timed, and executed to perfection."

She tilted her head. "*Executed*, Mort?"

"Possibly a poor choice of words. I take it back."

She started to make the bed. "What'll we do now? Stay here in Lovelock or go somewhere else?"

"We'll stick it out another day at least. The feds have the plane. Maybe forensics will turn up something useful and we'll be able to piggyback off that—if we or Vale can get close enough to a fed with loose lips."

"So we'll stay another day. Which gets me back to the question of what we're gonna do right now."

"Right now? I dunno. Gimme a moment here."

"That doesn't sound awfully professional."

"Who said I was a professional? I'm still in training. Didn't I mention that?"

"No."

"I've had almost nine thousand hours of training, but it takes ten thousand to get an investigator's license—plus a test administered by the state of Nevada, a test that has more to do with ethics and legalities than investigative procedures."

I didn't bother to tell her that ethics and legalities hadn't slowed me down much these past five years.

"I bedded down with a guy under false pretenses?" she said. "I thought you were a for-real PI."

I curled a forefinger at her. "C'mere, sugar."

She walked the three paces it took to stand in front of me. I pulled her down and got her sitting sideways on my lap. "You bedded down but you weren't bedded, so quit whining."

"I was whining?"

"I'm not an expert, but it sounded like it."

"Didn't mean to." She turned a little more toward me and in a quiet voice said, "You're a dangerously attractive man, Mort."

I didn't know how to respond to that so I didn't try.

She kissed my cheek. "You were talking on the phone with Harper when we first got here yesterday. Then you gave me the phone and went outside to check on the trailer and have a look at the RV park. Remember that?"

"Vaguely," I said.

"Yeah, right, vaguely, I'm sure. Anyway, she told me more about you and that lady, Dani, crammed together in a sleeping bag for fifteen hours. Naked," she added, as if I might've forgotten that part.

"Dani and I were naked?"

Ella kissed my cheek again. "Uh-huh. Unless I've been told a completely wacky fairy tale, which I doubt."

"Harper gave you more of that story, did she?"

"Uh-huh. Something about incidental touching that got pretty risqué toward the end. But that was all. Nothing serious happened. Which is amazing. Also amazing is that it didn't bother Harper at all. I had the feeling her telling me all of that was her way of letting me know that a bit of incidental touching, maybe even sort of a lot, didn't matter then and, well, maybe it still doesn't."

She looked into my eyes. "Thing is, that makes perfect sense in a sleeping bag, but not as much in this trailer—so are you *certain* Harper doesn't mind us being here like this? I don't want to cause a problem between you two. Not the littlest, tiniest speck of a problem."

"You won't. You can't. You know what Vale and I had to do last year to save Sue Kenny's mother, don't you?"

"I guess. At least I know what she put in the book she wrote. I had the feeling there was more."

"There was. Call it incidental touching on steroids."

"Oka-a-ay."

"I told Harper about that too. Like I said, I don't keep anything from her. Her response was a very slight lift of an eyebrow and a smile."

"That's all?"

"Well, she hustled me to bed and almost wore me out. We'd been apart for nearly a week and she's a very strong girl. But there was never a sign of jealousy. She's a lot like Jeri DiFrazzia, a wonderful gal I was all set to marry five years ago. I still remember what she said, word for word: "The tighter you hold onto someone, the less of them you get.""

Ella smiled. "I like that. I get it."

"Good. Harper gets it too. The past two nights with you have been very nice—sexy, too, in a low-key way—but it'll never be more than that."

"It's been a lot more than just 'very nice' for me, if you don't mind my saying. I like holding you and being held. It's comforting, feels safe, and, like you said, it's sexy. I'm not sure about it being low-key, though."

I smiled. "So we've got that out of the way?"

"Yes."

"That's good, because I have the feeling it'll be a while before we're done with this Ridel business."

She smiled. "That bodes well for tonight." She got to her feet. "Anyway, *now* what?"

"Most of the activity around here is at the Sage Inn. A limo was in the parking lot, which means a bigwig of some kind is in town, too important to ride around in a crummy Crown Vic. We might enhance our disguises and go over there to snoop around."

"Enhance how?"

"Little things. People have already seen us. Weight doesn't change overnight. Hair color can, but that would suggest a wig and therefore a disguise. I've got a Van Dyke. I can't suddenly have a full beard."

"Okay, so little things. What else do you have in that bag of tricks of yours?"

I waved a hand at it. "Have a look."

I would have to make do with non-prescription glasses with gray lenses in heavy black frames, a short-sleeve shirt with a collar and a string tie, red suspenders, the cane and the fake limp. So much for enhancement. A Richard Nixon mask was out of the question.

Ella rooted around in the bag for a while and surfaced with a pair of women's glasses with amber lenses and an Arizona Cardinals ball cap. She put them on. "How's this? I've got the T-shirt. I can be an Arizona football fan."

"That's good. Go with it. Just don't let anyone ask you how the team is doing."

"They're not doing yet. Season doesn't get going until September."

I stared at her. "Good to know."

She laughed. "I don't know all that much. My mother has a friend in Phoenix. They're the fans. I get reports."

"Whew."

"You're not into sports?"

"I only ask how the Giants are doing when some girl is partially or entirely naked and starting to get fresh."

She stared at me for a moment. "I'll remember that. If you mention the Giants tonight, I'll smack you. Hard, too."

No *wonder* I've got scars.

•   •   •

On the way to the Sage Inn, I took us through the Super 10 parking lot. No sign of the blue truck, so I parked on the street and fired up the app that would locate the tracker I'd attached to Vince Dolak's truck.

The app told me the truck was back in Reno.

"He's got an address in Reno," I said to Ella. "Looks

like he went back home."

"You think he went home? That's ... *amazing*. Ma doesn't pay you nearly enough."

"Was that irony or sarcasm?"

"Neither one. I'm not like that."

"You're a sweet kid."

. . .

I parked at the Sage Inn and 'Amber' and I got out and moseyed toward the casino entrance. Well, she moseyed and I limped, leaning on my cane. She looked forty-five. I'd passed fifty some years ago. She'd wrapped a towel around her midsection and pinned it in place under her T-shirt, adding another thirty pounds to her frame. I weighed close to three hundred. Two television vans were parked nearby: Channel Eight from Reno and CNN out of Sacramento.

Ella held my arm as we approached glass doors where a guy in a suit was eyeballing us as we got closer.

I nodded and started to edge past him, but he held up a hand and said, "Can I see some ID, folks?"

"To get a BLT and play a few slots?" I asked.

"Just a precaution." His voice was casual, but his eyes were Secret Service all the way.

I pulled out my fake ID. He gave it a good look, then said to Ella, "You too, ma'am."

She gave me a dismayed look. "I left my purse in the trailer, honey."

I grinned at the agent. "Wife's always forgetting it. We drove down from the KOA in Winnemucca. It would be a hundred twenty miles to go back and get it. Okay if we pop in to use the bathrooms and come right back out?"

He almost rolled his eyes. In fact, his lips did a kind of twist that replaced an eyeroll. "Go on in. Just keep out of the way of the official stuff goin' on in there. You'll see it."

"Official stuff?"

"This's the command post of the investigation." I gave him a perplexed look so he said, "Deputy Director Ridel's."

"Deputy director of what?"

"The FBI."

I turned to Ella-Amber. "You ever heard of 'im?"

"No. Should I?"

The agent stepped aside and ushered us toward the door. We were so far out of touch with events he couldn't take us anymore.

"Good work," I whispered to her when we were inside.

She smiled. "Thanks. You still need that bathroom? Prostate giving you fits, honey?"

Took all I had not to belt her one.

•   •   •

Not much going on in the lobby, just a few agents in suits, ties, and serious expressions walking around, three more in a federal huddle, but a conference room with open double doors was abuzz with activity, TV cameras visible with lights throwing a glare on a wooden podium where a jowly guy in his sixties with pink skin and thinning hair shuffled papers and checked his watch.

I checked mine. 9:59. A live update was about to kick off at ten this morning. News for a hungry nation.

A suit walked by. I said to him, "Who's that in there?"

"Director Gladstone."

"Director of what?"

He shook his head at my ignorance. "The FBI." But he was a man on a mission, kept going.

Okay by me. Now I knew who the limo was for. Dennis Wilke Gladstone was the FBI director Susan Kenny told me about last year. She was the US Attorney General at the time and Gladstone was the primary reason for her deep distrust of FBI's upper management—our supposed federal "law" enforcement agency—*law* with quotes, given their questionable activities the past decade.

I would've liked to stick around and hear what he had to say about the investigation's progress—in particular, the possible witnesses or killers whose cars had been torched and who hadn't yet been located. But a dragon lady in her fifties glared at us and closed the conference room doors almost in our faces.

So that was that. No sign of Vale in the place so I looked around, spotted what appeared to be a coffee shop.

"How about some coffee?" I asked my wife of recent

vintage.

"I don't drink coffee."

"Well, I do. You can have tea or a V-8."

"Maybe you laugh, but I like V-8."

"C'mon." I took her toward the restaurant.

We sat facing each other in a booth. I looked to one side and there was Gladstone at his podium on a TV on the wall, an American flag behind him supplying much-needed gravitas. His mouth was moving silently, eyes staring right into the camera. A waitress was headed our way, so we got menus we didn't need and I asked if she could get the sound going on the television. A small CNN logo was nestled at the bottom of the screen where a chyron scrolled across with the usual hiccups and misspellings.

The sound came on with Gladstone saying, ". . . the tragic and untimely death in the desert east of Lovelock, Nevada."

"Untimely?" I whispered. "It was timed right to the minute."

"You're awful," Ella whispered back.

"It's a knack. I've got a ton of 'em."

Gladstone continued: "Director Ridel's death is being treated as a possible homicide."

"A *possible* homicide? His hands were tied—"

"Sweetheart . . ."

"The FBI," Gladstone said, "in conjunction with the Secret Service, is following up on a number of promising leads on which I will not comment at this time, but I expect an arrest or arrests soon."

"Stuck his size-twelve in his mouth there," I said.

"You hope."

Gladstone: "Two possible witnesses, Mortimer Angel and Ella Kassel have not yet been located—"

"Knew that," I said.

"Hush, darling."

"—but it's expected that they will be found in the next day or two and that they will be able to shed some light on Director Ridel's death." He looked off to his right. "Do we have pictures of those two?" The screen went to picture-in-picture, Ella and I taking up most of the screen, Gladstone in a postage stamp off to one side—which was as it should be. "We're asking the public to be on the lookout for these two people. A reward of five thousand dollars is being offered to anyone who gives the FBI information regarding the whereabouts of either Mr. Angel or Ms. Kassel."

So we got thirty seconds of Warhol's infamous fifteen minutes of fame. I didn't need it since I had accumulated hours of it in the five years I'd been a PI, but Ella was now working on hers. Right then, the waitress came back.

Ella was still staring at the screen in shock. I snapped fingers in front of her face, startling her. "Tea, hon?"

She looked at me, then at the waitress. "Uh, yeah. Tea. Green if you've got it."

"Coffee for me," I said. "Black."

"You got it," the waitress said, and left.

"Five thousand dollars, Mort," Ella hissed, eyes boring into mine.

"Cheap bunch of so-and-so's in D.C. We'll be worth a lot more day after tomorrow when they still don't have us."

She stared at me. "That's . . . are you *serious*? I can't tell."

"I am, but I'm not. We'll be worth more but it won't matter since no one's gonna collect." I dropped two cubes of sugar into my coffee and stirred it.

"I'm just a *grad* student," Ella said in a low, intense voice.

"You want out of this?"

To her credit, she gave that some thought. Finally she said, "Yes, but I don't see how, at least not right now." She leaned back and stared at me. "Are we in trouble, Mort?"

"The name's Arnold, and what kind of trouble?"

"With the . . . the police or the FBI? Anyone?"

"We haven't done anything illegal. We had nothing to do with Ridel's death. The FBI wants to talk with us, that's all. You are guilty of accepting fifty bucks to write a note and deliver it to me—and showing up at that VOR station. If any of that is a crime punishable by more than a few hours in a stuffy interrogation room to tell them what you know half a dozen times, there are jaywalkers who are gonna get the death penalty."

She smiled. "Is this what it's like to be a PI?"

"For the vast majority of 'em, no, but it is for me."

The press conference ended, the public duly informed that the FBI, while clueless, was all over this case. Babble outside in the motel lobby swelled, and a gaggle of agents came into the coffee shop to get caffeine and Danish. Ella gave me a worried look as they poured in.

That intensified when, minutes later, Gladstone came in with two other suits, looked around, discovered that the place was almost full, finally took a table ten feet from us.

I leaned in close to Ella. "Smile, kiddo. Check out the new arrivals, look around, finish your tea. You and I are Mr. and Mrs. Nobody. We aren't in a hurry to leave. You've never tried to drink coffee through a fake moustache, have you?"

Her eyes brightened. "I don't drink coffee."

"That would explain it. Well, it's sorta irksome."

"You shouldn't've grown it, then."

"Nag, nag. I didn't know that about you before we got married. I'm starting to have second thoughts."

"No prenup. I would take you for all you're worth. You should've had a lawyer."

We sat there doing what people do all over this great nation: we stared at our cell phones, Facebooking, seeing what the kids were up to, checking email, flipping through photos, chuckling at riotous memes. We did all that using burners, which was impossible, but not one of our nation's finest noticed. All around us, the FBI contingent did pretty much the same but with iPhones and androids. Made me smile. Ella and I were vapor in their midst.

"Okay," I said after we'd given a roomful of serious-looking agents ten minutes to make us and get credit and promotions. "Coffee's pretty good here. Time to go."

I left eight dollars on the table, grabbed my cane and limped out with Ella-Amber holding my arm. We nodded to the agent at the door as we left the building, got in the truck and took off.

Chapter Nine

Back in the trailer we removed wigs, fake hair, shed a hundred pounds of bogus weight, and got comfortable. It was 10:42, Friday morning. Harper would be at Reno High in a classroom. No telling what Ma was doing, but keeping cell phone communication to a minimum only made sense. Ma, Harper, and Vale would have FBI agents hovering in the background, hoping to latch onto Mortimer Angel.

I didn't mind—much, anyway. I'd been there before. In particular there had been Ned Willis in the FBI's Reno office who'd been persistent in his efforts to prove that I'd murdered Julia Reinhart—U.S. Senator Harry Reinhart's loving spouse, who'd bludgeoned Harry and dumped him down an abandoned mineshaft in northwestern Nevada. Julia also murdered my fiancée, Jeri DeFrazzia, shot her point-blank between the eyes not three feet from me in the back of a Cadillac SUV then dumped Jeri down that same mineshaft. But there was no proof against Julia. She was going to get away with it. I couldn't let that stand. A month later, using fake IDs, Ma and I tracked Julia to a ritzy hotel room in Paris and we put out her lights, permanently. Ned had been right all along, but we hadn't left much of a trail to follow, not nearly enough for the FBI, but just enough, evidently, for Ned to pick at threads and insist that I was a murderer, even though I had an alibi for the motive part of his conjecture. The alibi was faked, but he couldn't prove that. The end result was that Ned got reassigned to FBI purgatory in Butte, Montana, for having been overzealous in pursuing a private citizen and making the FBI look bad, which was a spectacular case of the pot calling the kettle black—a cliché, but a useful one all the same.

Ella had never been under a media microscope before, but I had. I sat opposite her at the little dinette. "How are you doing?" I asked.

She shrugged. "I'm not sure. This is sort of crazy."

"Welcome to my world."

"This can't be what normal PIs go through."

"It's not, but it's still my world. I spent sixteen years as an IRS thug until I discovered I had a soul. So I told 'em to shove it and started a new career as a PI at my nephew's detective agency. That's when everything went off the rails. My very first day as a budding PI, I found the decapitated head of Reno's missing mayor in the trunk of my ex-wife's Mercedes."

Her eyes got wide. "You didn't."

"I did. I don't know how you missed that one. It made national news."

"When was that?"

"A little over five years ago."

"That explains it. I was a foreign exchange student in Argentina five years ago. But you found a head in the trunk of your wife's car? That's . . . unbelievable."

"Ex-wife's. Worse things have happened to me since then. I have been on a rollercoaster of strange ever since."

She pressed her lips together and said, "Tell me one of those things. Just one."

I thought for a moment, then said, "I was buried alive in the trunk of a Cadillac with an absolutely wonderful girl, Lucy, whom I later married. That was a week or so after I found the body of a gangsta rapper, Jonnie Xenon, strung up in the rafters of a garage with bullet holes in him."

"That was *you*? I remember hearing about that."

"That was me."

"You were buried alive in a car? How on earth did you get out of that?"

I told her, which took a few minutes, then I said, "You wanted to know. Trust me when I say that what's going on here, now, is weird, but not entirely unexpected given how my life has been going since I became a private eye."

Ella sighed. "How does Harper deal with all this?"

"She's tough, she's mellow, she lets the world flow around her, doesn't push back when she knows pushing would have no effect. It's pretty much a Zen thing."

"Which evidently includes you and me staying in this trailer together."

"It does, yes."

"That's almost the strangest thing of all."

I shrugged. "She's not the jealous type. Nor am I. A certain number of people will kill a spouse in order to keep them—which, oddly enough, doesn't work. The invisible truth behind good marriages is that people stay together because they want to, not because they have to."

Another sigh, deeper this time. "That sounds nice. I've never had anything like that."

"No current, uh, boyfriend right now?"

"Not for the past two years. I've been concentrating on running long distances and getting my advanced degree."

"Hard to catch you when you're still chugging along after that first fifty miles, huh?"

She laughed faintly, then looked around at the interior of the trailer. "This is cozy. I like it. But it's not getting us any closer to who killed Mr. Ridel or why anyone is chasing us, is it?"

"It's a way to stay out of sight when we're not nosing around. We'll hit a few bars tonight, maybe go back to the Sage Inn, see if we can pick up any more loose talk."

"That's hours away." She looked down at her hands. "Do you think it'd be safe for me to take a run? I sure could use one."

"It's your drug, huh?"

She smiled. "I guess. I feel out of sorts if I don't get a good run in for a few days."

"Should be okay, as long as you keep away from all the feds hanging around town. And you'd have to wear a wig, hat, dark glasses, maybe put on some lipstick."

"Maybe not. I thought about that. There should be dirt trails into the hills to the west. You could drive us south of town and drop me off if we see a place. Unless, of course, you want to run with me."

"How far?"

"Not too. Maybe twenty-five miles."

I smiled. "Just a quick little outing, huh?"

She returned the smile. "Sort of. It's kinda hot out so I wouldn't want to go too far."

"Sounds like a blast, but I think I'll pass."

She put on the gray wig, a ball cap, dark glasses, a hint of brown eyeshadow for the drive out, but she had no intention of being seen up close by anyone. I also wore my disguise. I took her six miles south before we spotted a two-track that went west toward dry empty hills, no sign of anyone around. I let her out with water, power bars, and a cell phone. She had on running shorts, a tank top, a small fanny pack. And long, long slender legs. Made me think of a deer.

"Be safe," I said.

"Always. I'll probably be about three hours."

"I'll get back here a little before that."

She chugged a pint of lemon-lime Gatorade, checked her Fitbit, then said, "See you," and took off.

I watched for a few minutes. Man, was I glad I wasn't going with her. I'd be left in the dust in the first quarter mile. She was going to run almost a full marathon in three hours.

I hung a U-turn and headed back to town.

• • •

Back in the trailer I set an alarm for two hours just in case, then stretched out on the bed and stared up at the ceiling, thinking about having been more or less invited out to the VOR station to be present when Deputy Director Ridel came down. But why? He had family in or around Reno, but I had never met the guy. I didn't remember ever hearing his name before I got dragged into this mess.

I was looking for a connection, but there might not be one. More than once in the past I had been targeted for being in the public eye for having found the bodies or body parts of famous missing people. This felt like that, like I'd been tagged simply because I filled the inside straight of a psycho's poker hand.

So, what else? In fact, I had a few past connections to

the FBI. Maybe that was it.

Ned Willis had been quarantined to FBI's leper colony in Butte, Montana, and I had been questioned by the FBI regarding Reinhart's death when his wife had dumped him and Jeri down the mineshaft. My latest run-in with the FBI was last year when Susan Kenny, the US attorney general at the time, had been stalked by a lunatic and forced to rob several businesses in Utah and Montana, wearing nothing but a semitransparent thong. Partway through that bizarre ordeal Vale had taken Sue's place, which is how Vale had ended up working for Ma. I had also sidestepped the FBI's assistance when Lucy and Harper were kidnapped by a guy by the name of Kyle Anza. I saved them without help by the FBI, which might've pissed off the Bureau since kicking in doors and shooting the place up to save kidnap victims is their bailiwick.

One thing that stood out from all the rest in this case was that several people were involved in Ridel's murder. I totaled it up: Red truck, blue truck, pilot, and the woman who had phoned Ella. Four people minimum, which meant this was a conspiracy. It's not easy to keep conspiracies quiet. The participants have to trust one another. Trusting inherently untrustworthy cohorts has a tendency to land all of them in prison.

But this was unquestionably a multi-person operation, so was it something personal, or had it been set up by a small number of people in the FBI? If the latter, how did it work? Bumping off their own deputy director would be a big deal. It could only involve a very few high-level people, or just one.

FBI Director Gladstone had come all the way across the country to Reno, then been driven a hundred miles in a limo to Lovelock. But why? He could have given a press conference right down the hall in the Hoover Building in D.C. Was it to show respect for a fallen colleague or to keep a close eye on the investigation?

Sue Kenny told us Gladstone hadn't gotten along well with Alden Ridel. Ridel wasn't "one of the team." Had that put a crimp in a cherished FBI operation? Did Gladstone feel a need to get rid of Ridel? In a way, that would make sense. Gladstone might be able to create a very tight team of highly trusted agents—but in another way that made no sense at all. None. Getting rid of Ridel would be a hell of a lot of exposure for relatively little gain—unless Ridel was about to blow the whistle on significant criminal acts by FBI's senior officials. His death had been choreographed in a way that would insure he made national news. And who was right there at ground zero when Ridel came tumbling down?—Mortimer Angel, well-known discoverer of famous missing people who end up dead, and Ridel couldn't have ended up any deader.

Shit.

But maybe that wasn't it. Ella and I had been shot at and then hunted by a pair of relative incompetents. That didn't have an FBI feel to it—unless that was intentional. Vince Dolak was local. He lived in Reno. Was he hired do what he did without knowing the whole story, perhaps by a cutout to prevent him from knowing he'd been hired by the FBI? If so, the cutout was likely the woman who'd phoned Ella. She'd set this thing in motion. Vince felt local, looked local. He was a nobody, a shmoo. I'd seen him in that bar, Whiskey River Saloon. If Vince was an FBI special agent, I was Grace Kelly, but he might be a hired dimwit.

Susan Kenny had distrusted upper management in the FBI—Dennis Gladstone in particular. Denny might have had a trusted third party hire local talent to eliminate Ridel when Ridel flew to Reno to attend a wedding a week ago.

All of which felt like a bad bowl of conjecture soup.

One last connection: Katherine Ridel Wells, Alden's younger sister, was the chief judge in the Nevada District Court in Reno and Susan Kenny was now an assistant U.S. attorney, Nevada District—a hell of a coincidence. I gave that a few seconds of thought, couldn't make anything of it right offhand . . .

Then I fell asleep.

•   •   •

The travel alarm woke me at 1:15. I donned a wig and hat, put on my belly fat, Van Dyke, sunglasses, took along a liter of water for Ella, then headed out. I stopped off at the

Safeway for a few more items, then rolled south.

No sign of her when I got to where I'd dropped her off, but I'd expected that. In fact, she showed up ten minutes earlier than I thought she would, hot, smiling, not much sign that she'd just run twenty-five point seven miles (she showed me her Fitbit) other than glistening with sweat and downing the liter of water I gave her in thirty seconds.

"That was wonderful," she said happily.

"I'm tired just looking at you."

"I'm *starving*, and I need a shower."

I drove her back to the trailer. She was tall and slender and looked a lot like the sought-after Ella Kassel for which there was a nice reward, so I parked in front of the trailer door to block the view as she hustled inside. Before leaving I'd set the thermostat at seventy degrees to cool the place. I figured she'd appreciate that.

Shower first. I turned my back while she stripped off sweaty clothes, and I whipped up two tuna sandwiches for her while she got wet and clean. While I was at it, I made a third one for myself.

She came out in a T-shirt barely long enough to cover things while she was standing, so sitting was not an option. She wolfed down the two sandwiches and a pint of milk, drank more water and a V-8 I'd picked up at the store on the way to get her, then she yawned and said, "I'm going to conk out for an hour or two. Join me?"

"Still awfully tempting, but no. I caught an hour while you were running. I'll keep an eye out for the bad guys and read a while."

"Your loss." She sat on the bed, stripped off the shirt, and got under the covers. And, as I'd suspected, she hadn't been wearing anything under the shirt.

"Yowzer," I said.

She laughed, then fell asleep in seconds.

•   •   •

Ma called at 6:20 that afternoon as Ella and I were making noises about heading off to a restaurant. Ella was anyway. Twenty-five miles leaves a hole in the belly that isn't easy to fill. I put the phone on speaker.

"Finally got the guy in the red truck," Ma said. "Took a while, but he was stopped yesterday afternoon by a police officer on Fourth Street for having a fairly obvious bullet hole in his windshield. Police are sensitive about that kind of thing."

"What's the guy's name, doll?"

She laughed, as did Ella. "Frank Dolak, boyo."

"Vince's brother," I said, sharp as always. That meant Vince was involved. Up to then, I wasn't absolutely certain, but this couldn't be a coincidence. This nailed it.

Ma guffawed. "Nothing gets by you, does it?"

"I get a raise for that?"

"For adding one and one and gettin' two? Don't you wish? Frank also lives in Reno. He's got priors. Assault and battery, domestic abuse, divorced now, did two years in Carson for the assault. Nothing in the past three years. I've got addresses for both him and Vince. We could go after these guys."

"We might, but not yet, certainly not face-to-face. I'd like to know who's running this shit show before we think about kicking ass. This is looking more and more local."

"Except the target was Deputy Director Alden Ridel of the FBI," Ma said. "Which is anything *but* local."

She might've been thinking along the same lines I had earlier. We would have to talk about that.

"There's that," I said. "Although Ridel had family in the Reno area. He could have local enemies. I think we're about done here in Lovelock. We'll head on back to Reno tomorrow if we don't pick up anything new tonight. We might tail the Dolaks, see if anything shakes out."

"Makes me *so* glad I hired you, boyo. I never would've thought of that." She laughed and ended the call.

"Sonofabitch," I fake-snarled. I texted Ma, told her to text me Frank and Vince's addresses.

Ella grinned. "She likes you."

"You think?"

"I know." She handed me my little girl's inner tube and said, "Put this on. I'm hungry. There's a Mexican food place eight blocks away."

"We had Mexican yesterday." My phone chirped and I

had Frank and Vinnie's Reno addresses.

"That was enchiladas," Ella said. "I want a burrito. I mean *two* burritos, and beans and rice."

"I hope you don't bloat up, sunshine."

She laughed. "Yeah, I worry about that *all* the time."

• • •

We ended up at a place called *El Borracho*, which I loosely translated as "The Drunk" or "The Drunkard." We ordered strawberry margaritas and pork burritos. Ella dove into a basket of tortilla chips and loaded them with salsa while the food was being prepared.

"How do you keep under a hundred and ten pounds?" I asked with a straight face.

She looked at me through one eye. "I burn it off. Not just by running. Don't ask me how, I just do. And I weigh one twenty-two, which I already told you. You should keep better notes." She stirred the slush of her margarita with a little red straw. "You told Ma we're gonna go back to Reno. Are you going to keep the trailer?"

"Yes."

"And me?"

"You, too, if I can't ship you off to Fiji."

She smiled. "Okay, good. Don't know what I'd do in Fiji. Is that in the southern or northern hemisphere?"

"Dunno. I'll Google it later."

She sipped her drink. "So where do you think we'll stay? In Reno, I mean. Or Sparks."

I shrugged. "We'll find a KOA somewhere. Why? Do you have a place in mind?"

"I do, actually. There's a place out in Verdi: Truckee River RV Park."

"Never heard of that one."

"It's pretty much out of the way, looks nice and quiet. I don't know what it's got in the way of amenities, but it's right by the river and it's shaded by trees."

"Sounds good. We'll look into it."

Verdi was a few miles west of Reno, small, and quiet. Might be a good place to park the trailer and keep out of sight while we try to get something on Vince and Frank

Dolak. Those two were our only leads into this tumult; the plane would be a nonstarter. With summer vacation over for students, and therefore their parents, the RV park in Verdi should have plenty of vacancies.

We left El Borracho in twilight, lights starting to come on, neon brightening along the main drag. We were in full disguise, no need to return to the trailer, so we cruised by the Sage Inn. At least half the Crown Vics and Suburbans had cleared out, and all the forensics vans and the limo. The investigation was starting to wind down in Lovelock, but a stripped-down team was still hanging around.

The first bar we came to was Bill's Buy-You Tavern, which would be an okay name in New Orleans, not so good for a bar in the desert. No obvious feds in the place, so we left without getting drinks. Next up was the Silver Spur Saloon. I parked the truck at the curb around the corner on a dark street a block from the bar. I went in limping on a cane with Ella holding my arm. Half a dozen likely agents were inside, so we took a table not far from a table of three who had their heads together, talking. I ordered a Moose Drool in a long neck and Amber had another gin and tonic. I looked around, trying to get a feel for the current social dynamic in the place.

Eight locals were scattered around, and two feds at the far end of the bar, one lone fed at the bar closer to us, and the three at the table who were keeping their voices down so I couldn't catch what they were saying. I kept an eye on the singleton at the bar for a while. His shoulders were hunched and his eyes were on his drink. He didn't look around. Might be an opportunity there, so I leaned in close to Ella and asked if she wanted to try something.

"Like what?"

I told her, and she said, "I can do that."

We got up with our drinks and she helped me to the back of the room where I played a pinball machine, scored eighty-one thousand points, then she helped me across the room, but as we passed the lone guy at the bar she held me back and took a barstool beside him, so I had to take the stool at her other side. We set our drinks on the bar.

She sipped her drink, let things go for a minute then

looked at the guy and said, "Do you . . . are you part of, you know, this investigation here?" Not the smoothest opening line, but that was intentional and well-played. If the guy was going to talk, he would talk.

He gave her a look, then said, "Uh-huh."

"Don't bother him, hon," I said.

"I'm *not*." She put a little pique in her voice. I liked that. She was a natural. God bless high school drama class.

I leaned forward to look past her at the guy. "Sorry about that. She's been bugging guys all evening."

Ella glared at me. "I'm *interested*, that's all."

"It's okay," the guy said, choosing sides.

"I'm Amber," Ella said to him. "What's your name?"

"Zachary. Zack," he amended quickly. A good sign.

"So, *are* you, Zack? I mean, this is *so* fascinating. It's been on TV and everything and it's right here in Lovelock where nothing ever happens, and I do mean *nothing*."

"It's something, all right," he agreed.

"Are you, what do they call it, a *special* agent?"

"Aw, jeez, hon," I said. "Leave the guy alone, huh?" I let it go at that and tuned them out. I'd established my position as a reluctant disinterested bystander. Now it was all up to Amber.

"I just wondered, that's all," she said.

Zack nodded. "I guess you'd call me that."

Ella lowered her voice. "Earlier tonight a guy told me that director guy fell out of an airplane. Was he *kidding*?"

We knew that hadn't made it into the news yet. This would either kickstart the guy, or shut him up.

Zack gave her a long look. "He said that? I thought we'd decided not to release that for another day or two."

Good goin', Zack. I masked a smile with a giant yawn. As a spy behind the Iron Curtain in the sixties Zack would have ended up in a gulag in Siberia, or worse.

"Uh-huh," Amber said. "He also said that's what killed him. The fall, I mean. Is that true?"

Zack thought about that, then shrugged. "Yeah."

Her eyes got wide. "That is *so* weird."

He laughed quietly. "You don't know the half of it."

"Oh, what's the other half?"

"Can't say. Sorry. It'll probably come out after a while but right now it's being withheld."

"Yeah, okay, I get it." She was quiet for a moment, then said, "Those two missing people that no one can find. Did *they* do it? I mean, if their cars were there, burned up, then they couldn't have been on the plane, could they?"

He pursed his lips. "That's a good question, miss."

"Seems kinda obvious. I mean, if it is to me it probably is to the FBI, right?"

He rolled his shoulders nervously. "It is, yeah. Right off the bat. We're workin' on it. We don't know exactly how those two are involved, but they are."

"I wonder how they managed to get away," Ella said in a musing tone. She took a sip of her drink and stared with unfocused eyes at bottles lined up along the back of the bar as if she were thinking about it.

"No idea," Zack said. He was silent for a moment, then said, "They made it to Fallon, then . . . vanished."

Ella tittered gaily, a bit drunkenly. "Like ghosts?"

Zack grinned. "Yeah, something like that." He swirled bourbon in his glass, knocked it back and ordered another. He turned toward her and said, "Some of that'll be made public in the next couple of days. Guess I could tell you a thing or two now. The girl left a bicycle at the scene. Three-thousand-dollar mountain bike. Serial number gave us her name, same as the owner of the VW that was torched out there. You've heard it: Ella Kassel. So of course we want her for questioning, and the guy she was with, Mortimer Angel. You might've heard of him. We know they got away on a dirt bike and ran out of gas up in the hills east of here, had to walk six or eight miles to a cabin. Cabin's owner drove them to Fallon. They ended up in a restaurant, got something to eat, and that's it. That's where the trail ends."

He was getting into it now, bourbon probably pushing him along, and a little loneliness. As I'd hoped.

"That's . . . strange. That they would just disappear."

"It won't last. We'll get him. And the dame, Ella."

"Dame?" Ella almost choked on a laugh.

Zack smiled. "Sorry. That just slipped out. Anyway, we know this Angel guy made a couple of calls from Fallon.

There's only one cell tower active there. One call went to a coworker of his, some lady last name of Marchant who was all over the news last year. He also called his wife, but the calls didn't last long, just seconds. Probably switched to burners—unregistered cell phones. Wife's a schoolteacher so we know she didn't go to Fallon. She was at school at the time those two disappeared. We don't know about the Marchant woman. She could've picked them up, but we got no indication she did. We found the phone calls nine or ten hours after the fact. For all we know, they could've called an Uber and taken it about anywhere."

He stopped, then said, "Listen to me, blabbing my fool head off. All of this is the kind of run-around crap you get from investigating every little lead, but not all of it is for public consumption, at least not yet."

"Yeah, well, *I'm* sure not gonna go public with it," Ella said. She laughed. "I wouldn't know how."

He smiled. "I wouldn't be giving away anything telling you I think the key to this whole thing is that girl on the run with Mortimer Angel."

"The girl? Ella something? *She's* the key?"

"Ella Kassel, yeah. Thing is, Angel's an oddball of the first order, but in spite of that he's pretty much a known quantity—or whatever you'd call it. At least he's a known oddball. Anyway, he's been on TV and everywhere else for finding missing people who always end up dead—senators, rock stars, famous people like that. No one knows how, but he's all over the place, no rhyme or reason to it. It's sort of like that guy I heard about, some park ranger who was hit by lightning seven or eight times. No way to account for it unless you figure God's got it in for the guy. But like I said, Angel's a known quantity, but the Kassel girl isn't. Not in this context, anyway. She's an outlier, an unknown, which I think means she's the key to all this—as does the Bureau. Of all the things about this case that make no sense, and I mean *none*, she makes the least. We find out how she's involved and we'll wrap this thing up pretty quick. All we have to do is find her—which we *will*. We always do. It's just a matter of time."

"All of that is just so . . . *fascinating*," Ella said, awed.

Zack smiled. "It is, this time. This is a strange case. I've never seen anything like it. Angel and Kassel are very likely still together, on the run, and there's Angel, calling his wife and a coworker, so he's obviously not the sharpest knife in the old drawer. All they said was Angel called them to let them know he was okay and not to worry. We're throwing an electronic net over the wife and the Marchant woman, *and* Angel's boss or partner. He'll call one of 'em again. We'll use that to get him and that'll get us the Kassel girl, *then* we'll see what's what."

"Wow," Ella said. "That's, I don't know, amazing, really." She finished her drink.

"C'mon, hon," I said to her. "My leg's killin' me here. I want to get a hot pack on it."

She sighed faintly. "Yeah, okay." She looked at Zack. "Hey, I wish you luck. I hope I didn't 'bug' you too much."

"You didn't. It sorta helps, talking it out. Sometimes I get new ideas that way."

"See?" Ella said to me. "I wasn't 'bugging' him. Not everyone is as easily put out as you, dear."

We got up and eased on out of there, didn't look back.

Chapter Ten

"You're a dame and an outlier," I said when we were back in the truck. "That sounds right."

She smiled. "Says the oddball who, according to Mr. FBI, isn't the sharpest knife in the drawer."

"He wasn't entirely wrong, but we had to get out of Fallon so I couldn't avoid that call to Vale. And Harper would've been going crazy with me missing and wanted for questioning. But Zack gave us some good intel back there. Now we have to use it."

"How?"

"For starters, like this." I called Ma on my burner. Unlike me, Ma *is* the sharpest knife in the drawer, so it didn't surprise me when she answered not with a word but with a two-second, single-note hum, then went silent. She sounded like a bad connection.

"Is this Red's Pizza?" I asked hesitantly.

"Wrong number." She ended the call, as did I.

Ella stared at me. "What was *that*?"

"Ma and I have been through a lot together," I said. "More than I can say. After what happened last year with Valentina she came up with an emergency procedure she calls Code Red. It felt a bit melodramatic at the time, but now it'll be useful."

"What's it do? This code red?"

The street was residential, dark. The night was quiet. I hadn't started the engine yet. I turned to Ella and gave her a serious look. "It's a way to communicate safely. The FBI either is now or is about to try to capture outgoing cell calls from the people closest to me—Ma, Harper, Vale. A certain kind of wideband receiver can get burner calls directly, before they go through a cell tower, but they can't really monitor a specific location of the outgoing call unless they reduce the receiver's sensitivity because Reno and Sparks will have tens of thousands of calls going in and out. But if they only pick up nearby calls, they can limit the number they have to record, so they'll camp out near Ma's office and try to capture calls within a very limited radius. What we're about to do is pretty simple, but do you really want to know the details? Sometimes it's better not to know. It's called deniability. Think about that before you answer."

She did, lips pursed, eyes unfocused as she looked into the middle distance at nothing. Finally she said, "It's not illegal, is it?"

"No. It's a bit slippery, but certainly not illegal."

"Then I guess not. At least not right now. But this code red thing is working right now? Now that you called Ma?"

"Yes. It's instant. There's nothing to set up. She'll tell

Harper and Vale and then it's done."

"This is . . . something else, Mort."

"Yes, it is. If we knew who to trust we wouldn't have to do this, but as things stand now, we don't have a choice. But I can tell you this much: by sending a certain kind of text, I'll be able to get Ma, Harper, or Vale to phone me in a way that will be all but impossible to intercept. The FBI doesn't know where I am, and I'm on a burner, so I don't have that problem. The bottom line is, our communication will be secure, but it'll be a lot slower."

She took a deep breath, let it out. "Okay."

"Okay?"

"I'm in this thing and I put myself in, so I guess I'm in." She turned to me. "And you're a nice guy, sort of an oddball, but nice. I could probably do worse. At least this isn't boring." She reached behind her back, then said, "By the way, this bra's kinda itchy, so watch out."

Before I could figure out what that meant, she had her shirt and bra off.

"Yowzer," I said. Good thing it was dark out.

She laughed, then put her shirt on, sans bra. "*That's* better."

"That shirt looks like a deflated zeppelin, though."

She slapped my arm, then gathered up wads of tissue. "Deflated. That's me. Always has been."

"Hey."

"What?"

"Since becoming a PI I've been engaged once, married twice, and all of those women were small-breasted."

She turned and looked at me. "Really?"

"Yes. You don't have any idea how sexy you are, do you?" I started the engine and pulled away.

The truck filled with silence.

I drove us to a Shop-n-Go I'd seen earlier as we were leaving El Borracho. I wore the cowboy hat I'd picked up in Fallon, glasses with thick black frames, made sure the Van Dyke and moustache were still in place, then limped inside with the cane *thonk*ing on the floor with every step, paid cash for a new burner, then limped and *thonk*ed back out, and got back in the truck.

"Sexy?" she said in a tiny voice.

"Hell, yes."

That's all I said. I figured it was enough.

Or maybe too much, what did I know?

I looked at her, saw a furtive little smile as she turned and looked out her side window.

Good enough.

•   •   •

Back in the trailer with the curtains pulled, I got the new burner charging then popped into the shower and sang, "I'm gonna wash that wench right outta my hair, and send her on her—" which is as far as I got because someone pulled the shower curtain back, stuck their pretty head in and said, "Hey!" then ducked back out.

"Whatever happened to privacy?" I called out.

She stuck her head back in and said, "Privacy? In a trailer this size? You gotta be kidding, mister."

"Get out or get in, toots."

"That's ... wow." She popped out, which meant anything could happen in the next ten seconds. She'd been wearing a T-shirt with nothing under it.

But I was left alone so we saved on propane to heat water. I got out and dried off. I sat at the dinette with the towel around my waist and fired up the new burner, got its number and disabled its GPS. Ella watched as I wrote the number down, did a bit of manipulation with pencil and paper that took a few minutes because it had to be done very carefully, then I wrote out a long string of numbers:

$$6152319352814492976138195246z$$

"What on earth?" Ella said.

"This burner's number is embedded in that number."

"How?"

"Magic. If I text this number to Ma, she'll be able to call this new phone."

"Magic, uh-huh. You wrote down a bunch of numbers and spaces then filled in more numbers. Are you sure Ma can get your new number out of that?"

"It's easier to get it out than to create the number you

see here. All you need is the key."

"Which you've memorized."

"Yup. It's not hard, but anyone else would have a devil of a time trying to get my cell number out of it."

She shook her head. "It looks hard. I definitely don't need details. I doubt that I could remember it anyway."

"There's more. A number like that and nothing else is suspicious. We don't send it in that form." I created a text that broke the number into pieces:

Ser. nos. 6152319352 and 8144929761 lot no. 3819
sold for $524.62

I texted that to Ma. If the FBI intercepted it, just one of tens of thousands of texts between two unknown phones, they would have to see it as an encoded number, not a business transaction, and if they got that far, a supercomputer couldn't pull my burner number out of it in a year. Ma wouldn't call me unless it was important, and then only from a public place, not her office or home. She would also sideline her old burner, then text me the encoded number of a new burner.

Ella stood up. "I know it's not late yet, but a good run still knocks me out. Are you ready for bed?"

"I could be sweet-talked into it."

She looked at the towel around my waist, smiled and said, "Harper told me you wore a towel to bed the night the two of you met, and she yanked it off you and tossed it all the way across the room."

"She told you that, did she?"

Ella kissed me. "Uh-huh. Something like that could happen again."

"Sort of a déjà vu thing?"

"Keep that towel on and you'll find out. By now I hope we're past all pretense of being modest with each other."

"Sweet talker."

She laughed.

I turned out all the lights except one, then dimmed it to a faint glow. "You first, lady."

She stripped off the shirt, then got under the covers. I draped my towel over the back of a chair as I had the night before, then slid into bed with her and tried to make the best of a tough situation.

• • •

She snuggled up close and rested a hand on my chest, breasts tucked against my left side. "Okay?" she asked.

"Yup." I am a master of pithy responses.

I felt her smile. "Good."

Then she draped her left leg over mine. "Still okay?"

"Not teasing me, are you?"

"I might be."

"Anyway, still yup. I'm tough. I can take it."

She kissed my cheek, got comfortable, then lay still.

I held her and said, "Sweet dreams."

She smiled again. "Sweet dreams, right. As if I could sleep like this, Mort."

"Like what? Lying on one side?"

"No. Kind of wound up, if you must know."

I was groping for a response when she said, "I know nothing's gonna happen, but this is pretty, um, erotic, so I hope that's okay."

"Yup." Back to pithy. Pithy is safe.

She laughed softly. "I can't believe you can do this and not get wound up, too."

"Who says I'm not?" Twisting the tail of this tiger.

She lifted her head and looked at me in the gloom. "Uh."

"Uh, yourself, kiddo."

She settled back down. "That's . . ."

"What?"

"Well, nice. If."

I didn't respond to that and she didn't pursue it, but she snuggled in closer so I held her in my arms and felt her warmth and the soft-hard strength of her body.

The snarl of eighteen-wheelers on I-80 came and went from a quarter mile away. I heard a bark of female laughter from an RV parked forty yards from ours, and someone snored so gently it was like a person breathing in another room.

She was out, gone. Running twenty-six miles has a

way of shutting things down.

I am basic male and a pig with a number of faults that apparently amuse Harper—one of them being that I like women. Couple that with a cosmic misunderstanding in which I often find myself in close proximity to a beautiful naked woman and the stage is set for interesting times. This does not bother Harper in the least, a fact I have come to understand, and has much to do with my amazing, now-deceased wife, Lucy. Lucy, who in the last week of her life gave me to Harper and Harper to me.

So I lay there in Ella's slow breathing warmth and registered the contact of our bodies and allowed myself a prurient yet hypothetical thought or two. Bony Moronie no longer suited her. Small breasts, yes, but although I have been accused of being partial to busty women due to the curve balls the universe has thrown at me, the truth is that I am partial to women who are easygoing, friendly, calm and even-tempered. Women without hard edges, who find a great deal of comfort and contentment in simply being held, especially when clothing is optional. Such women are sexy as hell, whatever their bust size.

• • •

I woke up before Ella. She was in my arms, molded to me. Faint daylight was visible at the margins of curtains. I lay there and thought about our situation, hers and mine.

We were wanted by the FBI. Presumably Frank and Vince Dolak wanted us too. I had their home addresses. I had the element of surprise. I could, in theory, capture one or both of them. But then what? All options were terrible. I couldn't kill them or keep them prisoner indefinitely. Just the thought of either of those made me shudder. I couldn't grab one of them and force him to tell me who was behind the note that got me to the VOR in time to witness Ridel's death, then turn him loose to come back at us. And what would I do if they didn't give up the person behind all this? I would have to release them regardless. They could then wait, bid their time, choose a convenient time and place to take me down—or, worse, harm Harper, Ma, Vale, or Ella. I wouldn't be able to live like that.

Miserable, intractable problem. I had never been in a situation like this. We were targets. We didn't know why or by whom because there were more people involved than just Vince and Frank. The more I thought about it, the less I liked it and the closer I got to wanting to simply eliminate the Dolak brothers. But I couldn't do that. I'd rid the world of Julia Reinhart, but once was enough.

So now what?

I didn't know. All I knew was, Ella and I were still on the run and I didn't see any end to it.

Shit.

So I backtracked and went through it again. Ridel had been dumped from a plane and Ella and I had "escaped" on a dirt bike. Those two things didn't add up to her and me being the ones responsible for dumping Ridel. It would be obvious, even to the fibbies, that others were involved. Maybe I would have to take a chance and go to them, tell them about the note and what Ella and I had done, what we'd seen, everything we knew. We were connected to this somehow, yet we were as in the dark as the FBI. We were little more than two people in the wrong place at the wrong time. We were wanted for questioning, that's all. No one had said we were armed and presumed dangerous. The FBI would assume, rightly, that we were unwilling to turn ourselves in, but *why* weren't we?

Because I didn't trust them, that's why. The FBI had managed to sabotage much of the trust of the people they were supposed to serve. That was on them. But I might have to make that leap of faith and tell them what Ella and I had done. If so, this case would make no more sense to them than it did to me. The parts of it were disconnected, like an exploded jigsaw puzzle. Nothing meshed. I . . . I—

—fell asleep.

•   •   •

I awoke when Ella lay on top of me, nuzzled my neck and said, "Morning."

I put my arms around her waist and pulled her harder against me. Which might've been a mistake.

"Oh, my," she whispered. "You're—"

So I kept rolling to my right and deposited her on the side of the bed nearest the kitchen, gave her butt a little slap and said, "Your turn to make breakfast, sparky."

My depositing her didn't take, however. She lay on her left side with the full length of her body against me.

"We could stay like this a while longer," she said. "I fell asleep and missed out."

"Missed out on what?"

"More of *this*, you fool. Especially with me on top and you being—"

I interrupted with: "How much more did you have in mind?"

She grinned. "How much more what?"

"Allow me to rephrase. How much longer, timewise?"

"What time is it? The clock's behind me."

I looked to my right. "It's six thirty-two."

"That's awfully early. We could stay like this until, say, eight o'clock."

"Like this, huh?"

"Well, yes. It's quite pleasant."

"Okay, if you insist."

"I don't, but it would be nice. Not to do anything more than this, just to . . . *be* here like this, warm and safe, and, you know, kinda wound up. Don't go away and don't you dare move. I just want to brush my teeth."

She got up, came back a few minutes later, so I did the same. When I slid back into bed she pulled me close, so I rolled her on top again and wrapped my arms around her. She got settled, molded herself to me and sighed softly in my ear.

"You're doing okay, then?" I asked.

"Better than that since you're still . . . happy. And so am I," she added. "In case you didn't know."

"I did. I do."

"Good."

That ended the talking. We lay there like that, letting the minutes tick by, aware of each other. It wasn't sex, but as she'd said, it was quite pleasant.

• • •

Wearing a T-shirt that would have been problematical if it were half an inch shorter, Ella made French toast. I loafed in bed, too comfortable, smug, and lazy to get up.

"You going to sleep all day?" she said.

"I'm not sleeping. I'm watching. You're a very good-looking critter."

"Critter. No one's ever called me *that* before. This is almost ready. How about you get up and out of there?"

"I might give it another minute or two."

"Oh? Do you have a problem, sir?"

"I wouldn't call it that."

"I could toss you your towel. It's dry now."

"Might not be a bad idea."

"Although it's not as if I haven't already . . ."

"Already what?"

"Never mind. Here." The towel hit me in the face.

•   •   •

Lovelock was done. I wasn't going to turn us into the FBI and take our chances, at least not yet. We weren't going to learn anything more here, and the Dolak brothers were back in Reno. Frank had been pulled over in the red truck in Reno for having a bullet hole in the windshield, and the GPS I'd put on Vince's truck told us he'd been in Reno since yesterday morning.

Time to move this investigation, such as it was, which wasn't much. I wanted to follow the Dolaks, see where they went, what they did.

Ella and I prepared the trailer for travel then donned disguises. I unhooked the power and water, cranked down the leveling jacks, paid Ralph Poda for the two nights we'd been at the Lazy L, then we hit the road, comfortably—I'd removed my fat pack, the Van Dyke, and Ella was braless in the tank top she'd been wearing at the VOR station.

Thirty miles south of Lovelock my new burner dinged. I was driving so I handed it to Ella.

"You got a text," she said. "Doesn't say who it's from, but the message is like the one you sent Ma. It looks like a bunch of sales data."

"What's the last number in the text?"

"One."

"Means it's from Ma. It'll give us the number for a new burner, not the one she's been using. She won't talk or text on it from her home or office where the FBI might have a receiver waiting to grab it as it goes out. That includes the number she just sent, so she's out somewhere right now."

"You can figure out her new number from this text?"

"Yes. Easy."

She smiled. "Like James Bond, huh?"

"Nope. I'm not as good looking as Jimmy, but I sleep with prettier women. Semi-platonically."

She slapped my shoulder, gently. "You are . . ."

"What?"

"I don't know. I'll have to think about it."

"Send a text to Ma," I said. "Just say, 'got it'."

She did, then didn't say anything for a while. Finally: "How long do you think this'll take? Figuring out this Ridel business?"

"Wish I knew. You in a hurry to get it over with?"

"Sort of. Not with you, but I've got a thesis that isn't getting done. And maybe a thesis advisor who's wondering where I am and what the heck I'm doing."

"The guy who tried to hit on you?"

"Yeah. Professor Zimmerman. Not lately, though. He evidently took the hint."

"Investigations like this have no time limit. They end when they end. I wish I could give you an estimate, but I can't. It could take a while." I didn't tell her it could take forever. We might never know who targeted us, and that wasn't the worst of a number of other possibilities.

She sighed and closed her eyes. "As long as I'm with you," she said quietly.

The thought was incomplete but I got it.

I liked her too, but I missed Harper.

A lot.

• • •

We arrived in Reno at 12:20, kept going west and got off I-80 at the Verdi exit and onto Old Highway Forty. We went half a mile and turned left onto County Road 112 and ended up at the Truckee River RV Park, partially hidden beneath huge cottonwoods. Before I got us a site I made certain we had cell coverage. We couldn't stay there if we didn't get a signal.

The park was small, thirty spaces, and less than a third full. We were a quiet middle-aged couple in a modest-sized trailer, keeping mostly to ourselves. Sixty dollars a day, 50-amp power, water, Wi-Fi. The place had a laundromat, bathrooms with showers, a small store in the office, a picnic area, walking trails along the river, birds in the trees, a mild breeze flowing through the channel of the river and through the park off mountains to the west.

I gazed up at the mountainside for a long moment. Up there, three years ago, I'd escaped a burning cabin and ran hell for leather down a dark slope at night to save Lucy's life and ended up killing two homicidal shitheads with a rock that weighed over three hundred pounds.

I didn't tell Ella any of that. That one hadn't made national news the way most of my misadventures had.

"What?" she said, looking where I was looking.

"Mountains with trees," I said, breathing deeply of the air. "Not like Lovelock. This is a terrific place."

She smiled. "I'm glad you like it."

I paid in advance for a week. We got hooked up to power and water. I leveled the trailer with the jacks, took a look around at our neighbors, the closest of which was sixty feet away in a fifth wheel the size of a cruise ship, then we went inside.

"Now what?" Ella asked.

"I'll text Ma, let her know we're in the area, then we'll see if we can get a look at Frank Dolak. He's the guy in the red truck who chased us into the hills."

I looked at the text Ma sent while we were driving to Reno. It read:

Ser. nos. 4721493866 and 5298978534 lot 2219
sold for $677.81

The area code would be for Northern Nevada. I broke the rest of it down to seven digits then sent her a text: *In reno will try to see frankie voice ok use mary burt hilda vicki emily*

Who are all those people at the end?" Ella asked.

"All of us. In order, that's Ma, Me, Harper, Vale, and you. Ma will get it."

"I'm Emily?"

"She'll know. The name starts with the letter E. Ma's a sharp cookie."

"Okay. So why is yours 'Burt,' of all things."

"My middle name is Burris. We didn't want two M names."

"What does 'voice okay' mean?"

"Means she can call and we can talk, but only from a mall or a casino where there's a lot of close-in cell phone traffic. The FBI would have to follow her, which wouldn't be easy, then try to figure out which cell phone is hers from all the chatter they scoop up since they won't know which number is hers, or if she's even actively using the phone, then we'd talk in circles and use the names I texted her."

"That's . . . wow. This's still kinda crazy."

"Necessary, though. It'll all go away once we get this crapola figured out."

"Wouldn't it be faster if we just told the FBI about the letter I had to type and give to you? I mean, at least they would stop showing our faces on TV and trying to find us, wouldn't they?"

"Yes, and if the highest rungs of the FBI were the ones who got rid of Ridel, they might be inclined to get rid of us as well to keep us quiet. It might not even be a conspiracy. It could be Gladstone alone, running this through a single trusted third party. It also might not be anyone at the FBI. We're completely in the dark here."

"Well . . . poop."

I smiled. That was Lucy's favorite pseudo-cussword. I didn't know what hidden force got me into situations like this, but I had the feeling Lucy was around, pulling a few invisible strings to help me out. How else to account for Ella and the kind of person she was? Luck? Who gets that lucky, time after time?

I didn't say any of that to Ella, however. Some things can't be explained rationally, but I've experienced enough weirdness that I don't discount the idea that I get hints or help from Beyond.

Ella and I donned disguises. In the bottom of my go-bag I found a wig with foot-long gray braids that hung down on either side in front. I put it on and looked at her.

"What do you think, dear? Makes me look like Willie Nelson back in '98. I end up having to give autographs."

She laughed. "Very nice, but I think it's a bit much. People will stare at you and try to see past the hair. And if you wear it once, you'll have to keep wearing it."

"Right you are." I took the wig off, found the next best thing: a white, inch-long grizzled beard and mustache that matched the gray wig I'd been wearing. I put it and the wig on, topped it with the black cowboy hat. "How's this?"

"Better. You look like an 1870's prospector. I suppose I could be married to that as long as you bathe regularly."

Good enough.

Ella went with the gray wig, middle-age makeup, a T-shirt big enough to fit a bit loosely around the D-cup bra. No one would have any idea how slender she was under all that. She put on a hat, dark glasses, and black jeans she'd bought at Walmart a few days ago.

"Let's go," I said. The time was 1:45.

I locked the trailer and we left in the truck. I had my gun on my hip, hidden by an untucked, unbuttoned short-sleeve cotton shirt over a T-shirt. No telling what we would run into on Frank Dolak's street.

• • •

What we ran into was his red pickup, parked in the driveway of a small single-story fifties ranch house with two bedrooms. There was nothing special about the place. It might've cost $22,500 back then; now it would be worth $390,000 in an insane but moribund real estate market due to mortgage rates that are past seven percent. Seven percent of its current market value would be $27,300 in interest per year—money tossed into the wind. That's what happens when Uncle Sam prints money like confetti. Trust the government to do precisely the wrong thing in every critical situation, *every* single time.

The truck's windshield no longer had a bullet hole in it. I slowed just enough to see that. Frank had already been to Fast Glass and had it replaced, but not fast enough. He should've punched the entire windshield out and left it in a ditch at the side of the road an hour after I'd put that bullet through it. If he'd done that, we wouldn't be here now.

I went two blocks past the house, then hung a U-turn and came back, parked eighty yards away with an oblique view of the truck. I shut off the engine. The neighborhood was quiet at 2:20 in the afternoon, kids in school, parents at work.

"Now what?" Ella asked.

"Now we watch and wait."

It took three minutes for her to say, "This's exciting. My heart rate's up."

"That's one reason why I left the IRS. I thought as a PI I would be skulking down dark alleys with a camera and a gun."

"Didn't work out that way, huh?"

"Not *that* way, but in the past five years my life has been like being stuck in a blender on puree."

"You said something like that in Lovelock. Tell me something else that happened to you."

"You sure?"

"Sure, I'm sure. It's boring here."

"A couple of years ago I saved Harper and my wife, Lucy, by tossing a shaped charge—that's an explosive—to a very bad guy and blew off his hand and half of his forearm. I was entirely naked at the time. He was going to kill all three of us, but blowing off a fair amount of his arm pretty much ended that nonsense."

She stared at me wide-eyed for several seconds. "I can't tell if you're kidding or not."

"I'm not."

"*Entirely* naked?"

"Wasn't even wearing socks."

"Oka-a-ay. *Why*?"

"Tell you later. But this, watching a truck with nothing happening, is typical PI work. It's like driving a big rig, an eighteen wheeler. I've heard that that's ninety-nine percent boring and one percent pure terror."

"I wonder which one of those kills the most people. People can die of boredom, you know."

"I could fire my gun in the air, stir things up a bit."

"Not yet. Let's wait a while."

Right then, a burly guy came out of the house and piled into the truck, backed out into the street and headed our way.

"Duck down," I said. "*All* the way down."

I heard the truck go by. Frank, if it was Frank, was on the loose. I started the engine and pulled into a driveway, backed out fast and looked up the street, saw him turn left. I went after him, but carefully. The last thing we wanted was for him to make us.

He got onto I-80 headed west, got off at Keystone and went east on Second Street. At the corner of Second and Bell he slowed, made an illegal U-turn, came back in our direction and parked a quarter block west of a bar called Shifters. I went past him without slowing. Ella turned in her seat and kept an eye on him through the rear window.

"He went into the bar back there," she said.

I went another two blocks east, came back and parked on Second a block east of Shifters. The bar had a hideous four-foot martini glass cantilevered over a dingy front entrance twelve feet from a 15-mile-an-hour school zone sign. Great mix of establishments in the neighborhood, but what impressed me most was that my house was half a block west and one and a half blocks south of Shifters. From home, I could walk to the bar in three minutes.

Coincidence? There's no such thing. My stomach did a slow roll, thinking about what this might mean.

As close as Shifters was to Harper's and my house, I'd never been in the place. It had the kind of bland, seedy look so many businesses on Second Street had, west of the downtown gaming district. Any sort of urban renewal had passed by Second Street without leaving a mark. Shifters was the front of one wing of the Midtown Motel—two long two-story buildings of dreary rooms with walkways facing each other across a too-narrow strip of diagonal parking. Several rooms on the east wing were right above the bar, a lousy place to try to sleep on a Friday or Saturday night, or would be if the bar were a nightspot, which was unlikely. It looked like a watering hole for alcoholics. Gunfire seemed more likely than music.

So, what to do?

The dashboard clock showed 3:05. No shade on the street, temperature just shy of a hundred.

I looked up and a blue pickup truck with old boards enclosing its back bed rumbled toward us from the west. It slowed and turned north on Bell Street right in front of us. Half a minute later a guy in jeans and boots, smaller than Frank, came striding into view. Long hair, ball cap, all we got was a side view of his face. He went into the bar. I used the app on my phone to verify that the truck was the same one I'd put the tracker on in Lovelock.

"That'll be Vince," I said to Ella. "The sniper."

"Are you sure?"

"Not that he was the sniper, that's just a guess, but I'm certain it's Vince. Shoulder-length hair, blue pickup like the one that came after us, tracker still on it, and brother Frank in the bar. I give it ninety-nine point nine percent."

"What'll we do now?"

I thought about that. This was an opportunity the likes of which we might never see again. It was also dangerous. Were our disguises good enough to go in there? I gave her a look. She was ... older, bustier, grayer, didn't look anything like the Ella Kassel whose picture had been on TV, or the girl who'd delivered the note to Waley's Tavern and started this ball rolling. And I didn't look like me.

"Going in could be risky. But maybe not a lot," I said.

"What are we learning out here?"

"Not much."

"What're we trying to do, following these guys?"

"Trying to get this goddamn shinola figured out," I said with some heat. I hadn't asked for any of this. Vince had lobbed bullets at us from three miles away, and Frank had fired a rifle at us as we'd escaped up into the hills. I was fed up with this. I wanted it over with.

She was silent for a moment. "Let's go in."

I gave her a look. "Sure you're up for that?"

"*I* am, and you don't look anything like Mortimer Angel." She hesitated, then said, "You look more like a guy who might hold up a sign at an intersection that says, 'Will work for food'."

I smiled. "*Really?*"

"Yes, really. Let's do this."

"Got a little moxie in you, huh?"

"Maybe. Let's go get beers and sit." She looked out at the street. "We look like we belong here."

I took a deep breath. It bothered me that we were so close to my house. I didn't tell her about that.

"Okay. You did good at that bar in Lovelock. We won't talk to these guys, but we might learn something. If not, it's hot out. A beer would taste good about now and there's nothing like alcohol to make a person think better."

She snorted and opened her door, got out, then looked back at me. "Moxie?"

Chapter Eleven

The interior was dim. I hadn't expected that since the front window faced due south toward the sun, but the glass was tinted and plastered with beer posters and other kinds of paper. A bar ran the length of the wall to the left, half a dozen tables with cheap straight-back chairs in the rest of the place, one TV, no booths, two restrooms in back. About as basic as it gets, and the television was dark and silent.

No other women there. A bartender in his fifties and a lone guy on a stool at the far end of the bar. Other than Frank and Vince, that was it. A morgue.

The Dolaks were at the bar with their heads together. Frank was the bigger of the two, thick neck, buzz cut, small ears, Vince four inches shorter, lean, wiry-looking, both in their thirties. I didn't know which one I'd rather tangle with, if it came to that. Vince looked faster on his feet with quick fists. Frank would probably be a bear, a barroom brawler. Maybe. Generalities like those can trip you up.

I had gone in with a limp, cane in my right hand, Ella holding my left arm. I gave the Dolaks a one-second look as I surveyed the room, as people do when they first come into a place like that. Ella and I took a table behind and to one side of the lads where we could see them; they would have to turn their heads to see us. I couldn't see their faces in the mirror behind the bar so they couldn't see mine or Ella's.

The bartender was jowly, balding, three-day stubble, small towel over one shoulder. He raised an eyebrow at me so I said, "Couple bottles of Bud Light."

He nodded, twisted off two caps, set two bottles on the bar. "Eight bucks, pardner."

Serve yourself.

"I'll get them," Ella said. I gave her a ten. She got up, stood five feet from the Dolak brothers to give the barkeep the ten, got two bills change, grabbed the sweating bottles and came back.

So we drank, and watched, and tried to hear what they were saying but their voices didn't carry. After five minutes of that Ella gave me a "what now" look. I gave her a "give it time" look back, which I think she interpreted as "dunno," which was also accurate.

Finally Frank raised his voice a notch and said, "The guy ain't *home*, Vinnie. What the hell's she want us to *do*?" He sounded angry.

Vince looked behind and to his right at Ella and me, then turned back to Frank and said something I couldn't make out, but his voice was a low growl.

Frank responded with, "Yeah, yeah," but that was all. Their voices were nothing but mumbles after that, but I pegged Vince as the one with the most brains, not that he was a likely Mensa candidate.

But "she?" What does *she* want us to do? Who was she? The only stray she in all of this was the woman who had called Ella and asked her write and deliver the note. I considered the other thing Frank had said: "The guy ain't home." *I* wasn't home, hadn't been in a while, and here we were, in a bar two blocks from my house.

So add it up, big guy. Two guys chase you in pickups, one of them snaps off a rifle shot at you from a hundred yards away and you put a hole in his windshield, and here they are, talking about some guy who isn't home and a 'she' who wants the two of them to "do something."

None of that sounded good.

But then, the world does not revolve around me. They could be talking about some other guy, and the "she" could be anyone, a mother, sister, wife, girlfriend, parole officer.

Time to go. I figured we got about all we were going to get and I wanted to follow one of them when they left, preferably Vince.

"C'mon, babe," I said to Ella. "Let's get goin'."

I picked up my bottle, she grabbed hers, and we went out the door.

"You hear what Frank said?" I asked as I headed west on Second. I dumped our bottles in a trash barrel outside the Midtown Motel office as we went by.

"I think so. Some guy isn't home and they think some girl or a woman wants them to do something. And why are we going this way? The truck's back the other way."

I didn't answer. "What 'he' do you know who hasn't been home lately?"

She stopped walking. "Well, *you*. You think they were talking about you?"

I got her going again. "I'd bet on it. We're going this way so I can show you something relevant to what we just heard."

We turned left at the corner and I took her one block south to First, across First and halfway down the block toward Jones Street, limping and keeping an eye out for federal agents who might be watching my house.

We kept going as I aimed a finger across the street at a two-story house with new siding and new windows due to fifty-odd bullets that had hit the place last year during a drive-by shooting by a moron with a semi-auto .22 rifle. "See the house there?"

She looked. "Uh-huh. So what?"

"It's mine and Harper's. Those two being at that bar this close to our house can't be a coincidence since there's no such thing."

Her eyes got wide. I kept her moving along. No sign of surveillance but the FBI tends to be good at that so they might be tracking the middle-aged couple who'd passed by the house. We went left on Jones, up to Ralston and back to Second. The red and blue pickups were still there, so we got in our truck, ran the windows down, and waited.

"They're still hunting you," Ella said.

"Looks like it."

"This's getting spookier. I don't like this."

"You and me both, toots."

She smiled faintly. "Toots? You can still joke around after what we just learned?"

"We old codgers are pretty resilient. But at this point I want you to seriously consider that cruise to the Bahamas, Fiji, Tahiti, Norway, wherever. I'm buying. Get out of Reno and away from this."

"No."

"I want you safe."

"So do I, but no, I'm not gonna hop on a cruise ship and bye-bye and leave all of this to you. Yes, this's sort of frightening, but you and me, dressed like this, look a whole lot less like the Mort and Ella everyone's looking for than you by yourself. Together we're practically invisible."

Exactly what I'd thought. She was a sharp one.

I tried one more time: "These guys look rough. I have a bad feeling about what they're up to. Take the cruise, kiddo."

"No. And I'm not a kiddo."

I have run up against more than my share of obstinate females. Lucy was one, Harper is another. Maybe the most headstrong was my fiancée five years ago, Jeri DiFrazzia, although Lucy was something else. But tough gals, one and all. Now I had another one to contend with. It's impossible to argue with karma.

"How about I insist?" I said, still arguing.

"Insist all you want, but—"

Frank and Vince came outside and stopped to check out the street. I grabbed Ella and kissed her, gave her an Academy Award, Burt Lancaster-Deborah Kerr, *From-Here-to-Eternity* kiss, but without the beach and bathing suits filling up with sand. My first thought was that I would keep one eye on the Dolaks, but it wasn't practical and the kiss was a good one. It got real and sort of sloppy and by the time it ended Frank was headed away from us toward his truck and Vince was no longer in sight.

"Whew," Ella said. "I haven't been kissed like that in, well . . . in forever."

"Your fault. Your lips are soft and you have a delicate Bud Light taste."

"Thanks, I think, but why did you do it—not that I'm complaining."

"Those two were looking our way. The kiss was mostly camouflage."

"Oh." Then she smiled. "*Mostly*?"

"It lasted longer than I thought it would."

"We could do it again sometime. Like tonight, if you're sure Harper wouldn't mind."

"She wouldn't, but that'll be a moot point with you up at thirty-eight thousand feet on a flight to Fiji."

"Where I'm *not* going. And incidentally, that red truck is pulling away in case you didn't notice."

I started the engine, but let Frank go. I wanted to get a good look at Vince's truck then tail him. Which began ten seconds later when his blue pickup nosed out onto Second Street for a moment, then turned right and headed away from us. By then I'd verified its license plate, first seen at the Super 10 parking lot in Lovelock. The tracker on his truck locked that down even tighter.

I waited a moment before going after him, surprised when he turned left onto Washington which would put him right by my house if he didn't turn left or right on First.

I hustled to the corner, looked down Washington, then went after him. He'd slowed at First, then gone on through. I made the turn, watched as he went slowly past my house. Too slowly, less than ten miles an hour, so I was in his sights. He turned right onto Jones, so I turned right onto First to parallel him one street north. I hit forty getting to the next intersection at Winter Street and looked left. Vince kept going toward Keystone. I tracked him all the way to Keystone where he turned north and went past us as we waited at the light at Keystone and First.

"Good work," Ella said.

"I got lucky."

"Doubt it."

I tailed Vince up Keystone past I-80 to Seventh Street, then up into the hills, watched him turn right on Munley Drive and pull into the driveway of a one-story house at most a decade newer than Frank's—weather-beaten, paint scaling, the front yard mostly dirt and patches of scabby lawn that had given up long ago. I waited at the curb fifty yards up the street, watched as Vince walked around to the side of the house and disappeared.

"Got him," Ella said.

"We already had him. Ma gave us his address. I just wanted to verify it and get a look at the place."

She stared at the blue truck. "Okay. Now what?"

"Now we watch his house for a while."

"I should've brought a book."

"That would make it hard to watch the house, flower."

She sighed, took my hand and we sat in the shade of a maple tree in a temperature of ninety-eight degrees.

"PI work is *so* much fun," she said. "I can see why you like it so much."

"Not this. It's the dames I meet that make it fun."

"Dames." She snorted a laugh.

• • •

I gave it twenty minutes then decided to leave. We were wanted by the FBI. A paranoid neighbor could call the police, wanting them to check out a suspicious vehicle parked in front of their house with people inside not doing anything. My fake ID would probably get us past that, but I didn't want to push it and had no reason to.

Before leaving, I called Ma. Safe enough. A cell tower would blast the call over its entire coverage area. The FBI could get the number of any calls being made, but they would have to zero in on ours among the thousands of calls active in the Reno-Sparks area, and they didn't have the number of my burner. That was worse than a needle in a haystack because Reno's haystack held twenty thousand needles that all looked the same, and the needle they were interested in might not even be in the stack. Ma would answer if she wasn't at home or in her office.

I let it ring four times, but she didn't pick up.

"Now what?" Ella asked.

I shrugged. "Grocery shopping, then we'll go back to the trailer."

"Good. I want to get this humongous bra off. It's been hours since I last saw my knees."

"Cool. I learn new stuff all the time."

•   •   •

Back in the trailer, we spent several hours reading. At least she did. By chapter seven I hadn't turned a page in twenty minutes. I'd been contemplating my next move. I had choices, none of them good and none that involved Ella, which might be a problem when the time came to leap into action—an image so wrong-headed it made me smile.

Ella looked at me. "What?"

Uh-oh. "What what?"

"You smiled."

"I did? I'm sorry."

She stuck a finger in her book to hold her place. "You aren't reading, Mort."

"I'm not?"

"You haven't turned a page in forever."

"You oughta be a detective."

She set her book aside. "What's going on?"

"Just trying to figure out how to handle the Dolaks."

"You're going to 'handle' them? How?"

"I'm working on it. I haven't come up with anything yet but something has to be done. I would put the FBI on them if I was certain no one in the FBI had set this thing in motion. But I don't, so I'll have to keep tailing those two."

"You mean we."

I ignored that. "If the FBI *doesn't* know about them, all the feds have out at the VOR are tire tracks and a bullet hole. And, of course, the burned-out shells of our cars, which won't get them one bit closer to who killed Ridel, although they don't know that so they're looking for us. This is convoluted, which doesn't make it easy for us. The guys chasing us probably aren't on the FBI's radar—not the entire FBI, meaning the rank and file agents who comprise 99.9 percent of the FBI. But an upper management bigwig could've hired the Dolaks or had them hired, in which case he'll be keeping a close eye on the investigation, probably controlling it somehow, reining it in as needed, and Frank and Vince won't be on the mainstream FBI's radar."

"When you put it that way, it sounds hopeless."

"It's not good. Not much we can do right now except keep after the Dolaks and hope something happens." I'd already allowed her to get closer to Frank and Vince than I should have. That was how I'd lost Jeri. I didn't want this to roll over Ella.

She sighed, then picked up her novel.

Right then, Ma called. I checked the time: 7:10.

"Is this Mary?" I asked. I put the phone on speaker.

"Yes."

"Did you give my number to Hilda and Vicki?" Harper and Vale. Ella smiled and put her book down.

"Yes, again. How're things with you and Emily?"

"Groovy."

"I bet. Vicki said the trailer's comfortable. Anyway, I got your text. What's up?"

"We checked in with Frank. He was home. Later he took off and met Vinnie at a bar. We followed Vinnie to the address you gave me earlier."

"That's good. Hilda's with me now. We're at a mall."

She didn't say which one. Good girl. "I want to talk with her, but before I do, you probably oughta know Vince drove by my house this afternoon."

Silence at the other end. Then, "*Did* he?"

"Yes. He didn't stop, but he went by very slowly. He

and Frank were at a bar two blocks from my house."

"That's not good."

"Understatement."

"Here, Hilda wants to talk with you."

"Hi, Burt," Harper said.

"Hey, there, cupcake. I hear you're at a mall."

"Yup. Shopping. How's Emily?"

"Good. I gave her a hell of a kiss in the truck when a couple of cretins looked in our direction." Ella gave me a wide-eyed stare.

"Good thinking," Harper said. "Bet that spun the bad guys around. Any other news?"

"Not much. I told Mary a few things. She'll relay it to you. We don't want to stay on these phones too long."

"Are you getting anywhere with this?"

"Little bits and pieces. Nothing as interesting yet as the dinosaurs dying out sixty-some million years ago due to a humongous meteor strike, but close."

Harper laughed. "You're still crazy."

"Yup."

"I like it. Don't ever change."

"Never."

"Keep in touch?"

"When I can. Text me your number or have Ma do it. Gotta go, Hill. Talk later."

I ended the call.

"Wow," Ella said. "That was . . . something. But what was that about *dinosaurs*?"

• • •

Since I couldn't drug Ella and ship her off to Fiji she also needed a burner. I broke a new one out of its package and set it up, sent its number to Ma, then explained our procedures to Ella in detail. "It's for emergency use only," I told her. "That's important."

She looked at her phone's screen. "This's okay, but do I really need it since I'm here with you?"

"It's backup. Just being safe. You can take a call and call out safely, but Ma and the others can't call us unless they're in a safe place, like at a mall or a casino."

"Got it." She set the phone on a countertop. "Thank you."

•   •   •

We ate dinner, read some more, watched the news at eleven. Those two rascals, Angel and Kassel, were still on the loose, then we showered, brushed teeth, went to bed. It had been a long day. I wanted sleep.

Which got delayed when Ella got close and we lay on our sides for a while holding each other.

Finally she said, "Could we kiss the way we did this afternoon? If you want to, that is."

"I imagine we could, but it might get us worked up."

"For sure it would, but would that be so bad? I mean, it feels good to get things humming. It doesn't have to lead to anything. That's if you could, you know, stand to be a little bit enthused for a while?"

I smiled. "A *little* bit?"

"Well, whatever happens."

"I can do that."

"It doesn't bother you to just stop like that?"

"For most runners, running is the reason they run, not the finish line. Being 'enthused' is often better than sex."

So we got that settled. I pulled her on top of me and let her position herself however she wanted, which turned out to be pretty darn close.

That and the next forty minutes got me another merit badge to sew on my sonofabitchin' Boy Scout uniform.

Chapter Twelve

I tried to sleep, but couldn't. I held the bedside clock a foot from my eyes to read its glowing numerals: 1:42. I laid back. Ella was in my arms while Frank and Vince marched through my head. I couldn't turn those two off—that idiotic sniper fire, the red truck chasing us across flat desert sand, more gunfire, Frank and Vince in Shifters. But the image that burned the brightest was that of Vince's truck gliding stealthily past my house not twelve hours ago. Over and over, that blue truck skulked by like a hunting cat.

I got out of bed without waking Ella. I looked down at her in the three-watt glow of a light at the far end of the trailer. Nice girl, sexy girl. I hoped she would find someone worthy of her someday. Twenty-nine years old. She still had time, but time was slipping away.

I dressed quietly. This was not a good idea, but it had the benefit of not involving Ella. Maybe she wouldn't kill me in the morning. If I lived that long.

Harper wouldn't like this either. Not one bit. But the Dolaks weren't through with us yet. I had to bring a halt to it. Or try to. This, tonight, could very well be wasted effort, but I had to check on my house.

I left Ella a brief note and set her burner on top of it, then eased the trailer door open, shut it soundlessly, and walked to the truck without a limp. No disguise, although I had my go-bag with me, which held wigs, facial hair, and other stuff, like a Glock 20 with two extra clips.

I started the engine and drove away.

• • •

I left the truck on Winter Street, turned off my burner so it wouldn't make a sound if Ma sent a text, and climbed a six-foot plank fence that separated my property from the house to the west. Safe enough. The Noffsingers, Doug and Cathy, were in their seventies and didn't have a dog.

I dropped into my backyard and stayed in a crouch for five minutes, peering into dark shadows, listening for . . . anything. Did the FBI have eyes on my house? No way of knowing, but at 2:15 in the morning, they might not. It had been four days since Ridel died. I gave it a fifty-fifty chance that the FBI had someone watching the place, about the same odds of Frank and Vince showing up in the wee dark hours. I had several zip ties coiled in a pocket in case they did and I got lucky.

The night was quiet. If nothing else, I might be able to get into the house and get another handgun from my gun safe. Or a shotgun. A shotgun would be good.

I crept through tree shadows to the south side of my house, then stood in darkness behind a shaggy lilac with a view of the street. I stayed like that for ten minutes, then crept closer to the street. I stood behind another lilac and gave it a while longer.

Which paid off, because a guy came walking along the sidewalk from the north. I slowly got a black balaclava out of a pocket of my dark blue windbreaker and pulled it over my head. I stood stock-still and waited to see what would happen.

The guy stopped, looked around, then came up the driveway, walking fast. It was too dark to see who it was, but I thought it was Vince, the smaller of the two. Vince, who had scoped out my house earlier.

He passed within four feet of me. When he was a foot beyond me I made a faint clicking sound with my tongue against the roof of my mouth. He stopped, turned to listen, and I punched him in the face, a snappy judo punch that rocked him back, almost put him down, but not quite. Like I'd thought, Vince was wiry and fast. He lunged at me and threw a right. It grazed my head as I ducked under it. I rushed him, clamped his jaw in my right hand and shoved back, hard, and yanked him off his feet with my right leg behind his. I went down with him, hand still gripping his jaw, and slammed the back of his head against the ground, then rolled over the top of him to come up behind him. As he tried to sit up, I hit the top of his head with a hammer fist. I could have killed him with it, but I pulled it. I didn't want him dead. I wanted him to talk, to tell us what this shit was all about.

The whole thing took no more than five seconds and made almost no noise. It was the kind of street fighting move you would never see in judo competition, something Rufus Booth taught me in his dojo after I'd earned my black belt. Judo and karate and all the other martial arts are all about repetition, the same move, over and over and over until it becomes second nature, no thought involved. Next time I saw Ruf I would have to thank him for making me do what I'd just done at least two thousand times.

I checked the guy on the ground, made sure it really was Vince and not some idiot joker off the street. He was out cold. I patted his pockets and came up with a little .22 popgun revolver. I left it in his pocket—evidence—and zip tied his hands behind his back, dragged him deeper into shadow. Frank might still be out there so I readied a Taser to deal with him. That was first choice, but I loosened the Glock in its holster just in case.

I zip tied Vince's ankles, gagged him, then stood deep in shadow and watched the street, listened to the night. Nothing moved. I gave it five minutes, then five more.

Still no Frank.

Okay, then. Now I was at a crossroad. I'd already thought about what I would have to do if it came to this, but now that I was here the decision was right in front of me. Police or no police? Police meant the FBI would be all over me. This would end up in an interrogation room. Ella and I couldn't possibly have killed Ridel, but we were at the scene when he died. At the least, she and I were in for an extended, unpleasant grilling.

I ran it through my head one last time. This would be annoying and messy. We would get disbelieving stares and hostility. We would tell our part of the story ten times, but there would be no hint of proof that she or I had anything to do with Ridel's death because we'd done nothing but see it happen, then dodge long-range bullets and get chased into the hills by two guys who knew what was going on, one of whom was on the ground beside my house bound with zip ties. We could give the feds that.

I texted Ma: *at my house got vince bif will get into it we need taber*.

"Bif" was the FBI.

I settled in to wait. I would give Ma half an hour to respond. If she didn't text or show up, I would have to call RPD Detective Fairchild and turn this mess over to him. Sadly, I was part of the mess, as was Ella.

• • •

Ma texted me with just six minutes to go: *on my way with taber*.

I breathed a sigh of relief.

Ulysses Morgan Taber was the lawyer who had yanked the foundation from under Ned Willis's accusation that Ma and I had traveled to Paris and murdered Julia Reinhart in her hotel room for having killed my fiancée, Jeri. Ulysses was fifty-four years old, a killer in a courtroom, trim, with the piercing eyes of a hunting wolf, charged four hundred dollars an hour out of the courtroom and worth every dime of it. I smiled, wondering if he charged more at three in the morning. I would.

Vince was awake at my feet, still gagged to keep from waking neighbors. I kept an eye on him.

I waited, knowing this circus was about to hit the big time. I hadn't slept since Ella and I woke up yesterday in Lovelock. I wasn't tired yet, but I probably wouldn't be getting to bed anytime soon.

I wanted caffeine.

I texted Ella. *hang tight stay put all is well*

That last part was a white lie with a fair bit of gray in it, but I wanted her to stay in the trailer and keep her head down. She might not get the text until morning, but if she woke up and I wasn't there it should keep her calm. Worth a try. I had no idea what would happen in the next six to eight hours. For all I knew I would end up in handcuffs on a flight to Guantanamo Bay.

I got Vince by the collar of his coat and dragged him over to my unattached garage, sat him on the ground with his back to a wall.

Ma arrived with Ulysses Taber at 3:08. She parked in the driveway and left the lights on, illuminating Vince and me from forty feet away for a moment, then the lights went out and they came over to us.

Ma said, "I gave Ulysses a rundown on what's been happening on the way over. Much as I could, anyway."

Taber grinned. "You lead an interesting life, Mort."

He and I had been on a first-name basis for two years, ever since he took down Ned Willis.

"You think?" I said.

On the ground, Vince shout-mumbled into his gag.

Taber stared at him. "Normally I would suggest that you remove the gag and the zip ties, but from what Maude told me, we had better let the police do that. That said, I suggest you call the police immediately if you haven't done so already. I'd rather not have this fellow's constitutional rights trampled any longer than necessary."

"You sound just like a lawyer," I said.

He smiled. Wolfishly. "Call Fairchild, if you have his number. It would be best to keep this official, but without the kind of overzealous police presence that prevents the kind of understanding among friends that might work well here. I understand you and Fairchild have a . . . past."

Did we ever. Because Taber was an officer of the court I couldn't tell him how much of a past Russ and I had. That was between me and Russ, but it bound us together in a way that had eventually resulted in real friendship.

I'd called Russ so often over the years I'd memorized his number. I used my burner, which wouldn't give him my name. He answered with, "Who the *hell* is this?"

"You're about to be famous, Russ. You can thank me later."

"Mort! Where the *fuck* are you?" I could visualize him sitting up in bed like Frankenstein's monster being hit by a bolt of lightning.

"My house, Russ. Get over here. Bring Day with you."

I was about to say more but Taber took the phone out of my hands and said, "This's Ulysses Taber. Do yourself a favor and don't make this official yet. Mort has asked you to come to his house and that's all you know."

Taber looked at me. "Who's Day?"

"Police officer, Russ's brother-in-law. A friendly. He'll be useful."

Taber nodded. "That's all," he said to Russ. "Get over here." He ended the call, gave me the phone, then looked down at Vince. "We'd better at least remove the gag. Also, people are often dumb enough to talk. There's three of us here. We're witnesses."

I untied the gag and Vince spouted off with a string of vile obscenities.

Taber shook his head. "Vapid, disappointing."

He took me and Ma twenty feet away, out of Vince's hearing. "What's the story here?" he asked quietly, giving Vince a long look. "I hope it's a good one."

I gave it to him. I couldn't sleep, came to check on my house, Vince Dolak came up my driveway, I made a little sound and he attacked me, didn't get past the judo move, and here he is in dark clothing with a gun in a pocket. He and his brother Frank were at the VOR station when Ridel came down. I explained how I knew that in some detail.

"You didn't actually see their faces out there?"

"No."

"Then his being here now isn't compelling. And even if you *had* seen their faces, that wouldn't be enough in a trial, not without corroborating evidence. What about the girl, Ella Kassel? Do you know where she is now?"

"In a trailer in Verdi. She's been with me all the time—except for this, here, tonight."

"Good. That's good. Knowing Fairchild, he'll be okay with us keeping this quiet long enough for me to get all the details. I'm your lawyer. You have rights. I've got the gist of what's happened so far but I'll want the whole thing, every bit of it, to be certain you're on safe ground."

"Ella too."

"Yeah. How did she get into this? I've heard that the FBI thinks she's the key to all this."

"She's not. Certainly not the key, anyway. But I think she's somewhere out on the periphery of this thing."

I told him about the note that sent me to the VOR, and how Ella ended up there. "I could be wrong, but I don't think she was picked purely at random to type and deliver that note."

"No proof either way?"

"No. And I think she's in the dark about that too."

"You still have the note?"

"She does. We do."

"Did anyone else see it and read it at the time it was delivered to you?"

"I did," Ma said. "And Valentina Marchant. In the bar, Waley's Tavern, the night before Mort went to the VOR."

"That's good," Taber said. He turned to me. "Now give me the rest of it. You've been wanted for questioning for the past four days. What've you been doing all that time?"

I told him about Ella and me escaping to Pete's cabin, the trip to Fallon, La Fiesta, seeing the prowling red truck with the bullet hole in the windshield.

"Do you have proof it was the bullet hole you put in the windshield?"

"No."

"We'll call it an identifying mark for now. Go on."

I continued with Vale driving us to Reno, buying the truck and trailer, staying two days in Lovelock to try to get a handle on what was going on. I told Taber about Ella and me sitting in the coffee shop surrounded by FBI agents and Director Gladstone himself.

"Not sure we'll include that in what you tell the FBI," he said with a grin. "But we might. I'll think about it. What else? In particular, why didn't you turn yourself in?"

I gave him my reasons, then told him what Ella and I had done all the way up to the time we got set up at the RV park in Verdi, followed Frank to Shifters where he met with Vince, watched Vince drive very slowly past my house yesterday afternoon, then having a feeling a few hours ago that I should check on my house.

"And here we are," Taber said. "It's a long story. This oughta be interesting. If what you just told me is accurate in every detail, I think you're in the clear except for putting a bullet through Frank Dolak's windshield. We'll talk about that in a moment. The FBI will try to run you and this woman Ella around the block about eight times, but I'll be there to rein that in. Trouble is, I think this guy, Vince Dolak, is also in the clear regarding Ridel's death. I didn't hear anything like proof that he's involved in that, but once the FBI hears your story they might find something. He's here on your property with a gun, wearing dark clothing, but none of that implies intent to harm you with enough oomph behind it to cause him more trouble than several unpleasant hours in an interview room."

"Is oomph a legal term?" I asked.

He smiled. "Yes."

My kind of lawyer.

Taber said, "At the Super 10 in Lovelock you spotted what looked like the blue truck that chased you. You got his license plate there, had Maude Clary find the name of the registered owner: Vince Dolak. There's more evidence against him of possible wrongdoing here, now, but it's still circumstantial and doesn't point to Director Ridel's death in any convincing way. It'll be up to the FBI to try to put that together with him being here tonight.

"From what you've told me, the guy in the red truck, Frank Dolak, is even more in the clear. That all depends on what the FBI can come up with out at the VOR station. Ella didn't see you put a bullet through his windshield. He had the windshield replaced because of a bullet hole, but that doesn't put him out there at the VOR station. If the feds don't have anything that puts him there at the time Ridel came down, he's home free. You and Ella never saw his face there. He might not have an alibi for that time frame, but without motive or opportunity he won't need one."

He gave that some thought. "You said you put a bullet through his windshield while he was in his truck. In other circumstances, that would be a felony, but not in this case since he chased you and shot a rifle at you. You have the right to defend yourself. We'll keep that in mind. It might not be something that needs to be mentioned.

"One last thing. You used the name Arnold Mercer in

the course of your travels because a senior FBI official was murdered, and a minimum of four people were involved in that murder. You therefore thought it possible—remotely, but still possible—that the Dolak brothers were connected to the FBI in some way, possibly hired by a senior FBI official to get rid of Mr. Ridel. In any case, you didn't know if the FBI could be trusted."

"Well said. That's exactly right."

"They'll be overjoyed to hear that. It's likely we won't be able to keep that out of your testimony. But using a false name to buy a truck isn't illegal. Buying a gun using a false name is an entirely different thing."

Fairchild and Day arrived together in Russ's personal car. They got out and hurried over to where all of us had gathered by the garage. Vince was sitting with his back to the wall, quiet now, but glaring poisoned darts at us.

Russ and Ulysses knew each other. Russ introduced Clifford Day to Taber.

I took Russ aside and gave him a three-minute version of the story, then said, "Ella's in a trailer out in Verdi. She has to be brought up to speed before the FBI or RPD gets into this. I'll drive you over there in my truck so we can talk. Ulysses can take your car." I nodded toward Vince. "I don't want him out there. Ma and Cliff can stay here with him. I'll fill you in on events as we go."

He nodded. "So far this sounds like a huge pile of bull pucky. Is it gonna stay that way?"

"Probably."

"That's terrific." He glanced at his watch. "Just what I needed at five minutes to four in the morning."

• • •

We arrived at the RV park in Verdi at 4:15. Russ and Taber waited outside while I opened the trailer and went in.

Ella was awake, dressed in a robe. Her eyes were wide, frightened. "Where'd you go?"

"There's been a development. Tell you about it while you get dressed."

"Are you okay?"

"Yes. Got some people outside who're gonna come in. You need to put on clothes."

She left the robe on, pulled on jeans, then shucked the robe, put on a T-shirt and covered up with a windbreaker. While she was doing that, I said, "I caught Vince skulking around my house."

She stopped and stared at me. "Why'd you go there?"

"I had a premonition, a feeling."

"You get those?"

"I get help. RPD Detective Fairchild is outside. I told you about him. He's a friend. Got a lawyer outside, too. Ulysses Taber. He has most of the story. Vince Dolak is in handcuffs at my house with Ma and a police officer."

"Well, shoot. This's gonna be a lot of trouble, isn't it?"

"Quite a bit. Ulysses will help keep it manageable."

I opened the door and we went outside under a porch light. I waved Taber and Fairchild over. First time either of them had seen Ella. Taber took charge. "I want to talk with Ms. Kassel alone inside, if I may," he said.

I stayed outside with Russ. Taber stepped up into the trailer with Ella and shut the door.

Minutes passed. I told Russ more of what happened at the VOR and afterward.

"Je-sus Christ, Mort," he said when I was finished.

"Yup."

"How do you do it?"

"Dunno. I think it's some sort of cosmic soup."

He stared at me. "Soup."

"Feels like it."

He turned and gazed at the trailer. "She's a looker."

"She is that."

"Wish I knew how you do that too, every damn time."

"It's cosmic sou—"

"Yeah, yeah, I don't think so."

Taber and Ella were inside for half an hour before the door opened and Taber came outside. "You didn't get any sleep tonight, did you?" he asked me.

"Not yet."

"Okay. Stay put here. Sleep. You need to be alert when you talk to the FBI. I want you and Ms. Kassel at my office at eleven sharp. I'll have the FBI there at eleven-thirty. You're only wanted for questioning. We'll do that on our turf, not theirs." He turned to Russ. "Odds are the media will get wind of this. Can you get RPD to control them, keep an open lane into my building?"

"Not a problem."

"Good." Taber faced me. "Anything in the trailer you don't want the feds to find? They'll get a warrant and be in there by early afternoon."

"Some stuff, yeah."

"Nothing to do with Ridel?"

"Not a thing."

"Round it up. Bring it to my office. We'll keep it there. I'll see you at eleven."

He and Russ got into Russ's car and took off. I went back inside the trailer, right into the arms of a warm, tall girl wearing nothing under a thin robe.

"I was so worried," she said. "When I woke up and you were gone."

"Sorry about that. I didn't want to wake you. I didn't want you in danger."

"Thanks, I guess. Ulysses is . . . intense. But he seems very nice. I like him."

"You told him everything we did?"

She smiled. "Not the sexy stuff, but the rest of it, yes. He seemed to know all of it already." She let the robe slide off her shoulders to the floor. "Come to bed and hold me."

I smiled. "Talked me into it."

Chapter Thirteen

On the way to Taber's office I cruised the streets near my house, searching for Vince's truck. I found it a block east of the bar, Shifters. I took the GPS tracker off his back bumper and put it in a pocket. I said to Ella, "This didn't do much for us and it doesn't have anything at all to do with Ridel's death. The FBI doesn't need to know about it. It would just make the questioning go on longer."

She took my hand and nodded. "I get it."

Media raptors had gathered on the sidewalk outside Taber's office building when Ella and I arrived at ten fifty-five that morning. Satellite antennas on raptors' vans were aimed at the sky, ready to provide live coverage of Angel and Kassel's "capture" to a hungry nation. I also saw half a dozen vehicles parked along the street that could only be FBI. I imagined several of them peeling out to unearth new evidence once we'd told our stories.

The police had held a spot vacant at the curb for us. Ella and I got out of the truck and hurried inside through a barrage of dumbass, fourth-grade questions shouted from fifteen feet away. I carried a travel bag that held fake IDs, two handguns, disguise paraphernalia, and a lot of cash. The FBI didn't need to see any of that.

Taber met us at the door, locked it as soon as we were inside, and took us upstairs to the inner sanctum, past a secretary in her fifties, Marie Trumbell, who might've been able to stop a Tiger tank from getting past her. Taber called out to someone named Sue as we went down a hallway and into his office.

"Whew," I said when we were inside. I could still hear the rasp of voices below in the street through the window.

He shrugged at the noise. "I could make the case that their development was arrested at about age ten."

Ella and I sat on comfortable chairs that swiveled and tilted, upholstered in dark green fabric.

His assistant, Susan Cano, whom I'd met a year and a half ago, came into the office. She was a year or two shy of thirty, pretty and competent. She took a chair to my right. Marie Trumbell came in, took orders for coffee and tea and provided cookies and catered sandwiches.

Taber locked my travel bag in a safe in a closet to the left of his desk. He sat behind the desk and looked at both of us. "You two ready for this?"

I snagged a sugar cookie and said, "Yup." I wasn't, but I didn't see the point in saying so. Due to karma, I was going to lose yet another day of my life to the Bureau.

Ella nodded, then said, "I guess."

"I've already heard your stories," Taber said. "Just tell it like you told me. They'll question you separately, but I'll be there for both of you. When one of you is being grilled, the other will be in Sue's office with Sue to ensure that no wandering FBI agents come in and try to get his or her hooks into you."

He gave us instructions that lasted a while, made sure we understood them, then sat back with a finger sandwich and a cup of coffee. It was 11:30. "FBI can cool their heels a while longer. It's good for them. All they know at this point is the people they have wanted for questioning as possible witnesses to Director Ridel's death are here in my office. Other than that, they're coming in blind." He produced a lupine smile. "Just the way we like them."

Yup. Definitely my kind of lawyer.

•   •   •

He let the FBI in at 11:40 with thin apologies and no explanation for the delay. He and I, two FBI special agents and an FBI lawyer, gathered around a conference table in the room I'd been in when Taber had run circles around Ned Willis, and Susan Cano had shown Ned and a pair of FBI lawyers a couple of videos that had been instrumental in shoving Ned's ill-advised investigation off a cliff.

Manly handshakes and direct eye contact all around set the mood. Coffee and leftover catered sandwiches were made available. Special agents Sam Ivers and Bruce Caton got coffee and finger sandwiches on paper plates before we got down to business.

Taber turned on a video recorder. George Hadley, the FBI lawyer, fired up one of his own.

Sam Ivers looked at me. "You've been out of touch for quite a while," he observed mildly—something he might've practiced at a Quantico in-service training: soft voice in an easy-going, "we're all friends here" tone to give the mark the impression that this would be just a friendly chat. He was the older, heavier, and shorter of the two agents.

I didn't respond to that. Taber had told me to respond only to questions and requests, and he would make certain those were legitimate attempts to get at the truth of what had happened to Deputy Director Ridel—and what I had done in the intervening five days since then. Keeping them in the dark about that, Ulysses explained, would only keep them anxious and digging into those five days.

"That was a statement," Taber said to Ivers. "You are here get Mr. Angel's story and to ask questions related to Mr. Ridel's death. I suggest you make the most of it. Time is of the essence since Mr. Angel is paying for my time and taxpayers are paying for yours. That said, I believe there is one question we should dispense with before we really get going here in order to speed things along."

"Which is?" Ivers asked, sipping coffee.

"What you hinted at a moment ago. Why didn't Mr. Angel contact you earlier?"

"Nailed it," Agent Caton said, leaning forward.

Taber got a bound sheaf of papers from a briefcase at his feet and tossed it on the table with a resounding thud.

"*That* is an FBI document asked for via a FOI request, *Freedom of Information* by a congressional subcommittee. It has been redacted to the point that it is, in effect, twelve ounces of poor-quality toilet paper. Over a thousand copies were printed and distributed. It says nothing. It gives no information. None whatsoever."

Ivers shrugged. "The FBI can't be giving out classified

information to anyone who asks for it."

"Including Congress?"

Ivers shrugged again and looked around at the walls.

Taber got another sheaf from his briefcase and let it fall with a similar thud on the table. "This is the same FBI document, unredacted. Try to find classified information in it. The redactions in the first response to the FOI were nothing but self-serving attempts to prevent the oversight committee from knowing just how much political bias has crept into much of what the FBI has been doing. If you'd like to see another redacted/unredacted document, it will demonstrate virtual criminal activity on the part of FBI's senior officials, redacted to keep congress and the public in the dark." He tilted his head at Ivers and at Caton, offering them to comment about that.

Neither of them said a word.

"Deputy Director Ridel was shoved from an airplane," Taber said. "Alive and drugged. He died on impact. As you are about to hear, a minimum of four people were involved in that act. *Four*. That's a conspiracy. As yet we don't know who was involved, but we're aware that Mr. Ridel was not well liked by a number of senior officials in the FBI and in the Justice Department. He was not a trusted member of the club. Therefore, it is not outside the realm of possibility that Mr. Ridel's death was at the hands of the FBI itself. I'm not saying that's likely, I'm saying it's not impossible. Big difference there, but critical."

At that, the FBI lawyer, George Hadley, shifted in his chair. He opened his mouth to speak, but didn't. I had the feeling he wanted to object, but didn't know how to frame the objection.

"Therefore," Taber went on, "Mr. Angel was exercising common sense and his right to remain silent. He had no way of knowing if FBI's upper management was involved in Mr. Ridel's death. But that was his concern, and in my opinion, personal and legal, the concern was valid. But you are now about to hear Mr. Angel's account of what he saw out there in the desert east of Lovelock and what he did afterward, so I expect to hear no whining by the FBI about his 'failure' to come forward until now."

"Whining?" Hadley said with narrowed eyes.

"Whining, redacting, CYA, it all stems from the same mindset. But it's my opinion and also Mr. Angel's that, as a whole, the rank and file in the Bureau do *not* adhere to the pseudo-criminal acts of a few senior FBI officials. We do not hold the rank and file responsible in any way for how the FBI is now perceived by many in this country."

Hadley's eyes narrowed further. "Pseudo-criminal?"

Taber's eyes bored into Hadley's. "A certain very high-ranking military officer was questioned by the FBI some years ago. Months later, he was asked the same questions, and when the answers were not identical, *identical*, that officer was accused of lying either when questioned the first time or the second time. A felony in either case. That tactic was what one expects in a police state, a totalitarian society. I could ask you, Mr. Hadley, where you were May first of this year, record your answer, then ask again in four months, and if the answer was not precisely the same, I could accuse you of lying and ram the legal system down your throat—*if* I were a senior agent of the FBI with the morals of a goat. This sort of thing does go on. No one in the country should ever, *ever*, speak to the FBI without a lawyer present. It would be good for people in power to act like adults once again, but I hold out very little hope that that will happen anytime soon. Now, shall we get on with it? If you have questions, ask." He leaned back and folded his arms.

Fifteen seconds of silence played out as both Ivers and Caton gave Taber long looks, then Ivers turned to me. "You were present at the time FBI Deputy Director Ridel fell from an airplane in the desert east of Lovelock?"

I nodded. "Yes."

"Was Ms. Kassel also present?"

"Yes."

"Okay, I wanted to get that out of the way so we're all starting on the same page here. Now, because I don't know what your story is, I can't very well ask questions about it. So I'll ask you to just tell us everything in narrative form, a story format, if you will. If Special Agent Caton and I have questions, we will ask, but we'll take notes and try not to interrupt too often. You might start by explaining why you were out there at that VOR station at that time. I've tried to think of a reason and I can't come up with one that doesn't . . . doesn't make you appear *culpable*, in some way." He gave me a hard, questioning look.

So I got into it. The note, driving out there the next day, leaving the truck at the ghost town and continuing on to the VOR station on a dirt bike.

"Sorry to interrupt," said Agent Caton, "but do you have a copy of that note?"

"I have the original." I took it out of a pocket and gave it to him.

Be at VOR Station WS61 at 1600 hours tomorrow. Come alone. No second chance. Ella**.**

He and Ivers read it, which took twenty seconds since they read it two or three times. "That's it?" Ivers asked.

"That's it."

"It's signed Ella. That would be Ella Kassel?"

"Yes, it would."

Ivers eyeballed me for a few seconds for having keyed off the way he'd phrased the question.

I'd only told them that I'd received a note, not where or when or how. Taber had asked me to do it that way. He wanted to see how they would handle it.

"Ella Kassel wanted you out there?" Ivers tilted his head at Agent Caton to indicate they were really getting somewhere now. Which figured. The agent at the Silver Spur Saloon in Lovelock had told us the FBI thought Ms. Kassel was the key to all this.

"No," I said. Might as well yank a chain or two since it was just hanging there.

"No?" Ivers glanced at the note again.

"You might ask her about that, but she said she got a phone call, that the caller dictated the note to her and told her to print it and deliver it to me."

He frowned. "She got a call?"

"Ask her about that. I'm only telling you what she told me. She delivered the note to a place called Waley's Tavern on Fourth Street in Reno. She gave it to the bartender and left. The bartender gave it to me. He's a witness. I was with Maude Clary and Valentina Marchant at the time. They're also witnesses."

"Valentina Marchant? *The* Valentina Marchant?"

"I wouldn't know. Are there several?"

Out of the corner of my eye I saw Taber smile.

"You know what I mean," Ivers said.

"I *do*? How do you know?"

He gave me a long look. "So you got this note and went to the VOR station at four the next day even though the note asked you to come alone? No second chance?"

"No." That chain was low-hanging fruit. Irresistible.

Ivers's eyebrows lifted. "*No*?"

"The note didn't ask me to come alone."

"Did I misread it?" Ivers said.

I shrugged. "Apparently. Give it another try."

Ivers frowned. He and Caton bent over the note one more time. Ivers looked up at me. "It very clearly asks for you to come alone."

"Where does it ask *me* to come at all? I don't see my name on it anywhere."

Ivers glanced at the note. "Uh . . ." He regrouped and said, "Because the note was delivered to you at that tavern, you felt it was meant for you, asking you to be at the VOR station at four o'clock?"

"That's correct."

He sighed faintly. I have that effect on people. It's one of my many knacks.

"Ms. Kassel was at the VOR when you got there?" Ivers asked—a question in the form of a statement, probably not taught at Quantico because it's that old "ass out of you and me" business, which I've always found silly since only one of the participants becomes the ass. In this case, Special Agent Ivers.

"No. I got there half an hour early. She came along on a bicycle about twenty minutes after I got there. I watched as she rode across the flats toward me."

"Why did she come, too?"

"I can tell you what she told me if you want hearsay,

but you might ask her when she tells her part of all this."

He sat back. "Okay, I'm doing what I said I wouldn't do, asking too many questions. Go ahead with your story."

So I did. Tried to, anyway. I told them about seeing Ridel fall from the plane, landing at 4:01, checking Ridel's body, finding his wallet and using nitrile gloves to take the wallet out to find the guy's name—

"*Nitrile* gloves?" Caton said. "Who carries gloves like that with them?"

"Physicians, EMT personnel, police," Taber said. "You might rephrase the question. Or drop it."

Caton gave Taber a narrow look. To me, he said, "Why did *you* have nitrile gloves with you?"

"I'm a private detective. I had a backpack with me. I'm always prepared. Also, nitrile gloves don't weigh me down. Their weight isn't a big consideration, like, say, gold bars."

Taber smiled. Caton shut up, but wrote something on his notepad. Probably not a smiley face.

I continued with the story. "I determined the dead guy was Alden Ridel. About then, someone in the hills to the west fired a big-bore rifle at us, might've been a .30-06—"

"Someone *shot* at you?" Agent Caton asked.

I knew that would get their attention. It also kept the narrative choppy, but *c'est la vie*. That was their problem.

"Yes. I didn't get it at first because the sniper was so far away. It took the bullet seven or eight seconds to reach us. The sound of the shot came about fifteen seconds after we saw the puff of smoke. So—roughly three miles."

"Jesus. That's nuts."

I smiled. "Yup. First bullet actually hit the VOR. Pure luck. The rest were pretty wild, except for the last one, but you might be able to find that first one somewhere in the VOR." I went on with the story, told them about the red truck that came hurtling across the desert toward us from the direction of the sniper fire.

Ivers frowned. "A truck?"

"A red pickup, might've been doing ninety across the flats, coming right for us. I got Ella on my dirt bike and we took off, headed east toward the hills where I could lose him. Which I did, barely. A few minutes later a blue pickup came across the flats, also going fast. It might've been the sniper since by then the bullets had stopped. Best guess, you'll see my dirt bike's tracks, and if either truck crossed my tracks you'll see that too. The guy in the red truck got out as we were escaping into the hills. He fired a rifle at us as we disappeared over a ridge. I got out and put a bullet through his windshield from about two hundred yards out to keep him away from us." I'd talked it over with Taber and we'd decided I should tell the FBI about the bullet in the windshield of Frank's truck since that was how Maude got his name and how we discovered that Frank and Vince Dolak were brothers.

"You shot at him?"

"More at the truck than the guy. But wouldn't you? Guy firing a high-powered rifle at you?"

Ivers smiled a bit. "Probably. Did you see his face? Could you recognize him if you saw him again?"

"Not then, no. He was too far away."

Ivers thought about that. "But later you saw his face? You could recognize him?"

"Yes, but nowhere near that VOR station so I doubt it would stand up in court."

"Can you explain that?"

"Yes, when I get to that part of the story. Right now it would make things jump around too much."

Ivers spun a little circle with an index finger. *Go on.*

I continued with our running out of gas and hiking up to Pete's cabin, staying the night, getting to Fallon the next day, eating at La Fiesta.

"Okay, you spent the night up there," Ivers said. "I can see why you couldn't contact the FBI. But you were in town the next day, so you could've called the FBI and—"

"Asked and answered," Taber interrupted laconically. "Unless you want to go round and round about trust issues again."

"Not hardly."

"You heard about the military officer I mentioned a while ago? He spent time in prison even though everyone at the FBI knew he was innocent. And now there's a rotten judge out there with egg on his corrupt face."

Ivers nodded curtly. "Yeah. Let's move on." He turned to me. "We tracked you and the girl to Fallon. That's where we lost you. How'd you get out of there? Where'd you go?"

I told him about Vale coming to get us, disguises, the trip to Reno, buying a truck and a trailer.

"You wore disguises?" Ivers said.

"Ella and I knew we were on TV—our faces. How else were we supposed to keep clear of the FBI?"

Ivers let out another little sigh.

Agent Caton said, "You bought a truck? We didn't pick that up."

"I paid cash and used the name Arnold Mercer."

"It's legal in this state," Taber said in order to head off any objection either agent might have to that. "Registering it in a different name is another matter, which Mr. Angel didn't do."

"Where'd you go after you got the truck and trailer?" Ivers asked.

I told him about buying supplies at a Walmart then driving to Lovelock.

"Lovelock?" Ivers said, momentarily stunned.

I smiled. "Best place to keep tabs on the investigation was right there, see if I could pick up anything helpful."

"Helpful?" Caton said.

"Helpful to me. Any suggestion of a conspiracy by the FBI regarding Mr. Ridel's death."

"Je-sus Christ," Ivers said under his breath. Later we heard it on the recording Taber made of the interview.

I went on, told them about seeing in the parking lot of the Super 10 motel what looked like the blue truck that had come after us in the desert.

"But you didn't actually *know* it was the same truck?" Caton asked.

"No. It was a Ford F450 stake truck, same color, and its bed was enclosed by old boards like the truck I saw that afternoon. It was distinctive, but I couldn't swear it was the same truck."

"Circumstantial," Caton said in a dismissive tone. "Go on."

"Circumstantial or not, it's what private investigators

do. I gave its license to my boss, and she came up with a name: Vince Dolak. At the time that was just a data point that might mean something, might not. But we're here now because I caught Vince Dolak on my property at three in the morning, so now it does mean something."

"Vince Dolak," Ivers said, squinting at me. "We could have used that name. The Bureau could have been all over that guy three days ago, not wasted all this time."

"Back to the conspiracy again," Taber said. "Mr. Angel had no way of knowing who was behind Dolak, pulling his strings." He gave Ivers a piercing look. "We still don't, nor do you, but Vince Dolak attacked Mr. Angel last night and he is currently in police custody."

Caton stared at Ivers. "That's—"

Ivers silenced him with a hand. He looked at me and Taber. "RPD gave us Dolak four hours ago. He's being held at the federal building. I was present during his first hour of questioning, before I was given this assignment, here. Dolak is lawyered up. All they're saying is that he couldn't sleep, took a wrong turn in the dark out walking early this morning, didn't have any idea he'd wandered onto private property. But"—he faced me—"you're saying you saw his truck in Lovelock, what, two days after Ridel was killed?"

"Evening of the second day."

"Which, if true, is also circumstantial," the lawyer, Hadley, said. "Did anyone else see his truck there?"

"Ella," I said. "Not sure if she saw his license plate, but you might check the registration at the Motel 10 there. If nothing else you might get him by his handwriting."

Caton pulled out a cell phone and began texting. He glanced at Taber. "This might change things—him being in Lovelock and here on Mr. Angel's property."

"I should think it does," Taber said. "But probably not enough. If Dolak has a lawyer I think he'll walk." He leaned forward. "What's the lawyer's name?"

Ivers consulted his notes. "Bertrand Hall."

"Dolak'll walk," Taber said, sitting back. "You realize that his arrest is the only reason Mr. Angel is talking to you now. We'll be very interested to see how the FBI handles Mr. Dolak. If he walks, he's a loose cannon."

Ivers gave me a look. "A guy in a blue truck appears to have chased you and Ms. Kassel after that red truck came after you, but you didn't see either of their faces, did you?"

"No."

"And even if you had, it would still be one of those he said, she said deals. Unless we find evidence that he was somewhere around the VOR at the time Mr. Ridel fell from the plane, we've got nothing on him. Even if we do find something that puts him there, it's unlikely he'd ever make it to trial." He glanced at Hadley. "That about right?"

"As things stand now, yes. But it's early yet. We're just getting started on Mr. Dolak."

Taber nodded to me. "Continue, Mr. Angel."

I told them Ella and I spent the night in Lovelock and got to the Sage Inn just in time to see Director Gladstone at the podium before his press conference began. I also told them Ella and I were in the motel's coffee shop when the conference broke up and the place was flooded with FBI agents, and Director Gladstone and two senior agents sat at a table ten feet from us.

Ivers's eyes bulged, then he shook his head and smiled wryly. "That'll make a few heads explode." He glanced at the two cameras recording the session, pursed his lips, and stared at his legal pad with a hint of pink on his cheeks.

"Continue," Taber said to me with a slight smile.

I told them about Ma finding the owner of the red truck via the bullet hole I'd put in its windshield—Frank Dolak—and discovering that he and Vince were brothers.

"That tightens it," Caton said. He got on his cell phone again and sent another text.

"Depends," Taber said doubtfully. He nodded to me to keep going.

I gave them the rest of it, up until the time Ella and I got to Verdi and we followed Frank Dolak to Shifters and he met with his brother, Vince. "That was the first time I actually saw Frank's face," I said.

"Which is problematical," Taber said to the two agents across the table from us. "Mr. Angel can't testify that either of the men he saw in that bar drove the trucks he saw at the VOR station. If Bertrand Hall is defending those two, he would tear Mr. Angel's testimony to shreds."

"Which means what?" Ivers asked.

"You don't have enough. Not yet, anyway." He nodded for me to continue.

I told them that after the Dolaks left the bar, Frank took off and Vince drove slowly by my house as if he were watching the place. Which is why I was up past two in the dead of night at my house and caught Vince coming up my driveway in dark clothing and armed with a .22 pistol. He attacked me, so I defended myself and took him down, then I called my boss and the police.

"And here we are," I said.

"Now's a good time for a fifteen-minute break," Taber said. "Mr. Angel will answer any questions you have after that. Bathroom's down the hall to your left."

Both Ivers and Caton had their cell phones out before they left the room.

Chapter Fourteen

I answered a few questions when they got back, but I'd already given them a reasonably comprehensive account, so they turned me loose and brought Ella in to get her side of things. I went to Susan Cano's office and spent the next hour chatting with Taber's better-looking half.

A special agent was stationed outside her office. I have always wondered what bureaucratic twit thought calling them special agents was a primo idea that wouldn't cause laughter. When I headed down the hallway to the men's room, Special Agent Torres came along, about to follow me inside, so I stopped in the doorway and said, "You might want to rethink coming in here with me."

"Yeah? Why is that?"

I held up a little recorder Sue Cano had given me. Its red light was on. "Because anything you say can and will be used against you, chief."

He gave me a hostile look, probably didn't like being called 'chief' since he was a long way from being in charge of anything but hallway duty, then strode back to his post without looking back.

Got a B+ for effort, though.

•   •   •

Ivers and Caton left Taber's building at 3:40 p.m. Ella and I sat in the conference room with Ulysses and Sue.

"The FBI picked up Frank Dolak," Sue told us. I had already heard that, but Taber and Ella hadn't.

Taber shrugged. "If the Bureau doesn't have anything more than what Mort and Ella told them, he'll be released sometime this afternoon. Unless, of course, he's a fool and doesn't have a lawyer with him."

"They've already cut Vince Dolak loose," Sue said. "He can still be charged with assault, but that's it. *If* Mr. Angel presses charges."

"Mort," I said. "Mr. Angel was my father."

Taber smiled. "Trying to get Dolak on assault would be more trouble than it's worth. Especially if Bertrand Hall is his lawyer. I wouldn't go there."

"Which," I said, "brings up the interesting question of who is paying for Vince's high-dollar pettifogger."

At that, both Ulysses and Sue lifted eyebrows.

"*What*?" I asked innocently.

"Pettifogger," Sue said, lips twitching a little. "Nice."

Marie Trumbull came in. "I got a call. Frank Dolak's been cut loose. He had the same lawyer, Bertrand Hall."

"Great," I said.

So we would have two loose cannons out there: Frank and Vince. They had chased us and shot at us, no idea why, but they were free to try again. I didn't like that, but that was how the system worked. Blind, but fair.

Except for politicians, in which case it's blind, stupid, two-tier, and a stacked deck, but that's a different story.

• • •

We gathered in the Green Room at 8:30 that evening, Me, Harper, Ella, Ma, Vale, Taber, and Sue. Also present were Russell Fairchild and the behemoth, Clifford Day. I call him the behemoth because he's six-six and is now up to three hundred sixty pounds. We would've made a lively crowd but for the somber undercurrent.

The topic was two-fold: What, if anything, to do about Frank and Vince Dolak—and what to drink. The second of those was the evening's primary consideration because the first had no apparent solution within the legal system.

The Green Room still had green track lighting, but the carpet was new, the bar top had been resurfaced in dark oak and the video slot machines previously imbedded in half the length of the bar's surface had been removed. New barstools of dark oak, upholstered in green leather, gave the place another little bump in class.

All nine of us sat around two tables pushed together in the middle of the room. Harper sat to my right, Ella to my left, Ma and Officer Day side by side which still had me wondering about those two. And I had the impression that Taber and his cutie, Susan Cano, were . . . close.

Harper had been holding my arm for an hour when she got up and pulled me and Ella into our own little group fifteen feet from the rest.

"Now what?" she said, including Ella in the comment. "What I mean is, are you two safe with the Dolak brothers out there? Do you think they're still after you?"

"Unknown," I said. "We still don't know what this was all about. Ma, Vale and I are going to keep working on it, but we don't have much of a handle to get hold of."

Harper looked at Ella. "You should stay with us at our house for a while."

Ella stared at her. "I couldn't. I mean, it feels like I've already come between you and Mort way too much."

"You haven't 'come between' us at all," Harper said.

Ella smiled. "I know you say that, but—"

"But it's *true*," Harper said. "Also, you've been at risk and you've helped Mort and you've kept him from being entirely alone in this. For all of that, I thank you."

I tried not to smile. This was going to get good. Maybe I should go to the bar and let them work it out alone.

But . . . no. I wanted to hear this.

Ella said, "That's . . . that's the part that . . ."

"That feels strange," Harper finished the thought for her.

"Yes."

"I know, because I've been there. Which is why I told you how Mort and I met and what we had to do only a few hours later when that woman took all our clothes."

Ella smiled, but didn't know what to say to that.

Harper lowered her voice. "He's got so many merit badges for something akin to chastity that the shirt of his Boy Scout uniform sags in front."

"Hey, hey, hey," I said.

"Hey, hey, yourself," Harper said. She looked at Ella. "He's a huggable old bear, isn't he? And safe as seatbelts. Anyway, the Dolaks are still out there so I'd really like it if you'd stay with us for a while, until, I don't know, until we know more about what's going on. We have a really nice spare bedroom all ready to go with its own bathroom."

"I would feel like a third wheel," Ella said.

"You wouldn't be." Harper leaned in closer. "At all. I want you to be safe. Also, you and I could talk."

"Uh-oh," I said.

Harper smiled at me. "Uh-oh?"

"Talk. *That's* trouble."

She pecked my cheek. "So you think. Anyway, I'd like to hear more about long-distance running." She turned to Ella. "Please stay with us, at least until we know those two Dolak shitbirds aren't going to be a problem."

Yeah, no problem. FBI guys falling from airplanes and guys firing rifles at us and chasing us in trucks. But I kept my mouth shut. This discussion about living arrangements was going to stay between the womenfolk.

"I could stay in the trailer," Ella said. "I mean, it's still out there in Verdi. Why don't I do that?"

"Because you'd be alone out there," Harper said. "And we don't know what the Dolaks know, and we don't know why someone picked you to write and deliver that note. I really wish you would stay with us for a while."

That's my girl. To keep up with the conversation I took another hit of Moose Drool.

"I don't know . . ."

"I'd like to insist without sounding pushy," Harp said.

"I guess . . . maybe . . . for a couple of days anyway."

"Good," Harper said. "Or longer if need be, but we can figure that out later." She turned to me. "Okay?"

"Two gorgeous women on hand to do the cooking and cleaning and bring me cold beers when I snap my fingers? Yeah, okay."

Harper smiled at Ella. "He's so cute, isn't he? But I worry about his death wish."

"I would too."

"Then it's settled. Are you okay for tonight? You and Mort could go to your apartment tomorrow while I'm at school and get whatever you need from there."

Ella sighed. "Okay, but it still feels kind of . . ."

"It'll be okay," Harper said. "You'll see."

• • •

And it was, for as long as it lasted, which was six days, but all was quiet, no sign of the Dolak brothers, no sign of anything out of the ordinary, so Sunday evening Ella said she wanted to move back to her apartment in the morning and get on with her life.

Which she did.

By then I had hauled the trailer to our house and set it up in back, beside the garage. I wasn't sure what to do with it. Maybe next summer Harper and I could go to the Grand Tetons, the Carlsbad Caverns, New Orleans, visit Mount Rushmore, ride the Gateway Arch tram in St. Louis. Lots of things I'd never done, places I've never seen.

In the days after Ella left, I stopped by her apartment around two p.m., about the time the last round of students were filing into Harper's classroom. After two weeks of that, I went by Ella's every two or three days, and after a month, by late September, I was stopping by once a week. In all that time she never once said a word about us having shared a bed those outlandish days in August, and I didn't either. That was over. I only wanted her to be safe.

The Dolaks were around. I kept track of them but I never caught them near Ella's or my house. Apparently the FBI couldn't find anything that would end up with lethal injection and canapés afterward, so all of us were in a kind of limbo, waiting for the other shoe to drop.

Then one Monday, October fourteenth, with the days getting shorter and cooler, Ella wasn't at her apartment. I knocked, got no answer. She didn't answer her cell phone. We didn't have a standing date, nothing like that, but she had always been there by two p.m. on Mondays, working on her thesis. I stared at her door, then left, but went back at six that afternoon. She was still out.

I tried the next day, still no Ella.

Wednesday, 2:05 p.m., I was about to knock on her door when my phone lit up with the first few bars of *Purple People Eater*, Ma's favorite ring tone whenever it kicked off in her office.

I answered, and a man's voice said, "If you ever want to see Ella Kassel alive again, leave Reno now, head east on Interstate Eighty. If you're not seen leaving Sparks in your truck in half an hour, Ella will be dead ten minutes later. If you call cops or the FBI, she's dead. Keep your phone on. Go east on I-80. You have half an hour. I'll be in touch."

click

I stared at the phone in my hand.

Ella? Dead?

My Ella?

Yes, she was my Ella. My friend, my responsibility, my girl. Somehow I had dragged her into this. She had gotten tangled up in my karma. Mine.

There were several girls I considered "my" girls. Jeri was one, but then she was my fiancée, a kind of upgrade. Same with Lucy, then I married her. Harper was one of my girls for quite some time, but I married her one year after Lucy died after she put me and Harper together. There was Holiday Breeze—Sarah Dellario—and Valentina and Susan Kenny and, finally, Ella. All of them were my girls.

I would give my life for any of them. Ma was also one of my girls, but in a different way. I would die for her too.

No time to call Harper. No time to do anything but get in the truck and go. And how did the guy know I was in my truck and not the new 4Runner Harper and I had bought?

No time to think about it. No time for anything. I got in the truck and headed for I-80. I checked the tank. Only a quarter full. I didn't know how far I would be going. I hit a gas station before getting on the interstate and pumped in fourteen gallons before I felt time slipping away.

I got on I-80, didn't get hung up in traffic, and went east past Sparks with only four minutes to spare.

Shit.

They got Ella. They wanted me.

And I didn't have any idea who "they" were.

None at all.

But there were at least four of them, and the SP101 .357 Ruger stashed under the front seat of my truck was the only gun I had with me.

And its cylinder only held five bullets.

Chapter Fifteen

Don't call the police or the FBI.

And yet, this could *still* be an FBI operation, which was shit. A senior official could have sandbagged evidence that put the Dolak brothers out at the VOR station, which was why they were still loose. Best guess, and only a guess, the voice on the phone I'd just heard was Vince's. Frank's was somewhat deeper and with a different timbre.

But Vince and Frank with their heads together didn't have half the intelligence needed to put together anything like Ridel being grabbed, drugged, and dumped out of a stolen plane. I still thought it was someone who'd had a professional or personal grudge against Ridel. Someone who had chosen me to be the dupe on the scene.

But more than just a dupe. They had Ella, but they wanted me. This wasn't only about Ridel. It was about him *and* me.

Someone wanted him dead, but they wanted me dead too, or so it seemed. I had been set up. I was supposed to have been alone at the VOR station, and the Dolaks had had rifles and trucks. Alone, I would have been dead.

This was still up in the air. They had killed Ridel and now they wanted me—whoever they were.

And they had Ella. They had Ella. They had Ella.

For her, I would ride right into their hands.

•   •   •

I had my cell phone and a burner. I called Harper on the burner as I passed by Fernley. The time was 3:05. She should be alone in her classroom except for a stray kid or two hanging around.

"Hey," she answered cautiously. "Why the burner?"

"They've got Ella," I said.

Silence. Then, "Oh, no."

"Yes. I was right outside her apartment when I got the call. I was told to drive east on I-80, not to call the police or the FBI or they'll kill her. That's all I know, babe."

"What can I do to help?" Her voice was shrill.

"Nothing. Stay out of it. I'm just calling to let you know this isn't over yet. I have to do this."

She started to cry, which broke my heart.

All I heard for the next thirty seconds was Harper's sobbing, then, "I love you, Mort," in a broken voice.

Which tore my heart in two.

"I love you too, cupcake."

"I know you have to try to save her, but please come back to me. Please." She had been in this situation before, but as the victim. Same thing: do not contact the FBI. She knew that if I had, she and Lucy would have died. Hostage situations often don't end well.

"I will. Gotta go. I'm gonna call Ma, get her in on this."

"Be safe. *Please* be safe."

We ended the call, and I called Ma.

"*Now* what?" she answered gruffly.

"They kidnapped Ella," I said.

"Oh, shit, no!"

"I'm on I-80, headed east. That's all I was told, except not to call the police or the FBI or Ella's dead."

"Where are you now?"

"A few miles past Fernley."

"Got a gun with you?"

"A .357 with five rounds in it."

"That's all?"

"Yes."

"Shit. I'll leave right away," Ma said.

"Don't. Stay put and find out everything you can about the Dolaks."

"I already got everything I could."

"Try harder. Put your hacker on it."

Silence.

"Ma?"

"Yeah, yeah, okay. Shit. Vale's right here. I'll get her on the road toward you soon as she can get going. With guns and ammo and other stuff."

"No. I want her to stay with Harper—every moment Harp isn't actually in a classroom. Whatever happens, I have to know she's safe."

"You need *help*, Mort."

"Vale stays with Harper, Ma. Do it!"

My cell phone rang.

"Gotta go. My other phone's ringing."

I cut her off and answered my cell. "Yes?"

"You better be near Fernley by now."

"Four miles past."

"Got enough gas to get to Winnemucca?"

"Yes."

"Gas up there. Fill it. Then keep goin' east. Set your cruise control on sixty-five so I'll have a good idea of where you are at all times."

"How'd you get my number?"

He laughed. "This Kassel bitch had it. She didn't like

the way I got it out of her."

click

Shit. I was going to have to kill that guy. I still thought it was Vince.

I called Ma, told her what he said, which wasn't much help, then I set the cruise control and kept going.

•   •   •

I filled the truck's tank at the Flying J in Winnemucca. I bought water, three red bulls, packaged sandwiches, junk food, got on the interstate and kept going east, sixty-five miles an hour.

I had been in tough situations in the past, life or death situations. I'd survived by the skin of my teeth, and had the puncture wounds and scars to prove it. This was different, except for the time I drove into the unknown to save Lucy and Harper from a Special Forces guy with a dishonorable discharge who was going to kill all three of us—and would have if I hadn't turned his weapon against him and blown his left arm off, halfway to his elbow.

So—driving into the unknown again. No idea who or what I was up against and all I had were five bullets in a revolver with a four-inch barrel. If I had time, I could try to buy more ammo on the way. Trying to reload a revolver in the midst of a gun battle wasn't my idea of fun, however. I missed my Glock 20 with its spare clips.

I passed Battle Mountain at 5:45. The sun was behind the western mountains, dark clouds in the east, forty-eight degrees outside, no contact by the kidnappers, plural. This was still a four-person operation, or more.

Ma called on the burner. "Vale's with Harper at my house. I sure wish Vale was with you, though."

"I've lost too many loves already. I can't lose Harper. I *can't*. That would kill me."

"She can't lose *you*, boyo. That would kill her. You'd better keep *that* in mind."

I didn't know what to say to that. "I'll be okay." As if I had a clue. I didn't know where I was going or what would be there when I got there.

Ma was silent for fifteen seconds. Then, "Shoot first

and ask questions later."

"Got it."

"Steve Dunn is on this. I'll let you know if he comes up with anything." Ma's hacker, nineteen years old and sharp as a Ka-Bar knife.

"Wish I could be there with you, boyo," she said. "I'm good with a .45." She'd saved my life three years ago with that gun, blew the brains out of a woman who'd shot me with a .38 and was about to finish the job.

"I want you right where you are, Ma. Keep after Vince and Frank. Come up with something."

"I'm tryin'. Don't know what good it'll do, but I'll keep goin' here."

"Thanks, Ma."

"Got a tracker with you?"

I thought about that. "No. I took one off Vince's truck, left it at home somewhere. It's been a while. I have my go-bag with me, but I know it's not in there."

"Shit. You coulda had it in a pocket so I'd know where you are at all times."

"Sorry about that."

"Water over the dam. Make those goddamn five shots count, Mort." She ended the call.

The daylight faded. I watched the interstate scroll by. Tire hum tried to lull me to sleep.

I reached Elko at 6:50 p.m. The sky was purple in the east. Still no call by the kidnapper. I had over half a tank of gas left. I passed Elko without stopping for gas or bullets. At sixty-five miles an hour, Vince would know right where I was supposed to be.

•   •   •

My burner rang. "How far from Wendover are you?"

"About eight miles."

"Gas up there. Keep goin' east on Eighty."

That was it. Same voice. No other information.

I drank another red bull.

•   •   •

I was past Utah and into Wyoming. "Location?" a guy on the burner asked. Different voice, deeper, gruffer. That would be Frank. I would have to kill him, too.

"Six miles west of Rock Springs."

"Right on time. Gas up. Keep 'er goin', dude."

Shit.

•   •   •

I went through Rawlins and reached Cheyenne at 5:08 a.m., having passed into Mountain Time. My burner rang.

"Where?" the deep voice said.

"Just got to Cheyenne."

"Cool. Gas up. Head north on I-25."

"How far?"

"Till I tell you otherwise, dude. Rock on."

click

•   •   •

I headed north toward Casper at sixty-five mph. I kept awake and amused by picturing a Brenneke slug blowing through Frank's sternum and punching a hole the size of a AA battery through his heart, taking bits of his spine with it as it came out.

Okay, so I'm not a nice guy. Sue me.

I was sick with dread about Ella, what she might be going through.

And I was getting goddamn tired of driving.

•   •   •

I went through Casper. No kidnapper contact as I slid by the city, but Ma called.

"You still on the road?" she asked.

"I think I'm being run around, Ma."

"Shit. Where are you?"

"Casper, Wyoming. Headed north now."

"That's a long fuckin' way. Okay, here's a bit of news. Don't see how it fits into any of this so it probably doesn't, but Ned Willis is dead."

Ned dead? Huh.

Willis was the FBI agent who spent three years trying

to pin Julia Reinhart's murder on Ma and me—the only
agent in the Bureau who got it right, but all he had was a
theory and the worst kind of circumstantial evidence, not a
lick of proof that would get past a half-assed grand jury or
federal or state prosecutors. Well, okay, a grand jury would
indict a loaf of moldy bread, so there's that.

"Dead how?" I asked.

"Coroner's report says it was suicide."

Huh. "Suicide how?" Not that it mattered.

"It doesn't actually say. Just suicide. But the place he
did it was called a suicide room, or *the* suicide room."

"Strange wording."

"Uh-huh. Probably the room where he shot himself, or
hung himself. Whatever he did."

"How long ago was that?"

"He was found June sixteenth, about four months ago.
How're you doin'? You've been driving a long damn time."

"I'm not seeing double yet. Getting tired of watching
this dotted line go by, though."

"Harper was here until one this morning. I finally sent
her home with Vale. She's got to teach tomorrow."

"Good. This has gotta be hard on her."

"On all of us, boyo, but her especially."

We ended the call on that note.

I kept going. Sixty-five.

•   •   •

I gassed the truck at a Conoco station in Sheridan, got
a microwaved burrito, a Monster energy drink, a red bull,
more water, all in fifteen minutes, then kept going.

At 11:15, my burner rang. "Location?"

"I'm about twenty miles east of Billings."

"You're slow. What's the holdup?"

"Needed gas in Sheridan. This truck doesn't get good
enough gas mileage."

A moment of silence. "You're good to go, then, dude.
I-90 dumps into I-94. Just before you get to Billings, take
Highway 87E north to Roundup."

click

The instructions were okay. I slid off I-90 onto 87E

and bypassed Billings, headed north.

I cranked the cruise control up to seventy-five and got to Roundup in fifty-two minutes, which gave me a few extra minutes. I found a small store that carried a little of everything: groceries, liquor, hardware, Bluetooth stuff, bullets. I was paying for a box of .357 ammunition and a cup of coffee when my burner rang.

"Where are you?"

"Just pulling into Roundup," I lied.

"Go west on U.S. 12 to Lavina," Frank said.

click

I glanced at a tattered map on a wall near the door. Like I thought, I was being given a runaround. They were trying to get me so tired I couldn't function. Which might work. I could barely focus on the map.

Fuck.

I got in the truck and headed west on 12.

Seventeen minutes later: "You near Lavina?"

"Two miles out."

"Get there, then go south on Three."

That got me back to Billings, right past Billings-Logan International airport and onto I-90 Business, then onto I-90 proper, headed west. I'd made a crap loop of 112 miles that got me nowhere. I gassed up at a Chevron station and left the Billings area at 1:35 p.m.

• • •

The burner rang at 2:10. It was Ma.

"You okay?" she asked.

"I've been better."

"Where are you?"

"Forty miles out of Billings, headed west."

"Are you east or west of Billings?"

I wasn't making sense, couldn't focus. "West," I forced the word out, blinking my eyes. "Headed west. I've driven over fifteen hundred miles, Ma."

"Shit. Okay, listen up. Steve came through. Maybe. Not sure what this means, but it's got to mean something. There's a Dinah Faye Jackson lives in Bemidji, Minnesota, formerly Dinah Foster, formerly Dinah Willis. She's got a younger sister, Evelyn Nestor, formerly Evelyn Dolak, lives in Blackduck, about twenty-five miles from Dinah."

I let that gel for a while, then finally got it. My brain was moving at one-quarter speed. "Ned Willis's mother," I said. "That Dinah woman. From her first marriage."

"You got it. Frank and Vince are her nephews. Steve's a wizard."

"Give him a bonus, Ma. What's all of that mean?"

"It's looking like a family deal. It's looking like revenge for Ned's suicide."

I blinked, felt sluggish. "How'd Deputy Director Ridel get into it then?"

"You got me, boyo. But we've got a handle on it now."

"We've got who and possibly the why, sort of, but not the where and what, since I'm being driven all over hell out here. I can't keep this up much longer."

Silence. "I don't know what to tell you, Mort."

"Yeah. Me neither." I stared at the road, mind numb. "Have you tried to call that Dinah woman?"

"Yes. No answer there, but I got hold of Evelyn Dolak. She's a hard bitch, said she 'don't know where Dinah's at an' she's busy so buzz off.' She hung up on me."

But she was at home in Minnesota. Dinah wasn't, or wasn't answering her phone. Ma didn't say anything for a long moment, nor did I, then I said, "Who flew the plane, Ma? It wasn't either of the Dolak boys."

"I don't know."

I closed my eyes for just one second and felt myself starting to fall asleep. I jerked the wheel, took a very deep breath, tried to focus. I like my eight hours' sleep a night. I don't do well on six; now I'd been up for thirty-four hours and didn't know when I'd be able to sleep again.

"Mort?"

"Yup."

"You okay? Felt like I lost you there for a moment."

"Just tired, Ma. You must be, too. You get any sleep last night?"

"No."

"Get some. And get some for me."

She laughed, but it sounded forced.

We ended the call. I tried to think about Dinah Willis, now Dinah Jackson, but it didn't take and I didn't think it'd get me anywhere if it did.

I kept driving.

• • •

The burner rang at 3:00 p.m. "Where?"

"I don't know. Five, ten miles east of Livingston."

A dark chuckle. "You sound tired."

"I'm a long-distance trucker. This ain't shit."

Another chuckle. "You're a PI. You're dead in a truck dude. Keep goin'."

click

Dead in a truck. I didn't know what that was supposed to mean, but it sounded right. Red Bull was just making me sick so I was drinking water, slapping myself to stay awake. Thinking about what Ella must be going through was depressing, but it also kept me angry, kept me going.

I was going to seriously kill two shitheads.

• • •

My cell phone rang at 4:45 p.m. "Where?"

"About ten miles east of Butte."

"Right on target. You got a cell phone that'll give you directions if I give you a place?"

"Yes."

"Put in Bull Run Gulch Road. That'll get you through western Butte, through Walkerville, and into open country north of Butte. Four point seven miles up Bull Run Gulch you'll see a tree with two yellow ribbons around it. Turn right a hundred yards past the tree onto a trail with a *No Trespassing* sign on it. Go in one point two miles. Stop in the yard outside an old shack and get out."

"I want to talk with Ella."

He laughed. "And I want a Lamborghini. If anyone but you turns off Bull Run Gulch Road, this Ella babe gets her throat cut and I've got a dozen ways out of here."

click

• • •

My cell phone told me when and where to turn. Good thing I had it because it took a lot of awkward turns to get through Walkerville and onto Bull Run Gulch Road.

The sun was behind the mountains but the sky was still blue as I climbed up into the hills on a winding dirt road. I saw the tree with the yellow ribbons on it at 5:18.

I turned to the right and bounced the truck up a rocky trail that meandered between fir trees. It reminded me of the trail to another cabin where Harper and Lucy were being held and where none of us were supposed to get out alive.

Déjà vu. I wasn't supposed to get out of this alive, and neither was Ella. This was going to be a terminal run, which meant I had to take chances. I was tired, but awake now, humming with adrenaline. The trail wound upward through forest. I had the .357 Magnum on the seat beside me. When I saw the shack up ahead, I shoved the gun in the waistband of my jeans behind my back where I could get a hand on it in half a second. And I had a razor-sharp CRKT M16 knife with a four-inch blade in one pocket, a small handful of bullets in another.

Best I could do.

"Lucy," I whispered. "If you're here, I could use a bit of help, honey."

I didn't hear anything, but the world got brighter for an instant and I felt . . . love.

Maybe we were about to be together again.

My burner rang.

"Stop," the gruff voice said. Frank.

I hit the brakes, stopped forty yards from the shack. Frank's red pickup was parked to one side in a clearing to the left. It had an old camper on it, big enough for a double bed over the truck's cab, a tiny kitchen and dinette. A guy in jeans and a blue flannel shirt came out the door of the shack. I recognized Vince. He had a big-bore rifle with a telescopic sight in his hands. Not the best gun for close-in combat. He was followed by Frank with a cell phone to his ear and a handgun aimed approximately in my direction.

Give them a sporting chance? Let them shoot first so I could claim self-defense? Queensbury rules?

Not hardly. I would use a machine gun if I had one.

Vince held the rifle in both hands, ready. The two of them came closer then stopped, weapons aimed at me.

"Get out," Frank shouted, pocketing the cell phone.

They had what they wanted. Me. I was probably about to die.

I could either die easy or hard.

I chose hard.

Chapter Sixteen

"Hands where I can see them," Vince yelled. I was still in the truck. His rifle was aimed at me through the truck's windshield, but he wasn't using the telescopic sight.

I opened the door and got out, put my left hand up as if I was doing what I was told, came around the open door and pulled the revolver as I dropped to the ground and snap-rolled to my right, ended up facedown with the Ruger aimed at Vince, twenty-five yards away. He got off a wild shot with the rifle. I took an extra quarter second to line up the sights, then shot him in the chest, center mass. He went down. I shot at Frank as he jumped sideways, crouched and ran like a broken-field runner, like a football player with the ball through a chaotic scrimmage line.

He didn't get off a shot. He didn't head for the shack's door. He ran like a jitterbug toward the shack's right side. I fired two more times before he made it around the side of the shack, but didn't get a hit.

Then I was the sitting duck. I got up and sprinted to the left side of the shack with bullets whining past me like hornets. One of them burned a furrow across my ribs, right side. I almost went down, but that would have been death. I was about to continue to that left side of the shack, but changed direction at the last instant and charged inside instead. I had only one bullet left in the cylinder and no time to reload. I couldn't be caught standing there with the cylinder out if Frank barged in through the door.

One window left side, one window to the right. Several gaping holes in the roof. A wall with a door separated the shack into at least two rooms. No sign of Ella. I spun and covered the front door then watched the righthand window as I ran to the door in the far wall, slammed through it and found Ella gagged and bound to a chair with nylon rope.

No time to do anything about that. She looked unhurt. There was a window and a back door in the back wall. I kicked the door at its lock and it blew open. I didn't go out. Frank fired a shot across the back of the shack. Jumpy. But it gave me an idea.

I released the cylinder of the Ruger and spun it one click counterclockwise so the single live round was under the hammer, slapped it back in place. I leaped out the door and pulled the trigger four times, the action clicking loudly and futilely as if all the rounds had been fired. Doing that rotated the cylinder until the last live round would be next. I crouched low and yelled "Shit!" as I aimed the gun at the righthand corner of the shack. Frank rounded the corner quickly, gun aimed high, a smirk on his face, "You're dead, mother—" then his eyes widened as he tried to lower his gun at me and I shot him in the bridge of the nose, blew out the back of his head.

I got his automatic, a SIG Sauer P226, ran around the side of the shack and checked on Vince. He was still alive, but down, dying. "Frank's dead," I said. "So are you." Vince blinked at me, tried to say something, didn't make it, then his eyes went blank and he stared beyond the farthest edge of the universe.

•   •   •

I looked around. No one else was in sight. I ran into the shack, into the back. Ella's eyes were wide, frantic. "It's okay," I said as I got the gag off her. "They're dead."

She began to cry.

I opened the M16 knife and cut the rope binding her to the chair, lifted her to her feet and held her close.

She clung to me, sobbing, trembling.

We stayed like that for two minutes. Finally I held her face and kissed her. "Are you okay?" I asked.

"I don't know. I mean, I'm not hurt." She looked into my eyes. "They're dead? Really?"

"Yes."

"I want to see."

I led her outside. Vince was on his back, still staring up at the darkening sky, seeing nothing.

"Good," Ella said. "Good." She looked around. "I want to see the other one, Frank."

I took her around the side of the shack. Frank was also face up. Mercifully, he only had a little hole an inch above the bridge of his nose. The back of his head wasn't visible. She didn't see the blood and brain matter glistening in the needles of a small fir tree eight feet away.

"Good," she said again. She wiped tears from her eyes. "They were talking. They didn't care if I heard. They were going to kill you as soon as you got here, then me. They were going to get twenty-five thousand dollars each."

I didn't say anything. I got her away from Frank, kept her from looking at Vince, and held her again, out in the yard in front of the house. I kept an eye on the trail in and listened for anyone, any sound of a vehicle approaching, but all was quiet. The forest had gotten darker, shadows deeper, daylight starting to go.

"It's like a miracle," Ella whispered. "They had guns. There were two of them." She stepped back and looked at me. "You're hurt!"

I looked down. Blood on my shirt, right side. Not a lot, but enough. I untucked the shirt, unbuttoned it, had a look at a three-inch furrow maybe an eighth of an inch deep. Now that I saw it, it hurt. "This is nothing," I said. "Just another little scar is all."

"It doesn't look like nothing."

"Antiseptic and a bandage'll do it. It's not a cut and it isn't deep enough to put in stitches." I buttoned the shirt, tucked it in. I ejected the spent brass onto the ground and reloaded the revolver. "We have to get out of here. I got two of them, but we know there's at least four. Do you have anything here we need to get before we go?"

"A purse with a wallet in it. One of them had it. I don't know which one. They grabbed me as I was leaving to go to the university. That was Monday morning. What is it now, Wednesday or Thursday? I've lost track."

"Thursday. October seventeen. It'll be dark in another half hour."

No sign of Ella's purse in the shack. The only furniture was the chair Ella had been tied to and a bed of rusty angle irons and springs, no mattress. A pizza box, beer cans and sandwich wrappers littered the floor amid pine needles and forest debris. No bathroom facilities of any kind in the place and no outhouse that I could see outside. Primitive. I asked her about that and she said, "Don't ask. You don't want to know. Also, I've been wearing the same clothes for four days, so don't get too close to me. I mean, again. I'm sorry about the hug. I feel totally gross."

"I didn't notice. I'm in the same boat."

"Not like me, you're not."

I found her purse inside Frank's truck under the front seat, passenger side. Her wallet was still in the purse.

I kept Frank's SIG, took the rifle, a .30-06, Frank's cell phone, found another cell in the shack, didn't see anything else worth taking, so I guided Ella to my truck.

And stopped dead. Green water had turned the dust to mud beneath the engine. I crouched in front of the hood. Vince's lone rifle shot had blown a hole in the radiator.

Perfect.

But I didn't want to leave the truck. Not here, with a couple of dead bodies lying around. I wasn't about to load them up and haul them anywhere. I still didn't know what I was going to do about what had happened here. I would call Ma, have her ask Ulysses Taber what should be done.

I nodded toward Frank's truck. "Can you drive that thing with the camper on it?"

"I guess. If it's an automatic. I can't drive a stick."

"It's automatic."

"Okay, then. Probably. If I have to."

"My truck is going to overheat. I don't know how long it'll run, but I want it out of here and to a repair shop or at least to a place where I can leave it in Butte."

I put the rifle in the camper of Frank's truck, kept the SIG and the two cell phones in case one of the Dolaks got a call, not sure what I would do if that happened. It might be best not to answer. Answering would give the caller more information than I was likely to get, but either way I might get the caller's number.

I took a few forensic photos of Vince and Frank where they lay, then dragged them into the shack and shut and blocked the doors to keep animals out. Maybe. Some of the windows were broken and a few holes in the roof were big enough for birds the size of ravens to get in. The place looked as if no one had used it for the past thirty years.

I led the way back downhill to Bull Run Gulch Road. I had been at the shack for about forty minutes. The engine was warm, temperature gauge down some from its normal running temperature. It climbed up to normal by the time I got to Bull Run Gulch Road with Ella behind me, and I had five miles of dirt road to get to Walkerville, Butte not far beyond that.

I didn't push it. Ella wasn't familiar with the weight of a truck and camper. The temperature gauge hit red a mile before I got to Walkerville then kept rising. I reached West Daly Street, turned left and came down North Main Street with steam billowing from under the hood, turned left onto a side street and got lucky, pulled into the back parking lot of a Motel 6 using wipers to squeegee hot water off the windshield and parked the truck. I shut the engine down, got out in a rumble-roar of pressurized steam that looked like Old Faithful was about to blow under the hood.

Ella pulled up alongside my truck. I locked the truck and scooted her over, got behind the wheel of Frank's rig. I was about to take off when I had a thought.

"Wait here," I said. "I'm going to get a room."

"No."

"No?"

"I can't keep wearing these clothes. They're filthy. And

you need clean clothes. And a doctor, or at least bandages and some kind of antiseptic cream."

She was right. The only thing immediately salvageable in the way of clothing were her shoes and my boots. But I wanted misdirection. Two people we hadn't identified were still out there. Or more than two.

"Stay put," I said. I trotted into the motel and got us a room using a credit card with my name on it. If someone had a way to track my card, this might pull them off us.

Back in Frank's truck I fired up the engine and handed Ella my cell phone. "See if you can find us a Walmart."

Took her thirty seconds. She gave me directions while I drove. I parked and we went into the store. We hadn't been in the news for nearly two months, so the looks I got might have been due to blood on my shirt and an overall scruffy demeanor, and the looks she got were because she looked like something the cat dragged in.

I didn't tell her. Women don't like to hear that.

We bought basic clothing, all the way down to socks and underwear. I grabbed alcohol, Polysporin, Advil, gauze bandages, tape. Ella found body wash, a hair brush, comb, other stuff, and we got toothbrushes and toothpaste.

Inside the camper, I removed the bloody shirt. The groove in my side looked worse than it was. Ella washed it with alcohol which stung like a son of a bitch, slathered it with antiseptic cream and applied a gauze bandage. I drove us south and east, stayed within the city limits of Butte, got us onto a busy commercial street, Harrison Avenue.

"Stop," Ella said. "There's a McDonald's. I'm *starving*. I haven't had anything to eat for two days."

"They didn't feed you?"

"They . . . no. They gave me one slice of pizza when we got to that horrible cabin on Tuesday. That's all."

She was starving; my problem was different. All traces of adrenaline had worn off and I was so tired I was about to slip into a coma, but I am a sympathetic, sensitive guy, so I fought through my fatigue and turned the truck into the McDonald's parking lot.

"Let's get the food to go," I said. "I've been up thirty-six hours and I've driven over seventeen hundred miles."

She stared at me. "It's not that far to Reno."

"Trust me. Those assholes ran me all over the country trying to tire me out, soften me up for the kill." I looked at her. "Which didn't do them any good."

She smiled uncertainly. "Good thing."

We went in and ordered five Big Macs, two for me and three for her. And fries and shakes for both of us.

Across the avenue I saw a Best Western Plus. It would have beds. I wanted a bed above all else on earth. I drove into the lot, made certain the camper with its rifle in back was locked and we went in, got a room for two nights. I paid using a credit card I dug out of a semi-secret Velcro compartment in my go-bag in the name of Harvey Orkaza, a credit card I had never used before.

"Who on earth is Harvey Orkaza?" she asked.

"That would be me, hon."

"Harvey. Are you serious? *Harvey*?"

"Laugh and I get all the Big Macs."

"Nuh-uh. You could lose an arm that way."

Good. She was feeling better.

We got a room on the second floor overlooking a few acres of pine forest. Nice room, a gorgeous king bed with pillows and everything, shower, forty-inch TV, Wi-Fi, all the amenities. And a terrific-looking bed. Spectacular.

Which I didn't get to use right away in spite of the fact that it was whispering sweet nothings to me. I called Ma.

"Where are you?" she answered.

"Butte. All is good, so far. Ella's with me. We're safe, and Frank and Vince are . . . they are no more, Ma."

"No more. That what I think it means?"

"How would I know? But they are out of the picture and God's hands."

"Good. Are you okay?"

"Got a minor bullet wound, nothing serious."

"Shit. *How* not serious?"

"Three-inch groove, not deep. No doctor needed. The Dolaks are a different story. Docs wouldn't be a bit of help there."

"Still good. But you said all is good 'so far.' What does that mean?"

"It means two down, but four were running this thing, maybe more. I got us a room at a Motel 6 under my name, but Ella and I are in a Best Western Plus using the Orkaza card. I'm driving Frank's truck because the radiator of my truck took a bullet."

"You've got a story. Better tell it so I can call Ulysses, see what he thinks."

So I did, quickly, ending with the current disposition of Frank and Vince—decomposing in a rundown shack. I didn't try to describe the location of the shack. The route I'd taken was too convoluted and I was too tired. I figured the Dolaks would keep for at least one day.

"Okay," Ma said. "I'll tell Ulysses."

"Do that. I gotta sleep. I'm seeing triple. Try not to call before noon tomorrow."

Ella looked at me and took the last bite of her second Big Mac. She looked like a feeding wolf.

"Before you go," Ma said. "Harper and Vale are right here. Here's Harper. She couldn't talk right away, but I had you on speaker so she heard everything you said."

She was crying. Her voice sounded liquid. "You made it," she said. "I was *so* . . ." She bawled. That went on for a while, I heard voices and the sound of the phone trading hands, then Vale was there.

"Nice shooting," Vale said. She sounded teary too.

"Thanks. It was kinda close."

"Sounds like it, since you said you got shot."

"Just grazed. It's nothing. A doctor wouldn't be able to do any more than what we're doing. Bandage, antiseptic, a few ibuprofen."

She didn't respond to that. I didn't know what else to say and my eyelids were heavy, so I said, "I'm exhausted. I've got to sleep. Am I still on speaker?"

"Yes."

"Then good night, all. I love all of you. I'm okay, Ella's okay, but I'm absolutely dead tired right now. I'm about to drop. Bye, everyone."

That got a chorus of 'byes' and the call ended.

Ella was almost through her last Big Mac. "I know you're tired, but we can't go to bed like this. I'm disgusting, you're ripe, and you'll need a new bandage after a shower."

"What do you suggest?" I asked deadpan. Twisting the tail of this tiger one more time.

"How about this?" She took the last bite, pulled off her T-shirt and shucked off her jeans and underwear.

"Yowser," I said.

She smiled. "Your turn."

"My turn for what?"

She gave me a tortured look. "How many women have you showered with, Mort?"

"Accurate total or ballpark figure?"

"Now I know why Ma calls you a shithead."

I started counting silently on my fingers.

"Oh, for heaven's sake." She unbuttoned my shirt and pulled it off me, removed my boots and socks, unbuckled my belt, took off my pants, hauled my Jockeys down and off, led me into the bathroom and got the shower going, all without saying another word.

I got in with the bandage on, used water to soften the tape, then pulled the sodden mass off gingerly. The water stung like hell, which woke me up some.

"This doesn't look good," she said.

"Really? Exactly what're you looking at, lady?"

She slapped me.

"It looks worse than it is," I said. I dabbed the wound with a washcloth, didn't rub it, then we soaped up and got clean. I didn't fall asleep, but the warmth made me woozy. Ella looked terrific, once the four-day sludge came off.

Sludge? I kept that to myself, too.

So I showered with Ella, an activity with which I was familiar, having acquired quite a bit of expertise in the past five years. I am particularly adept and subtle in the vicinity of nipples, and she was adept in other ways, so we used a good amount of water and got pretty doggone clean.

•   •   •

I toweled off carefully, with help, and she got dry and hit me with more alcohol, patted it dry, then applied a long line of Polysporin, put on a new bandage, then slapped my butt and said, "You're good to go, cowboy"—all while I ate two Big Macs and a dozen fries.

I led her over to the bed. "Don't expect too much." A clock on a nightstand read 7:25 p.m.

"All I expect is snoring, Mort."

"Which is exactly what you're gonna get."

She gave me a tentative look. "Do you think you could fall asleep with a girl in your arms?"

"A warm, clean, extremely naked girl?"

"Yeah, one of those."

"Let's give it a try."

Which we did. But 1,788 miles of driving took its toll and I was gone in thirty seconds. A very nice thirty seconds it was, too, with a nude girl gently nuzzling me. I was even sort of aware that long silky legs were involved, and much appreciated.

. . .

When I awoke the room was dark. Ella was tucked against my left side, one slim arm slung across my chest, toothpasty breath rhythmic on my neck, pubic hair lightly brushing my hip. *Tall* girl. The green glowing numerals of a bedside clock read 3:55. Except for the bullet groove in my side I felt more or less human again but still tired. I put my arms around her and let my hands gently roam her body, down her back, over her waist, over an unbelievably taut rear end. I finished copping a feel with one hand still cupping a rounded butt cheek, closed my eyes, and . . .

"Don't stop," she breathed in my ear.

So I didn't. For a while. She purred, then I was gone.

. . .

I woke up when she came back to bed and kissed me, snuggled up against my left side again. I checked the time. 10:22. I'd slept a little over fifteen hours. Daylight filtered into the room past heavy curtains.

"Morning," she said.

"You're going to make some guy very happy," I said.

"But not you?"

I smiled and said, "I'm not the only one who knows how to twist the tail of this tiger."

"Huh? What tiger?"

"I *am* happy, lady. Very."

"Good. I'm glad."

I pulled her all the way on top of me.

"Oh, *that's* nice," she murmured. "Now I know what you meant by 'very'."

"This is still as far as we go. Is it enough?"

She was quiet for a moment. "Yes. I mean, I would like more, but this will do if it doesn't end too soon. It's kind of got me worked up, though. Us, I mean."

"It's supposed to. That's how nature works."

"Do you think your boss, Ma, really isn't going to call until noon?"

"Guess we'll find out."

"Are we going to stay like this until then?"

"Unless you have to be someplace."

"I'll let you know."

She snuggled in closer, as if that were possible, and we walked a fine line without slipping over the edge.

Ma didn't call until 12:25.

Chapter Seventeen

"Other than a freakin' bullet wound you seem to think isn't worth writing home about, are you okay?" Ma asked.

"Couldn't be better," I said.

"Does that mean what I think it means?"

Ella was sprawled on top of me, about like a starfish trying to open a clam. I rolled to my left, depositing her on the bed. "I could answer that better if I could read your mind."

"Uh-huh. That's what I thought."

"Cryptic, Ma."

"Good, you sound okay. Ulysses says you need to talk with a lawyer there in Butte. Got something to write with?"

"Hold on." Blackout curtains were pulled, so I turned on a bedside light, had Ella get out of bed to locate pen and paper. She looked better than she had when we checked in yesterday evening. A lot better.

"Okay, shoot. I'm ready," I said. Ella slid into bed and snuggled in close, the fingers of one slender hand touching in a way that could hardly be called incidental, which made talking with Ma quite a bit more difficult.

"James A. Carbon, LLC," Ma said.

"Do I need to write the LLC?" I gently removed Ella's hand, but it returned in a way I found hard to ignore.

Ma gave me Carbon's address and phone number. I wrote it down because Ella didn't offer to, and I needed both hands to hold the pad of paper and write so I couldn't do anything about her wandering hand. Bad girl. I would have a talk with her about that later.

"Ulysses says Jim Carbon is the best mouthpiece in Butte," Ma said. "He contacted him, so Carbon is expecting your call."

"Should I tell him I need a mouthpiece?"

Ma sighed. "Get that bullet wound looked at. It might be infected. Sounds like you're running a fever."

"I'll do that after I call the lawyer. And after breakfast, if that's okay." My voice lifted a quarter octave on that last word, which was Ella's fault.

"You two've been in bed all this time?" Ma asked.

"Who wants to know?"

She guffawed, then ended the call.

"Oh, my," Ella said softly, fingers still roving. "This is more than I'd expected."

I didn't ask, but I knew it was time for me to give as good as I got, so I did—more, actually—incidental touching be damned.

It was 1:08 when we finally crawled out of bed.

· · ·

We ate onsite in the motel's restaurant. Steak and eggs, English muffins slathered with butter and strawberry jam for both of us. A side of pancakes for me, fruit bowl for her, coffee, tea.

"After we talk to this lawyer, if I get a chance, I could use a loosen-up run," she said.

"Loosen-up's how far? Fifty miles? Eighty?"

She smiled. "Twenty would be nice." Her smile faded. "I was tied to that chair for two days, except when they had to . . . let me go outside. On a kind of leash."

I didn't ask her to explain that.

She looked down at her plate. "I had a rope around my neck. It wasn't very long. Not long enough, only about ten feet. I tried to run once, thought I might yank the rope out of Frank's hand, but he about jerked me off my feet. If I'd been able to get free they never would have caught me."

She looked up at me. "Yesterday I was glad you killed them. Now . . . I don't know. They were going to kill us, but now I wish they were alive so they could spend the rest of their lives in a little prison cell."

"They're probably in a worse place than a prison cell right now."

"I imagine so."

We went up to the room to freshen up before heading out to talk to James Carbon, LLC. It was likely we would be in Butte another two or three days. Police ask a lot of questions when you shoot people, and then there's all that paperwork to fill out and file.

We had an appointment to see Jim Carbon at 2:30. I locked the room and we left at 2:10, plenty of time to drive the three miles to Jim's office.

We went outside into cool air, bright sun. The parking lot was less than half full. Vehicles were parked on either side of Frank's truck. I should've paid attention to that. I opened the truck door and a bolt of lightning hit me, my vision went white and my legs gave out.

I don't remember falling, but I must have.

• • •

I came to in Frank's camper with Ella beside me. We were on the floor, trussed like Christmas turkeys.

Road rumble came up through the camper's floor. We were headed somewhere. It took a moment to get my mind working again. We'd been captured, right out there in the open, in broad daylight.

It must've been a Taser that put me down. Ella would have gotten the same. Vehicles on either side of Frank's truck, people in them, windows open, fire a Taser out the window, get out and load us into the camper, go in after us and tie us up. It had to have been something like that. Very fast and efficient and quiet.

"Ella?" I said.

"Mort? Thank God you're awake. Are you okay?"

"Don't know yet. Sort of, anyway. How about you?"

"I'm . . . I don't know. Kinda sick feeling."

"If we were tased, it'll wear off."

"What's going on? Who's doing this?"

Questions I couldn't answer. I tried to think but it was hard. The left side of my head throbbed. I might've hit my head when I fell, or I might have been hit with some sort of a sap to make sure I was completely out before they loaded me into the camper. They. It would have taken two people to put us down the way they did. I had been on one side of the truck, Ella on the other.

Frank and Vince were dead. Who else was left? Of the four we'd more or less identified—not by name but by what they had done—two remained.

I said, "It could be the pilot of the plane that flew over the VOR station. And, possibly the woman who called you to write and deliver the note. Those're the only two others we know about."

None of which did us any good that I could see. I had rope around my wrists. I tried to reach the knot, couldn't so much as feel it.

"Can you get untied?" I asked her.

"I've tried. I can't." She began to cry. "I'm sorry, I'm *so* sorry I got you into this."

"You didn't. I did." I was fairly certain this was about FBI Special Agent Ned Willis. Ned was dead. Suicide. He'd been cast aside by the Bureau. Stuck in Butte's purgatory, he'd killed himself. Someone was getting even, probably a family member. Best guess, it was his mother, Dinah Willis years ago, now Dinah Jackson. Ella was collateral damage. She got in the way, not sure how that happened, but this was my fault, my doing, not hers. Ned was reaching out from beyond the grave to try to take me down again, but it had all started the day Julia Reinhart murdered my fiancée Jeri in cold blood in the back of a Cadillac SUV.

I tried to get at the knots holding my ankles, but my hands were behind me and the knots of the cords holding my ankles were in front. I could see them, couldn't touch them.

"Can you untie my hands?" I asked her.

"My fingers are numb, but I'll try."

I shuffled around so she could get at my wrists. She'd only been working on the knot for a minute when the truck tilted up in front, then slowed, leveled out and stopped. I heard the rumble of a garage door starting to go down. The truck's engine went off, doors slammed.

Shit. No time left.

The back of the camper opened. I looked out the door and saw the steel framework and hinged panels of a basic residential garage door. A big guy in his forties looked in at us and grinned. He looked like a weightlifter. He wore a T-shirt with the sleeves cut off. His biceps looked like the kind of snakes you try to avoid in South America.

"Nice ride, folks?" he said. "It's a one-way trip."

Great. A comedian. Just when I thought this couldn't get any worse.

•   •   •

He held up a Taser. "This little puppy has two settings, two hundred thousand volts or five hundred thousand. I gave you two hundred back there in the parking lot. If you want all five hundred, just give me a hard time."

He hauled me out by my feet and turned me around before standing me up. I would've tried for a head butt if he wasn't standing beside me, but he had anticipated that. Maybe. Maybe he just got lucky.

He shoved me, hard. I couldn't stay upright with my feet tied. I twisted my body before crashing into the wall of the garage and landing crumpled on the floor.

"Stay down or I'll break something," he said. "Maybe a leg."

I felt the presence of someone else, like a kind of heat. I craned my neck, looked toward the front of the truck and saw a woman, gray-haired, short, and huge. She was five-four, weighed at least three hundred pounds. She stared at me with eyes that held no life in them, just death. She wore a dress that looked like a circus tent, colorless, no style, nothing but a covering. Her upper arms were bare, pale, wrinkled, flaccid, bigger than the arms of the guy who'd dragged me out of the camper.

The guy reached in and slid Ella out, took her under the knees and upper back and carried her to where I was on the floor, set her down sitting with her back to a wall.

"You're the pilot," I said.

He grinned and bowed slightly. "FBI Private Charter," he said. "At your service."

Still not funny.

"C'mon, Cole," the woman said to him. "Let's get 'em inside,"

"You're Dinah Jackson," I said.

Her eyes bored into mine, then she glared at Cole as if it were his fault. "He's got my damn name. I gotta get back home." She looked at me. "I'll be back, though. Count on it, not that you'll know. By then you'll be rotting in hell."

"Home," I said. "That'd be Bemidji, Minnesota." She didn't like it that I'd known her name. I wondered how she would react to my knowing where she lived.

Her eyes went cobra-flat. "I would have Cole kick you to death, except I got something a lot better in mind." She turned to him. "Take him downstairs. I'll watch the girl." She held a Taser in one pudgy hand.

Cole picked me up and slung me over one shoulder. I weighed two hundred four pounds. He picked me up like I was a sack of dog food. Fucker was *strong*.

"Try to bite me and I'll knock out every one of your teeth," he said. "*And* your girlfriend's."

There wasn't much I could bite, but this guy sounded like he would do what he said he'd do, so I was carried into the house and along a dim hallway as I stared at the floor and the back of Cole's legs. He carried me down a flight of wooden stairs into a basement, propped me against a four-by-four post and looped a length of rope twice around the post and my neck and tied it off.

"Stay put," he said, then he trooped up the stairs.

I tried not to stay put, but I couldn't get loose. I had a view of a shop set up for woodworking. A table saw, jigsaw, bandsaw, drill press, woodworking table with wood-faced vises, wood lathe, routers, belt sander, a workbench with every kind of hand tool imaginable for working with wood, drill bits and a set of Forstner bits. Sheets of plywood were leaning against one wall, different sized dowels, plain two-by-fours and racks of good stuff: walnut, oak, mahogany, cedar, ready to be turned into something useful.

A skin of sawdust littered the floor. A clock read 2:36. I'd been unconscious no more than ten or twelve minutes. This house was probably still within Butte's city limits.

To my right a dim hallway was blocked by a horizontal two-by-four at knee level, like a low hurdle. Strange.

Cole came downstairs with Ella in his arms, sat her in a handmade oak chair and untied her hands. Her feet were still tied. "Stay put or I kill your boyfriend."

Ella gave me a terrified look. I didn't know what to say or do to help her. I just shook my head slightly. *Don't say anything. Don't antagonize this guy.*

Cole went to the top of the stairs and helped Dinah navigate the steps down, which took a while. She paused at the bottom for a while to catch her breath. "You know who I am and where I live," she said to me.

"Just a lucky guess," I said. I should learn when not to open my mouth.

"Hit him," Dinah said to Cole.

Cole punched my solar plexus. I couldn't breathe. My mouth gaped open. I couldn't suck in air. My vision started to go dark before I got the slightest hint of air.

Ella cried.

It took several minutes before I could breathe almost

normally again.

"You know who I am," Dinah said, staring at me.

No smartass reply this time, but I wanted to keep Ma out of this so I didn't tell her Ma had found her. "I heard Ned Willis died. I found a newspaper account of his death. It gave his mother's name as Dinah Jackson, not Willis. I looked into that, which took quite a while because you had remarried a time or two. I spoke with Ned some years ago in Reno. He mentioned his mother's name: Dinah," I lied. "Seeing it in the newspaper rang a bell."

She smiled. If Satan arrives on Earth as a woman, she will smile exactly like that.

She turned to Cole. "I gotta get home. If he knows that much, so do others. I ain't goin' down for this."

"So let's get goin' here," Cole said.

"Not until this stinking rotten sonofabitch knows what he's in for. And why. I want him thinking about that while he's dying. Can you move him closer this way so he can get a better look at the door?"

"No problem." Cole got a big eyehook out of a drawer full of various kinds of hardware. He found a drill and a rack of drill bits, held a bit up to the screw threads of the eyehook, selected the next bigger size, then walked over to me and stared at my neck.

Gave me the willies. He was six-one, weighed at least two-forty. Made me feel small and weak even though I was three inches taller and a good size myself.

But he only went ten or twelve feet down the hallway and put a hole in the wall after thumping it to find a stud, then put the eyehook in deep. He untied me from the post and half carried me down the hallway, looped the rope around my neck and through the eyehook and tied me in place again.

"Stay put," he said, grinning.

"Get her over here where she can see," Dinah said.

Cole slid Ella across the floor in the chair to within a few feet of me, then stood watch over us.

Dinah said, "Cole's my youngest sister's boy. Did you get his name too? You go all though my family tree?"

I tried to remember what Ma told me. Finally I came

up with a last name.

"Cole Nestor. Or Cole Dolak."

She smiled at Cole. "He don't know you. You're okay."

"I'm okay any which way," he said. "This guy's dead."

Dinah looked at me. "Evelyn isn't my youngest sister. That'd be Jenna, 'cept she's my half-sister. Got knocked up when she was sixteen. Cole's her boy. Cole Keeler. At least she knew the guy's name. But Jen died when Cole was just a year old. I ended up with Cole when Neddie was two. I raised 'em both, didn't change Cole's last name, though. No reason to."

Cole Keeler. Ma and her hacker hadn't found him. He was buried too deep in the family's underbrush.

"You fly planes?" I asked him.

"That I do. Landings can be a bit rough, though. If you fly FBI United, that is. It's not a full-service airline."

Ha, ha.

"Cole's been in prison fifteen years. Got out only eight months ago."

"Hey, c'mon, Dee," Cole said.

"C'mon, what? He ain't gonna tell anyone. *Or* her." She glanced at Ella.

Cole shrugged. "Got my pilot's license when I was twenty-two," he said proudly. "Always did like flyin', being free like that. Prison sucked the big one. I'll die before I go back, take a few cops with me, you bet."

"What were you in for?"

He stared at me. Then said, "Murder, second degree."

Figures. Except first degree seemed more likely. There must have been a plea bargain in there somewhere.

"You're the one who grabbed Ridel."

"Yeah. Fat sloppy pussy son of a bitch. He didn't put up any kind of a fight. I held him for seven days, had to gag him to shut him the fuck up without killing him. Dipshit gets himself a law degree, thinks he can talk his way out of anything. Hardest part was gettin' him into that little plane in bright daylight, trying to make it look like he wasn't out cold at the time."

"On GHB," I said.

Cole rubbed his chin. "Feds got that, did they?"

I didn't answer. I looked at Dinah. "How'd you find us at that motel?"

"Tracker on Frank's truck. I told him to put it there so I would know where he was all the time."

Cole grinned. "And you're the big private eye? Kind of a joke, aren't you?"

Felt like it, yeah.

Dinah made an impatient sound. She waved a hand at the basement, ceiling, the entire building. "This's Neddie's house. I signed the papers, not Neddie, so this place is in my name—Jackson. He paid a third of the down. That was all he could afford after you got him tossed out of the FBI." She glared at me, daring me to contradict her, to tell her Ned's assignment to Butte wasn't my fault.

Because it was, more or less. But I wasn't about to go to prison for having sent Julia Reinhart over the River Styx because justice *had* been served. It was just too bad that Ned had been too intuitive and unyielding for his own good. I'd never wished him ill or wanted him dead. I only wanted him to quit trying to get me into a prison cell or into a little room for a lethal injection.

"Not tossed entirely out of the FBI," Dinah said. "Just stuck in this rathole city in a deadend job in the FBI, which is the same thing. They put him in charge of records in the office. *Records.* They made him a *secretary*. And who do you think did all of that to him?"

I didn't respond. I waited for her to blame me and go off on another rant.

"Alden Lund Ridel," she said, surprising me.

"Ridel?"

Her eyes glowed with hatred. "Ridel was Executive Assistant Director for Human Resources at the time. Since then they made him deputy director. But back then he took over Neddie's case personally, assigned him to Butte when Neddie was made a laughingstock by you and that lawyer in Reno, Ulysses Taber—who is *also* going to end up dead as soon as I can make that happen. But you're first, you're number one on the list, you miserable piece of *shit*."

She looked at Ella. "You just got in the way. Too bad, but that's life."

"Why her?" I said. I had to know.

"There is no *why*," Dinah said. "My sister, Evelyn, was married to a George Zimmerman before she married Bruce Dolak then Harold Nestor. Zimmerman didn't last long, barely a year. She had it annulled." She glared at me. "We had nothing but crap luck with husbands."

I didn't tell her we make our own luck, every one of us. She probably wouldn't respond well to that.

"Evie had a kid, Jason Zimmerman. She was going to change his last name to Nestor, but didn't." She gave Ella an unreadable look. "Jason was smart. He went to college, first one in the family, ended up teaching at that college in Reno you were at."

"My thesis advisor," Ella said, looking at me.

Dinah shrugged. "Whatever. I asked Jason to suggest someone he knew and trusted to write a note and deliver it. I didn't know anyone in Reno and I didn't trust Frank or Vince to know anyone reliable enough to write a note and put fifty dollars in a mailbox, so I asked Jason. All I wanted was the name and phone number of a student he trusted since he would know someone. I sent him fifty bucks to put in an envelope with a note saying they would get a phone call, and I told him to put it in the mailbox of whoever he chose. *Your* mailbox, as it turns out." She stared at Ella. "You wrote the note I told you to write. If you did it right it told Angel to go to that VOR thing *alone*. But then what happens? *You* showed up. Why *hell* did you do that? You screwed everything up royally."

Ella didn't answer.

"Well, what's done is done," Dinah said. "You're in the shit now, girl, along with Angel here. If it hadn't been for you, Frank and Vince could've handled Angel that day out at that VOR place. It was supposed to be just him and Ridel out there. Two dead assholes who ruined Neddie's life. I was gonna call 911 and get the cops out there to find them. It would've been a sensation, especially with that dimwit Ridel missing an entire week like he was."

I looked at Cole. "The VOR was your idea?"

"Uh-huh. In the middle of nowhere and I could beam in on it, drop Ridel right on top of you. It was a white speck in the desert, nothing else around."

Figured that, too. Not that it helped us any. I took a risk. "Ella didn't ruin this for you," I said to Dinah. "Vince did."

Dinah's eyes swiveled toward me. "How's that?"

"He fired a rifle at us. From three miles away."

Silence. Then: "He didn't tell us that."

"He wouldn't want you to know. Three miles was too far for him to actually hit anything, but if it hadn't been for him, we would've stayed where we were when Frank came out in the truck. Maybe. By then, Director Ridel had been dumped from the plane. That'd get anyone spooked about a truck headed our way, but we were expecting something at four that afternoon, so it could've been the truck. Vince might have thought pinning us down was a smart move, not that it would have worked in any case, but from three miles away all it did was scare us away."

"Vinnie surely loved his goddamn guns," Dinah said. "The idiot." She looked at me for a while. "I saw what you did up there at the cabin. Killed 'em both. I don't know how, but those two boys were as dumb as a short row of stumps. I thought Vince was the smarter of the two, but he got caught at your house at night, the dumb shit. I never should've used 'em, but I didn't have nobody else and they were right there in Reno."

She looked around again. "Anyway, here we are and I gotta get back to Minnesota, so let's get goin' here." She waved a hand at the woodshop. "Neddie was a genius with wood," she said. "You'd never know it, him bein' in the FBI and all, but he was. He made the chair that girl's sitting in. He made my dining table and chairs at home. He made all kinds of stuff, all of it professional grade, not enough to make a real living at it, and not so much after you got him sent out here to Butte. It's like the fire in him just about went out.

"But here's something he made," she said, indicating the two-by-four across the hallway, which reached from a wall on one side of the hallway to a door on the other. "It's a trap." She glared death at me. "A place to go in and . . . and just die. I cry every time I think about him building this goddamn horrible thing."

She lifted the two-by-four. One end was held in place by a big hinge attached to a wall. She lowered the free end and it came to rest on a piece of wood screwed to the door —a beautiful door made of oak with six huge hinges on one side. The two-by-four, lowered across the hallway, locked the door in place. Dinah lifted it and pulled the door open.

It was two inches thick, made of oak planks layered vertically and horizontally, held together with wood pegs. The craftsmanship was beautiful. Inside was a nine by seven room with a single light bulb and a small ventilation cover in the ceiling. Nothing else that I could see.

"Watch," Dinah said. She shut the door partway and lowered the two-by-four until it leaned against the door. Then, slowly, she closed the door. As she did, the free end of the two-by-four slid down the face of the door. When the door shut, the two-by-four was horizontal across the hallway, locking the door in place. No amount of pushing on the door by any human on the planet would dislodge that barrier. Two thousand pounds wouldn't open the door a tenth of an inch.

I shuddered slightly.

"Imagine," Dinah said, "going into that room and just shutting the door. That's all. Just shut the door and . . . die. No way to raise this board from inside. No way out. Can you imagine Neddie *building* this thing? Putting so much time and energy into making this solid goddamn door, installing this simple lever, knowing what going in and just shutting the door would *mean*?

"*Do you?*" she screeched, eyes bulging. "*Imagine how Neddie must have felt, making this horrid fucking thing! And it's all your fault. YOURS!*"

She was breathing like she'd run ten miles. Or, in her case, forty feet. I thought a stroke was a real possibility.

But, no such luck.

Cole grinned at me and waggled his eyebrows. He was probably a laugh a minute on his cellblock.

It took a while for Dinah to get hold of herself. Then she latched the killing lever against the far wall with the kind of hook and eye catch used on screen doors.

"Put 'em inside," Dinah said to Cole.

"No!" Ella cried.

"Do it," Dinah said.

Cole shrugged. He grabbed Ella under the armpits and lifted her straight up, carried her into the room. He set her down against the far wall. "Stay put or I kill Angel and toss him in with you."

He came out, punched me in the solar plexus again and untied me, hauled me into the room and dumped me on the floor. I couldn't stand, couldn't breathe. I tried, but I was paralyzed; I felt like I was drowning.

Finally I got a smidgeon of air, just enough to remain conscious. Ella crouched beside me, wanting to help, but there was no help until the paralysis wore off. My hands and feet were still tied. Ella's hands were free, but her feet were bound.

Dinah came into the room. Cole stood in the entrance. "Look around," Dinah said. "This used to be a storeroom. Neddie lined its walls with inch-thick plywood then lined that with sixteenth-inch sheet metal. There's nothing to get hold of, nothing to grab. It's just a metal box. The only way out is through the door and if that wood latch comes down, there's no way out. None. Then one day he just . . . went in and shut the door. That's all. I was in Minnesota. I hadn't heard from him in over a week. He wasn't answering his phone. He'd taken time off from the FBI here in Butte. He didn't have friends here to worry about him. No one ever came by to visit. Finally I flew out to talk with him, find out what was wrong, and . . . I found him. In here."

She broke down and cried. In other circumstances I would have felt sorry for her, but I wasn't in the mood. My empathy had dried up. I knew what she was about to do with Ella and me. I only wanted her dead.

"He was *shriveled*," Dinah said savagely. "And he was . . . corrupt. I can't imagine dying like that. My Neddie. My precious Neddie." She murdered me with her eyes. "He was the best of us, of all the family, and you killed him, you horrible, wicked, *evil* . . ."

She broke down again.

Well, shit, lady. I didn't mean for that to happen. I

didn't tell her that, but the words went through my head. I was all done with empathy. Every last drop. She was going to murder Ella. And me, but my thoughts were on Ella.

But I thought about Ned, too, dying by inches in this appalling room. I'd never wanted him dead.

"It took two days to clean this room," Dinah said. "But I did it after the police and everyone left. I wanted it clean, for *you*." She stared at me. "For *you*. I saved it for you. I didn't want a trace of Neddie in it. Ten days from now this room will reek of what's left of you, *and* you," she said to Ella, "but there's no help for that."

"There is," I said. "Let her go." I was still on my back on the floor. My midsection throbbed.

Cole laughed. "Then what? She has a life? She doesn't think about you, doesn't go to the cops? We just watch her scoot off into the sunset, no worries?"

I had no answer to that, nothing that had any hope of getting through to him.

"I'm through here," Dinah said. "Cut 'em loose and let's get out of here."

Cole crossed the room to Ella and cut the rope from around her ankles. Then he turned to me. "You want to tussle, hero, go ahead. Last time I broke anyone's legs was in the joint." He gave me an appraising look for a moment, then nodded to himself and rolled me over, cut the nylon rope holding my hands and feet, then stepped outside, leaving the door open eighteen inches. He left my sight for several seconds, then returned with an automatic in one hand, a Glock or a SIG.

"Toss your shoes out the door," he said to Ella and me. "And your belt, Angel."

No point in resisting him. We took off boots and shoes and tossed them out into the hallway. I did the same with my belt.

Dinah leaned the two-by-four latch against the door, then said, "Shut the door, Angel."

I didn't move, not that that laughable bit of resistance would hold up for long.

Cole aimed the gun, not at me but at Ella. "Shut the door, dude. You do it, not me or Dee, or I kill the girl and you can watch her decompose while you die in there. Or if you want, I can shoot you and she can watch you rot."

I had the thought that if there was a God, He would blast those two right there where they stood.

But nothing happened.

"Fuck you, Cole," Ella said.

Cole smiled. "Gutsy. Close it, stud. Last chance, unless you want me to go eenie meenie miney moe." The barrel of the gun shifted between me and Ella.

No choice. I staggered to my feet.

The door had a half-inch dowel sticking out an inch on the inside as a handle. I gripped it, then looked at Dinah and said, "You have a soul. Everyone does. Yours will have problems. Cole's might have bigger ones, hard to say."

Cole chuckled. "Close it. *Now*."

So I did. I pulled the dowel. The door swing inward and the latch scraped down the face of Ned's tremendous oak door. It locked in place with a terrifying terminal thud.

The sound of absolute death.

Chapter Eighteen

Ella stared at the door, then at me. Tears leaked out of her eyes. "I'm sorry, Mort."

"It's not over yet." Big words that rang false and got caught in my throat. I would never see Harper again.

I looked around. There wasn't much to see. Overhead, a forty-watt LED bulb glowed. A whisper of air came out of a four- by sixteen-inch vent of louvered steel screwed through sheet metal into the ceiling. The door didn't have an airtight seal. Air came in and leaked out. We wouldn't

suffocate in there. We would die slowly, as we were meant
to. As Ned had, four months ago. I could still smell a hint
of the Clorox Dinah used to clean the room.

I listened at the door. The sound of footsteps on stairs
was faint but they came through. Slow, heavy steps—Dinah
going up with Cole's help.

Finally they stopped.

"Cheers," Cole called out, probably from the top of the
stairs. The door above closed with a muffled thud.

Then nothing.

No dogs barking, no birds chirping, no cars, traffic, no
distant television, no airliner overhead. Just nothing. Then
I felt a slight rumble in the room, a shiver in the floor and
walls. Then it stopped. It took a while for me to realize the
garage door had gone up. A minute later the rumble was
back and Dinah and Cole were gone.

For a moment I just stood there. The psychological
impact of the sheet metal walls and that impervious door
was horrific. I felt a knife blade of claustrophobia slide into
my soul. This was a coffin.

I hit the door with a shoulder, but it was like hitting a
brick wall.

Ella sank down on the floor with her back to a wall
and put her face in her hands. She didn't make a sound. I
couldn't tell if she was crying or . . . or what. I pulled her in
close and hugged her. She held me tight.

We stayed like that for a while, then Lucy said, plain
as day and in an astonishingly loud voice: "Save her, save
yourself. Get *out* of there, big guy."

I heard her, but Ella didn't react in any way. I looked
around. No sign of Lucy, no ethereal light, no ectoplasm,
no more sound, but she was there. My Lucy was with me
wherever I went—had been from the day she died, almost
two years ago. She was my true soul mate.

"How?" I asked, but silently, in my head. I didn't want
to alarm Ella, but I knew Lucy would hear me.

I got a glow of pure love, like heat. It filled me, made
my heart swell, gave me hope.

I stood up and surveyed the room. It was just a box
with metal sides, a concrete floor, a solid oak door, a light

bulb and an air vent in the ceiling. Nothing else. The only way out was through Ned's terrible door.

I considered it, tried to visualize what I had seen of it and the latch when I had been outside. Dinah had leaned the latch board against the door then closed it. The end of the board scraped down the face of the door and came to rest on a horizontal piece of wood screwed to the front of the door roughly knee-high off the floor. The latch didn't hit the middle of the door. It was closer to the non-hinged side, about a foot in from the edge.

The door's hinges were huge. Two near the top, two at the bottom, and two more spaced evenly between top and bottom. Six big hinges. Ned didn't want anyone kicking the door in at the hinges. If it had been a typical interior door I could've kicked the screws out of the bottom hinge and used the door as a big lever to rip the rest of them out of the wall. I could've been out in ten minutes, but that wasn't going to happen here.

Ned was great with wood. *Had* been great.

So, what else? The only thing I could think of was to make a hole in the door at just the right place so Ella, with her smaller hand, could get an arm through far enough to lift the latch. I couldn't make a hole with my fingers. I needed metal. And the only metal I could conceivably get any kind of a hold on was the air vent screwed to the ceiling. It was anodized brown steel with fixed louvers that were tilted one way through half its length, the rest tilted the other way to diffuse incoming air throughout the room.

Ella looked up at me. "What're you doing?"

"I'm going to kill Cole and Dinah."

Her lips compressed in what might have been a smile, but I wasn't sure. Her eyes still glistened with tears.

"Really?" she said.

"That's right, but first I have to get us out of here."

"How?"

"Don't ask. I don't want to make a fool of myself."

She stood up. "Is there anything I can do to help?"

"I don't know. Not yet, anyway. Unless you have an idea. I'm willing to listen to any and all suggestions."

The ceiling was eight feet high. I'm six four. I could

just touch the vent flat-footed, and on my toes I could get a reasonably decent grip on the louvers.

Which I did, and the little bastards were tough. They didn't want to bend. But I had built up a lot of strength in my fingers slamming a sixteen-pound steel bar into earth like concrete while digging fencepost holes at a woman's sheep ranch in Borroloola, Australia. A mile of fence posts, one every eight feet. I lifted that iron bar up two and a half feet and slammed it into the ground 300,000 times, more than twelve million foot-pounds of work. Since then I had worked on retaining my grip strength. It had been useful in the hallway of an old apartment building when I'd shaken hands with a shithead and brought him to his knees. Later, however, I'd had to kill him and his psycho friend because they tried to kill me and were going to rape and kill Lucy.

I grabbed one of the louvers between thumb and the first two fingers of both hands and twisted. It bent slightly, rotated maybe five degrees, so I twisted it the other way five degrees which gave it a full ten-degree rotation. Then back and forth, back and forth, standing on my toes.

Hard work. Miserable hard fucking work. I had to rest often to ease the cramping in my fingers. But after a while I was bending the louver a total of about twenty degrees. Then thirty. The twisting got easier toward the end as the metal crystalized, then snapped at one end. From there it was easy to get a four-inch piece of sheet metal out, half an inch wide. Best guess, it had taken thirty minutes.

"That's . . . amazing," Ella said.

"It'll be a crappy knife. Or a crappy razor blade. But it has to be sharpened before I can work on that damn oak door."

"How?"

"Grind one of its edges on this concrete floor into a blade. Not an entire edge, just a quarter inch or so of the edge at one end."

"I can do that."

"Bevel it fairly steeply. If it's too thin it'll bend."

She stared at the door. "It'll take a long time to make any kind of a hole in that."

"Yes, it will, so let's get started."

She sharpened the "knife," and I watched, gave her a few pointers because I knew what I would need. Once she got the hang of it, I started to remove another louver.

After a while she held up the tool she'd made. "Is this gonna work?"

I kissed her. "It won't be easy, but we sure as hell are gonna try. Now we have to decide where to make the hole. Point to the place on the door where you think the end of that latch board is touching on the other side."

"I didn't get a very good look at it."

"You saw how it worked, didn't you?"

"Yes. It was horrible. And so simple, considering what it does."

"Close your eyes. Visualize what you saw. How high up on the door was the latch when the door closed, how far in from the edge opposite the hinges."

She did. Her eyes moved under her lids. She took a few deep breaths. Finally she looked at the door, crouched down, and touched a spot. "Here. About. Maybe."

I smiled. Then I did the same thing: got an image of where the latch hit the door. Moved my finger up not quite two feet and to my left about ten inches.

My mark was higher than hers by almost four inches, a bit further in from the edge. I scratched a little X at a spot between our two estimates.

I held my hands out to her, trying to form a rectangle using my thumbs, middle fingers, and palms.

"Try to put your hand through this box I've made," I told her.

She did, easily enough, so I shortened the rectangle's height but kept its width the same. "Try again."

Better.

"Now try to put your arm through, all the way to your elbow."

She did—after I made the box half an inch wider. It ended up roughly three and a half inches high, two and a half inches wide.

I considered the latch board on the other side of the door. As the latch lifted, the end of the board would ride up the face of the door. At some point the door itself would lift the latch as the door was opened, but not until the angle of the latch overcame friction of the latch against the door.

Tricky.

She would have to lift the latch throughout the entire sequence. I visualized her hand going through the hole and reaching down to get hold of the latch, then lifting it high enough to get past that friction point. Making the hole was going to be a bitch. I didn't know if we could do it before we couldn't work any longer, so it had to be the smallest possible hole, yet big enough. She had slender hands and arms. Mine wouldn't look out of place on sasquatch.

I scratched an outline of the hole on the door, nine inches above and a couple inches to the right of where we thought the end of the latch was hitting the door.

"Are you sure that'll work?" she asked.

"Nope. It's only my best guess, sweetheart."

"Sweetheart. I like that."

I wanted another louver out while my hands were still strong enough, so I continued working on it. With the first louver out I had more room to hold it and twist, so it didn't take quite as long. When I had it out, she went to work sharpening the tip of one of its edges.

While she did that, I went to work on the door.

• • •

I gouged a vertical line along the right side of the box I had drawn in the oak. It was just a scratch. It might've been a hundredth of an inch deep, if that.

I shuddered. Oak is hard.

I ran the knife down the same groove. It still looked like a scratch, not much more than that. I kept at it until I had a thin groove an eighth of an inch deep, then I made another groove next to it, same depth and a sixteenth of an inch to the left of the first. Then I used the dull end of the louver as a lever in one of the grooves and snapped off a bit of oak. It looked like a thin toothpick. It had taken seven or eight minutes to do that.

"That's awfully small," Ella said.

"This is how they built the pyramids," I replied. "One brick at a time."

"Except we don't have twenty years."

"Patience. The tortoise won the race."

"Pyramids and tortoises. You're something else. Let me try it. Your fingers can't do all of this."

I gave her the knife and she went to work. It took her at least twelve minutes to get another little toothpick out of the wood.

I came up with a different routine. I made two parallel grooves a quarter inch deep and an eighth of an inch apart, then snapped off the piece. It was twice as deep and twice as wide as first piece I'd removed, which was four times the volume—and excavating this hole was all about removing volume. Four times the volume in twice the time meant we could go through twice as fast.

Got some use out of my high school math.

"That's better," she said. "But this is still gonna take a long time."

• • •

An hour passed. Then another, and another, and yet another before the hole was a quarter inch deep in the shape of the template. We were roughly an eighth of the way to getting out. But the deeper the hole got, the harder the job would get, because we wouldn't be able to get our fingers in while we worked, so we would lose leverage. My fingers had cramped often. I couldn't work continuously. I'd ripped an inch-wide strip off the cuff of my jeans and wound it around the shaft of the knife to make a kind of handle to keep the edge of the louver from biting into my fingers. We had a long way to go. I didn't want to literally work my fingers to the bone. Or hers.

"If we trade off and don't stop," I said, "this'll take at least fifty hours, maybe more."

"Then we trade off and don't stop," she said. "And one of us has to rest and maybe sleep while the other works."

She was sounding tougher, more determined. Good.

"I'll start the next ... next whatever it's called," she said. "The next quarter inch of this hole. You rest."

• • •

We were half an inch into the door and starting on the next layer when she crouched beside me and said, "I'm sorry, Mort, but I *really* have to pee. I can't hold it."

I figured that was coming, for both of us, and I wasn't looking forward to it. It would produce complications and embarrassment. Bodily functions were not going to stop.

"We knew this was coming," I said.

"I know. But still, this is . . ."

"Nothing we can do about it, hon."

She sighed. "I know, I *know*. I've thought about what we need to do and what it'll be like if we get out of here."

That didn't make sense. I looked at her. "What do you mean? And it's not if, it's *when*."

"Okay, yes, *when*. What I was going to say is, we can use clothing for toilet paper, starting with underwear, and we can pee on clothing to keep it from running all over the floor. But we don't know what we'll find in the house to use for clothing if we use up what we're wearing now."

"That's a bridge we'll cross when we come to it."

And that was all we said about that. But we were adult about the situation, not children.

We kept digging.

•   •   •

As I worked, I thought about Ned and this room he'd built. It spoke in obscure whispers. Why die *this* way? Why not end it all with a gun or a rope? Too classic? Or were those acts so specifically suicidal that he couldn't face them, couldn't hide them from himself? This room was different. All Ned had to do was turn off his thoughts for five seconds, come inside and . . . shut the door. That's all. An everyday act that didn't hint of suicide. Do that and it was done. Was that its appeal?

Something I would never know.

I kept digging into the oak by tenths of millimeters.

•   •   •

We were working an inch deep in the hole, having to cut the oak into horizontal pieces because Ned had layered the middle boards horizontally, when I heard a voice on the other side.

"How y'all doing in there?"

It was Cole. Twenty or twenty-four hours had passed since he and Dinah had left us. By then both Ella and I had given up our shirts for use as pee sponges, and our socks and underwear had been used for toilet paper. But without food and water, that problem was slowing down.

"We need water," I yelled. Not because I expected to get water, but to make him think we were doing nothing in there but dying. If he opened the door and saw the hole, we were dead.

He laughed. "Good luck with that, *señor*."

I heard him clump back up the stairs, then all was quiet again for a few minutes until I heard a faint rumble as the garage door went down. I hadn't heard or felt it go up. I would have to listen for that more carefully.

"This is trouble," I said. "Cole coming around."

"Why?"

"If we get the hole partway through and he shows up and sees a small hole in the door, he'll know what we're doing and that we're close. That would end this."

Her face got pale. "How do we work around that?"

"Timing," I said. "He might not come again, but we can't count on that. He'll probably come in the daytime if at all, hopefully at the same time, so we need to get all the way through the door and out during the night."

"How will we know when that is?"

"Timing," I said again. "He came now. Odds are he'll be back in about twenty-four hours if he's keeping track of us. He might be reporting our progress to Dinah. If we can break through in the next thirty to thirty-six hours, we should be okay."

She took a deep breath. "Let's do it."

Tough lady. She didn't say anything about food and water. We were dehydrated, exhausted, and the air was foul, but hunger pangs had stopped. No use talking about any of it. She was topless, but that meant nothing. We were in survival mode. Nothing else mattered.

My bullet wound didn't look too bad. A bit raw still, and maybe a little infected, but it wouldn't kill me in the next few days like this room would if we didn't get out.

We kept going.

•   •   •

My fingers were raw, as were Ella's, when Cole came back the next day. This time I heard or felt the garage door go up, so I was expecting his voice when he said, "How're you doing in there, guys?"

I thumped on the door with a fist. "Help," I called out in a weak voice, partly faked, partly real.

That got a laugh.

Then he left—still checking up on us, but there must not have been anything in the house to keep him hanging around.

We had a little over half an inch left to go. It could be as much as three-quarters of an inch. Hard to tell.

"We better get this done before he's back again," Ella said.

•   •   •

The blade went through sometime during the night, or what we hoped was night. It was hard to get a sense of time in that room. A few minutes might feel like an hour. When the blade went through, a sliver of light was visible on the other side—electric light or daylight, we couldn't tell which but we knew then that we had to go all out and finish the hole before Cole returned.

It was hard, frustrating work, measured in millimeters or less. I could only hold onto the last two inches of the knife, which didn't give me much leverage. Ella didn't have my finger strength so her progress was even slower, and we were both getting weak.

Finally I was down to no more than the last eighth of an inch and the knife had gone entirely through one side of the hole, and both the top and bottom, so I stuck my right thumb into the hole and punched out the last thin panel of wood and its splintery lefthand edge.

Ella cried. I cried.

But we did it without tears. We were dry.

We still didn't know if the hole was in a place where

Ella could reach the latch board and lift it.

"You're up," I said. "It's all up to you now."

"Kiss me."

I did, then said, "Do it, hon. Get us out of here."

She put her hand in the hole, then her wrist. If we had the hole at the right elevation, she would have to reach down nine or ten inches to touch the latch.

Her forearm went in five or six inches. She angled her arm down and groped around.

"I feel it," she said, excited. "It's to my left."

"Can you get your fingers under it."

"I'm . . . trying."

She pushed harder, got her arm in another inch.

Silence for a moment. Then, "The tip of my middle finger is under it but the others don't reach."

"Can you lift it, sweetheart?"

She was silent, then, "It's not moving."

"Pull back a little. It'll be a lot harder to lift the latch if we're pushing on the door." I helped by pulling the bit of dowel handle as hard as I could.

"Try it now, honey. Hard as you can."

"It's . . . heavy."

"Lift."

"I . . . it moved. I've got two fingers under it now . . . it's up a little bit."

"Keep going. We're almost out of here."

She was crying while she lifted. The latch scraped the outer face of the door at first as it went up, but I held the door closed so she could lift it without fighting friction. Then she twisted her arm above the hole and kept shoving. The outer edge of the door opened an inch, then two, two and a half. I gave the door an experimental shove but the latch hadn't gone past that critical friction point yet.

"Higher," I said, easing off the pressure.

"I can't. That's . . . it's as high as I can reach." Her voice filled with tears.

"It's okay." I pushed the door, which held the latch in place. "Pull your arm out and trade places with me."

When she got her arm out I saw deep lacerations an inch and a half long in her arm over halfway to her elbow where she'd forced her arm past splintery wood. She hadn't said a thing about it but it had to have hurt.

The door was open a little over two inches. My arm would never fit through a gap that narrow, but hers might. "Reach through and around and see if you can reach the latch," I said. If she couldn't, we were in big trouble.

She stuck her arm into the gap, getting her arm all the way through to the elbow. "It's here," she said. "I've got my fingers under it."

"Lift."

She did. I removed all pressure from the door to make it easier for her. The latch scraped upward and suddenly it went beyond the friction point. The door swung open and we almost tumbled out onto the basement floor.

Out.

Out.

Out.

Chapter Nineteen

We cried, we hugged, and we kissed, even though our lips were dry and rough.

"Omigod, omigod," Ella wailed. "We did it!"

If I'd tried to speak I would've sounded four years old, which would've played hell with my dumbass gravitas.

The light we'd first seen came from two LED bulbs in the ceiling. I glanced at the clock I'd seen on a wall a few days ago. 8:34. But was that a.m. or p.m.? I'd lost all track of time. The basement had no windows.

No underwear, no socks, no shirts, but we still had pants and we were out. *Out.*

My belt, boots, and Ella's shoes had been tossed into a

corner. First thing I wanted was a weapon. I looked around the woodshop, finally found a heavy framing hammer with a long handle and a claw so straight it looked almost like a pickaxe.

A decent weapon, but a Glock would've been better.

I led the way up the stairs. Blood ran down Ella's arm and drops fell off her fingertips. The door to the first floor wasn't locked. We went out into a hallway, saw daylight at windows to the left and right. It was morning. Cole could be on the way.

"I want water," Ella said. "And a bathroom."

A bathroom was off the hallway. She turned the faucet and water came out. Blessed water, beautiful water, not yet running clear, but it probably would in a minute or so. The house hadn't been used in months.

"Don't drink too much right away," I told her. "Only a few ounces. Let your stomach adjust."

"Okay." She let the water run. I found the kitchen and got water there, taking my own advice. The windows only gave me a view of the back and side yards.

Cole.

He could show up any moment.

I went down the hallway past the bathroom where Ella had the door closed. A short hallway led to the right and I was in a laundry alcove with a door at the far end. I opened the door, looked into the garage, which was empty, closed it again. I went down the longer hall and into a living room with a view out the front through dirty windows. A thirty-foot driveway to the right would give access to the garage. An ordinary street was beyond that. I watched as a Prius rolled silently by. Pale sunlight slanted through maples and elms that were starting to lose their leaves.

We had to get out of there.

But I didn't want to only get away. I also wanted Cole dead, and he was going to return sometime to check on us. I wanted him gone forever so I didn't have to keep looking over my shoulder.

Therefore I was conflicted.

But he would have a gun, I didn't, so my thoughts got tangled in what's laughingly known as conflict resolution.

I didn't resolve a damn thing.

Ella came out of the bathroom. She'd washed her arm and wrapped it in paper towels. The towels were pink with blood. She'd saved our lives, forcing her arm through that ragged hole.

"There's no hot water," she said, "but you can wash up a bit. I did."

"I'll do that. Keep an eye on the street. Let me know if you see Cole coming." I showed her the view out the front.

I washed as best I could in the sink using water and an old bar of soap, but a full-on shower would have to wait. We couldn't be there when Cole arrived—if he did. I had a little voice telling me to get us the hell out of there, just go, but the same little voice was also telling me to stay and end this. Stupid little ambiguous voice.

But if Cole did show up, he would expect us to be half dead in Ned's room by now, maybe unconscious, so at least I would have the element of . . .

"*No!*" Ella cried. "No, no, *no!*"

I both felt and heard the rumble of the garage door as it went up.

Ah, shit, no. We should've gotten out of there.

I hustled Ella into the kitchen where I'd seen a door to the back yard. "Stay here. Don't make a sound. Open the door but don't go out yet. If you have to run, run. You're a deer. He'll never catch you."

"What about *you*?" she wailed.

I hefted the hammer. "I've done more with less than this. Now go, and be *absolutely* quiet. Don't say a word no matter what. He doesn't know we're out and loose. Do not make a sound, *none.*"

She went.

I hustled to the door that led to the garage. The sound of Frank's truck was audible from inside. Then the engine shut down and the truck's door opened, slammed shut, and the garage door went trundling down.

I had a framing hammer and surprise on my side. And anger, and thoughts of Harper and Ella. I made certain the hammer's claw was faced in the right direction and I stood behind the door, but not too close. If the door touched me as it opened, he would know something was wrong. I lifted the hammer over my head and waited. I had one chance to get this right. Just one.

The door swung open and Cole came in. He jerked at the last instant, alerted to danger, possibly a whisper of air as I swung the hammer, but, too late. The hammer's claw went almost three inches deep into the top of his skull.

Poleaxed him, just like Lucy had done to a nasty little shit named Joe Anza three years ago and saved our lives.

One more of these guys down. One more to go. Unless there were a few we hadn't detected yet.

• • •

"Ella!"

No answer.

Cole was dead at my feet, the claw of the hammer still embedded in his skull. I headed for the kitchen.

"I got him," I called out, immediately wishing I'd come up with something more heroic than that puny comment. I had, after all, slain fucking Goliath.

She peered around a corner as I entered the kitchen. "You got him? Really?" she said in a quavering voice.

"He's dead."

Rather anticlimactically, too. Cole hadn't had a chance to fight back. Surprise and a hammer's claw wedged deep in the skull bone will do that.

She wanted to see, to be sure, just like she had up at the shack when I'd taken out Frank and Vince.

She almost fell when she saw Cole. Her legs got loose and she started to slump. I held her up. Then she turned to me and hugged me as if clinging to life.

I get that a lot. It's not bad. She needed a shirt, as did I, but we all do the best we can, whatever the situation.

• • •

But now what?

I wanted to call Ma, and the lawyer, Jim Carbon, LLC, and Harper, and 911, and find Ella and me something to eat, drink more water, and maybe find shirts, though that could wait since she seemed to be okay with what she had on and the house was warm enough. It wasn't easy to prioritize all that. All of it was important, but it had to be done in the proper order.

I felt weak. Ella looked weak. I had a headache and my eyes wouldn't focus properly. I wasn't a hero. I could tell a tall tale with the best of them but I realized I'd been damn lucky to take Cole down the way I had in my condition.

Food and water.

Water first, then food. Ned Willis had been gone a long time. Would there be any food in the house?

I took several deep breaths. Cole was dead so we had time. We didn't have to get everything done all at once, but water was easy so we needed food.

Nothing was in the refrigerator. It had been cleaned out and the door propped open. We checked shelves and came up with a ragtag collection of canned stuff: tuna, black beans, tomato sauce, chicken noodle soup, a six-pack of V8, garbanzos, black olives, lentils, condensed milk.

Better than nothing, which is what we'd had for the past—I totaled it up, which wasn't easy—sixty-seven hours.

A drawer held utensils and a can opener, other things. I wanted to call Ma, but I didn't have a cell phone. I picked up the house phone, got no dial tone.

"What's for breakfast, sweetheart?" I asked.

Ella smiled. "Chicken noodle soup first—if the stove works since it's gas, and if we can find a pot."

Which it did, and we did. She heated the soup while I went in search of a cell phone, and if I came across a shirt I would snag it for Ella. But I had an idea where to look for a cell phone: in one of Cole's pockets.

He was leaking on the floor where I'd left him. I had searched more than my fair share of bodies in the past five years so it didn't give me the willies. In a pocket of a denim jacket I came up with a burner—not one of mine. Cole had found mine and Ella's before tying our hands and feet in the camper three days ago. As soon as I thought of that, I realized how sluggishly my mind was working. My burner might be in the camper, which should be in the garage. Before checking that however, I picked up the SIG that had fallen out of Cole's hand. That I hadn't noticed the gun at the time I'd put him down, or right after, was an indication of just how utterly exhausted I was, and how dehydration affects a person's ability to think.

I dialed Ma's number using Cole's phone, then went in search of clothing. I found a bedroom just as Ma answered.

"Yeah?" she said cautiously.

"It's me, Ma," I said. The bedroom had been stripped of personal stuff. No sign of clothing and the mattress on a double bed was bare.

"Mort! Where the *hell* are you? Last I heard you were in Butte. Are you okay?"

"Still in Butte—probably. Ella and I are more or less okay. Got a lot to tell you and it'll take a while to give you all of it, but we've been locked in Ned's suicide room for the past three days."

"Suicide room? What the hell's that?"

"Tell you when I get a chance. It's ugly. Right now, you need to know we're okay, but we could use help."

"You said you're *probably* in Butte. You don't know?"

"Pretty sure. Let's go with that for now."

Ma sighed, then said, "None of us heard from you in so long I finally decided to head your way. I'm in a rental. Vale's still with Harper, so they're good. Right now I'm at a little town called Monida just inside Montana on I-15. I got too tired to keep going so I got a motel room last night."

"How far is Monida from Butte?"

"Hang on. I'll Google it." Twenty seconds of silence, then, "A hundred twenty-seven miles."

Two hours out.

"Not too far," I said. "We'll try to hang tight here until you get here."

"Where *is* here, exactly? Butte's a big place."

"Well, shoot, I don't know. It's Ned's house in Butte, but Dinah bought it so it's in her name: Jackson. She and Cole brought us here. I was out cold for most of the trip so I don't know exactly where we are."

"Who's Cole? And you were out cold?"

"Cole Keeler. Dinah's possibly-adopted kid. I don't know if the adoption was legal. He's one year younger than Ned Willis. Got out of prison eight months ago. He flew the plane and shoved Ridel out over the VOR station. He tasered me, Dinah tasered Ella, they captured both of us. I'll tell you about that later. But if you're wondering about him, he's in Ned's house twenty feet away from me right now with a hammer embedded in his skull."

"Did you put it there?"

"Nope. Carpentry accident, Ma."

"Mort, for *Christ's sake*—"

"Yeah, I did it. Shades of Lucy using that tomahawk to put down Joe Anza in that basement."

"Well, good. Can you get me an address for the house where you're at?"

"Ella can't go outside without a shirt, but I can. Hold on. I'll see if the house has a number on it."

"You two aren't wearing shirts?"

"We would, but they're full of urine." Yanking Ma's chain is one of my favorite pastimes.

"Urine? What the *hell*, Mort."

"Later. It's a long story and I'm still a little out of it. Ella and I haven't had anything to eat or drink for going on seventy hours."

"Oh, lord."

"You might find a Walmart and pick up a shirt for her. Phone Vale if you're not sure about Ella's size. I could use a shirt too. Underwear and socks would be appreciated. In fact, a whole new wardrobe for both of us would be great."

"She's topless and both of you are missing clothes?"

"I'll explain when you get here."

I gave Ma a little more of what had happened while I went outside and walked down the driveway. I looked back at the house. Brass numerals were screwed to the garage wall beside its door, which was down, concealing the truck Cole had arrived in.

"House number is 1615, Ma."

"Great. What's the name of the street?"

I was at the street. A street sign a hundred yards away was too far for me to read. A woman two doors down at a mailbox stared at me. I didn't think an unknown shirtless guy should saunter up to her to ask the name of the street. That might bring the cops and I didn't want that, at least not yet. I waved to her and she looked at me for a moment, then returned the wave. Ned's mailbox was empty. No help with the street name there.

"Don't know," I told Ma. "See if you can find a house that belongs to a Dinah Jackson with a street number of 1615. If I find anything in the house like a letter or bill that has the street name on it, I'll call back."

I ended the call and went back in the house. Chicken noodle soup was ready. Best chicken noodle soup *ever*. I'd never had soup of any description a tenth that good.

"You're still topless, miss," I said conversationally.

"I ordered a shirt from room service, but the service in this place is lousy. If it bothers you, don't look."

"Doesn't bother me one bit."

She smiled. "Figures. I opened two cans of tuna. We need protein in addition to liquid and calories." She passed me a fork and a can of tuna.

"Room service looks pretty good to me," I said. "Kinda hot, actually."

"You *would* say something like that, wouldn't you?"

"Testosterone is a powerful drug, miss."

"It must also have a defective nose. We stink. I really, *really* want a shower."

. . .

A shower. Well, shit, we had electricity and water. My brain was still grinding along in low gear. I found a breaker panel in the garage. A breaker was flipped off beside the words WATER HEATER. I flipped it on, then looked around for the heater. It was in a corner by the door into the house, hissing very faintly, just getting started.

Back in the kitchen I said, "Hot water comin' up. But it's starting from scratch so it'll take a while."

"You're a lifesaver." She smiled. "In more ways than one. I don't suppose you came across any clothes in here?"

"I've been prioritizing. That's low on the list."

"Uh-huh. You're a brute. Let's look around."

We went through the bedroom I'd seen earlier. It had a chest of drawers, empty. Nothing in a closet. A flight of stairs off the main hallway led up to a small bedroom and bathroom over the garage. Those were the only two rooms upstairs, a terrific place for a kid. No clothes there either, but a towel was hanging on a rack in the bathroom.

"Dibs," Ella said, grabbing it. She wrapped it around her chest, tucked one end in to hold it, then gave my bullet wound a close look. "I wish we had something for that."

Which once again told me how slow I was processing things. I took her downstairs and into the garage where Frank's truck still had the camper on the back.

I went through the camper and found my wallet in a cabinet drawer. It still had both my IDs, my real one and the one for Harvey Orkaza. No money in it, but I thought I could fix that by checking Cole's pockets for a wallet.

I wouldn't be able to use the Orkaza credit cards or ID until Ma okayed it. No telling if Cole had tried to use them. If he had, they were burned.

We found Ella's purse with her wallet in it. Cole had removed the money but her license and credit cards were intact. I also found my .357 Ruger and our cell phones.

In a kitchen drawer in the house I found an electric bill with the full street address: 1615 Burgess Lane.

I called Ma and gave her the address. She was still an hour and a half out of Butte. Ella and I drank more water, ate more food. We had a lot to catch up on.

Finally the water was hot. We had a bar of soap and Ella found a bottle of shampoo beneath the bathroom sink. She turned on the shower in the downstairs bathroom, stripped off her jeans, then looked at me.

"You're not naked yet," she said.

"Beautiful *and* observant."

She smiled. "Strip, Mort. I'm getting wet."

So we both got wet, and it felt good to be clean again after what we'd had to do in Ned's terrible room.

• • •

When we got out we had another problem. Ella picked up the jeans she'd been wearing, and said, "Yuk. I can't put these on again. And you can't wear yours."

I smiled. "Which means what?"

"Which means I get the towel and I hope Ma shows up

soon with medical stuff and clothing—not that I mind the view here since you've been ogling me."

"I don't ogle. And, shit, there's gotta be something left lying around this house I can wear."

She smiled. "*Now* you're concerned about clothing."

We hiked down to the basement, I shut the door to the suicide room, hooked the latch against the wall, then we continued along the hallway and found a kind of storeroom full of boxes and crap furniture—and a pillow with a pillowcase. So I cut leg holes in the closed end of the pillowcase and put it on, tied a cord around the waist to keep it up, and it was the ugliest fuckin' thing I'd ever worn in my life.

"And me without a camera," Ella said. "Maybe Ma can take one with her cell phone when she gets here."

"Nope. I've got a gun, sweetheart. *Two* guns."

"You think *that'll* slow Ma down?"

Well, no.

We ate more, drank more, and watched the street from the living room. Ella wanted to clean up the poop and urine-soaked clothing in the suicide room, but I told her it was part of the story, like the pile of sawdust and splinters we'd managed to carve out of the door to get free. In truth, I didn't want to go back inside that room for any reason.

"It's *horrible*, Mort," she said. "And embarrassing."

"It's life. Anyone stuck in that room would have done the same thing, one way or another."

"I don't care."

She prevailed, but we didn't do more than gather up the soiled clothing, stuff it into a plastic garbage bag, and set it outside the kitchen door. In time the police would get here and I wanted the story to be as visual and complete as possible, so I left Cole where he lay, blood congealing around his head, hammer still stuck in his skull. We didn't try to clean the suicide room further. It would tell its own story. I was actually proud of that—the way Ella and I had burrowed out of that impossible room. Frank and Vince were dead in the hills, and my truck was in Motel 6's back parking lot with a bullet hole in its radiator—unless they'd already had it towed. All part of the story.

Chapter Twenty

Ma showed up at 11:20. My pillowcase shorts were a big hit, but I'm a good sport, so I let her take the picture. Harper would like it. Later, Ma would notice the unusual configuration of the middle finger of my left hand at the moment she took the shot.

Ella and I dressed in new clothes while Ma called Jim Carbon. He said he'd be there in fifteen minutes, at which time he would call the police, not us.

I showed Ma the suicide room, the hole we'd made and the tool we'd used to make it. She made no comment about the rest of the room. It was self-explanatory.

Then Carbon showed up and he got the tour. He was fifty-two years old, white hair, trim, looked like a runner. There's a lot of that going around.

"Suicide room," he said. "I heard about that guy Ned Willis and a suicide room, but I didn't expect anything like this. This's a real sonofabitch." He was impressed by Cole's body and the location of the hammer, and sanguine about what I told him the police would find at the shack in the hills if Cole and Dinah hadn't disturbed the scene. If they had, I had taken pictures of Vince and Frank where they'd fallen so the authorities could compare that to the story I would have to tell. But Cole probably hadn't done anything with those two. They were only cousins, after all.

Jim Carbon called the police and gave them a brief description of what they were about to find so they could send everything they would need, then we waited for local law enforcement to roll over us—over me, actually, since I had rid the world of three homicidal retreads.

Which it did, and the resulting circus was pretty much what I thought it would be. The lead investigator, a guy in his late forties, Mike Roeder, sallow, bald, sharp-eyed, and competent, was first through the door, followed by a very female detective, Ann Trenner, and four uniformed officers of various ranks, ages, and sizes. Roeder and Trenner had a good look at Cole's body and an explanation of how that happened. Roeder stared at the body for a moment, then said, "That's gotta hurt."

Trenner rolled her eyes at that, then smiled. I figured those two had seen worse in their day.

Trenner caught sight of the torn flesh on Ella's right arm. "How did that happen?"

"You need to see what's downstairs," I said.

We hiked down to the basement and had a gander at the suicide room, its latch and the hole that had taken us sixty-five hours to scratch through the oak. It was ragged. It looked as if it had been done by mice.

"Ella had to shove her arm through that," I told them. Drying blood was visible around the hole.

Roeder took a closer look at the hole. "How the hell did you do this?"

I showed him the tool we'd used.

"Je-*sus*, you went through this door with *that*?"

"Had to. It's all we had." I showed him the vent in the ceiling with its missing louvers.

"Sonofabitch." He operated the latch several times to watch it work. "Christ," he muttered once he realized what it would mean to go into the room and shut the door. Ella turned away when he actually went into the room, shut the door, and the latch fell into place. Seconds later he hit the door with his shoulder, hard. It didn't so much as quiver.

Ten seconds of dead quiet followed, then he knocked on the door, a plaintive sound. Trenner lifted the latch and Roeder came out with a bead of sweat on his forehead.

Then a forensics crew arrived and after surveying the scene they began photographing, dusting for fingerprints, measuring with tape, the whole nine yards. I started to sag with fatigue. My eyelids drooped.

"You okay?" Jim Carbon asked.

"Ella and I are probably still dehydrated. I got maybe eight hours' sleep in the past seventy hours, and she has those tears on her arm and I've got this." I lifted my shirt and showed him and Roeder the bullet wound.

"Holy Christ," Roeder said. "How'd you get that? Why didn't you say something? Medical attention takes priority. Let's get you and Ms. Kassel to a hospital."

Before Ella and I were whisked away, I gave Roeder an account of where Ella had been held and how I'd been shot by Frank as I ran toward the shack after I'd managed to put Vince down. I showed him and Trenner the pictures I'd taken of the bodies. They would have to get up there to see if those two were still there, decomposing. It had been four days.

So that ended the questioning, at least for a while. I ended up in an emergency room in St. James Hospital with a good-looking female doctor, Paula Jensen, who gave the wound one look and said, "You should've been in here four days ago."

"Got here as fast as I could, doc," I said.

A deputy sheriff who'd accompanied us to the hospital gave me a grin. He'd seen the hole Ella and I had made in the door. He knew the story.

"Where *were* you?" Paula asked. "The North Pole?"

"Right here in Butte, but I was held up." For that, the deputy gave me a thumb's up.

Exhaustion started to set in with a vengeance and I fell dead asleep on the examination table while Paula was doing her thing. Sometime later she woke me up and said, "All done." She gave me a closer look. "You need sleep. I heard what you did, digging a hole through a solid wood door with a tiny bit of metal. How long did that take?"

"Sixty-five hours. I might've got eight hours of sleep. The girl with me, Ella, she needs sleep too."

The deputy was still there. "FBI is here," he told Paula. "They want to talk to the two of them."

"That's not happening," she said. "Maybe tomorrow or the next day. We patched the girl up but we're keeping her and Mr. Angel overnight for observation. They're suffering from the effects of dehydration. We're monitoring vitals.

And right now this old boy's getting a mild sedative."

Old boy? Me? I would have swatted her rear end if she hadn't been holding a hypodermic needle.

So I got an overnight stay in the hospital to be certain the infection didn't get worse and to keep the FBI at bay. I didn't get a private room because Ella got the bed next to mine, which took some verbal shoving but we got it done.

Before being discharged the next day I got a small plastic bottle of antibiotics with instructions, a lime sucker that turned my tongue green, and a ride to the exit doors in a wheelchair that didn't feel the least bit necessary. But it was a terrific ride because Harper did the pushing while Vale and Ella walked along with us. A few of the hospital staff—males—had signed the bandage on Ella's arm.

No one signed mine, but I got the sucker.

• • •

Harper. My life, my love. I felt whole again. She got to my hospital room at 9:25 p.m. the day I'd been admitted, a Monday. She had bailed out of school at noon when she'd heard I'd finally been found after having been missing the past four days, and that I'd been shot but it wasn't serious. She and Vale had flown into Butte's Bert Mooney airport after a four-hour layover in Denver. Ma had driven them to the hospital and come up with them to room 408, then she had taken off to go somewhere.

We left the hospital without the FBI knowing. It was noon, so they were probably off finding donuts and coffee. Life is all about timing.

The day Harper arrived, Ella and Harper had hours to get to know each other. They became instant friends, as I'd figured. They were two of a kind.

"Where's Ma?" I asked Harper as I was about to get into a rented Chevy Equinox in the parking lot. She and I were going to stick around Butte—a lovely city, really, I swear on a stack of IRS regs—while my truck got a new radiator and a clean bill of health. She was taking a week off from teaching. She didn't get much of a hassle from the school administrators when they heard her husband had been shot. As excuses go, it was one of the better ones.

"Don't know," Harper said.

I looked at Vale and she said, "Don't ask."

So I looked at Ella, who said, "Don't look at me."

So, no Ma, but Vale's comment stuck with me.

•   •   •

FBI agents—*Special* Agents, but aren't they all?—flew in from D.C., nudging aside the Butte FBI guys and gals to interrogate me and Ella. Swift as eagles, they were, but it didn't set well with them that I'd done their job for them, taking down Vince and Frank, *and* Cole, who'd never been so much as a blip on their radar, so to speak—telling them who'd actually murdered FBI Deputy Director Alden Ridel. Embarrassing, no doubt. If they'd been a tad sharper, they would've left it to the Butte agents to look bad, but they'd been too eager to swoop in and grab the credit, so they got the short end of that stick.

That took place at the Copper King Convention Center in Butte where Harper and I had an excellent suite on the second floor and Ella and Vale had a similar suites right down the hall. Ella and I told our story a number of times in a small conference room with Jim Carbon in attendance to keep our rights from being trampled. My homicides were deemed to be self-defense, especially when the agents visited Ned's suicide room and saw how we had escaped.

Ma was still missing. Harper, Ella, Vale, and I stayed at the Copper King two full days before Harper and I drove back to Reno in the truck Ella and I bought the day after Ridel died. I liked the truck and it had a new radiator so why get rid of it? It could pull the trailer. Ella flew back to Reno with Vale—via Denver, of course. Everything goes through Denver.

•   •   •

First day back in Reno, I stopped by the university and caught the tail end of a lecture by Jason Zimmerman. I sat in the back row of the lecture hall. It might've thrown him off to see me there because he dismissed the class with five minutes left to go in the period. He knew who I was. I was famous. My picture had been on television again. Our story, Ella's and mine, was now public knowledge. Most of it, anyway.

But back in August Jason would've known she'd been wanted for questioning by the FBI, and he knew he'd put a note and fifty dollars in her mailbox, but he hadn't gone to the FBI with that. He could have given them Dinah's name. He could have short-circuited this entire mess.

I was the last person he wanted to see. He would know it was likely he had put Ella in harm's way. It may have been intentional, but probably not. We might never know how close Jason was to his Aunt Dinah or what he knew of his cousins, Frank and Vince. But as a married man and Ella's thesis advisor, he shouldn't have hit on Ella. That was a no-no for which he could have lost his professorship and ended up in . . . Muncie.

He gathered up lecture notes, then said, "I didn't have a thing to do with it."

I gave him a lifted eyebrow. The guy doth protest too swiftly and too much, I thought. "Tell it to Dinah," I said.

He left without another word.

About what I'd expected.

• • •

Five days later, at 10:58 p.m., we were around a table in the Green Room of Reno's Golden Goose Casino: Ella, Harper, Vale, and me. And Ma. She didn't say where she'd been since the evening of the day Ella and I had scratched our way out of Ned's room. "Had somethin' to do, boyo," was all she said. "Have another Moose Drool. I'm buyin'."

Good enough. I had another Moose Drool. My excuse was residual dehydration, but that was wearing thin.

Ella and Harper evidently had a lot to talk about. The girlish laughter I heard when they and Vale got their heads together probably had nothing to do with me.

Sure.

I had another scar to add to the collection. Scars were manly, but might also indicate a certain level of ineptitude. My only concern at that point was Dinah Jackson. I hadn't heard a thing about her. The FBI might've picked her up and beaten a confession out of her. Or they might've tried to get something on her, but couldn't. If she was running around loose, all of us still had to watch our backs.

Which meant this might not be over yet.

News came on the TV over the bar, twenty feet away. It looked like the same old nightly rehash of crap going on here and there that none of us could do anything about. I don't know why anyone watches the news.

The bartender, Traci Ellis, came over and asked if we wanted anything, so Vale ordered another gin and tonic, and Ma got another double bourbon.

Drinking kinda heavy that evening, I thought.

Then I heard the name *Dinah*. It came from over by the bar. I looked that way and a photo of Dinah Jackson was on the flat screen, so I got up and went over to watch. Maybe the FBI had managed to get something on her.

"... mother of Cole Keeler, the man who held Ella Kassel and Mortimer Angel in a containment room in the basement of a house in Butte, Montana, was discovered late this afternoon several miles from her home in Bemidji, Minnesota. An FBI spokesman said Mrs. Jackson had been sought in connection with Kassel's and Angel's kidnapping and captivity a week ago that made national news and was connected to the murder of FBI Deputy Director Alden Ridel in August of this year."

Ma came up beside me to watch.

The news continued: "Mrs. Jackson had been shot at close range with a .45 handgun and her body had been left in a roadside ditch several miles from the town of Bemidji. The FBI is asking anyone with information that might lead to the person or persons who killed Mrs. Jackson to please contact their nearest FBI office."

The picture of Dinah Jackson lingered on the TV for several seconds. Ma lifted her shot glass to the screen and said, "Here's to you, honey bun."

GUMSHOE NOVELS BY ROB LEININGER

Humorous, bawdy, deadly.

1) Gumshoe (nominated for a Shamus Award for "Best PI Novel" in 2015 by the Private Eye Writers of America, and a finalist in the USA Best Book Awards.)
2) Gumshoe For Two
3) Gumshoe on the Loose
4) Gumshoe Rock
5) Gumshoe in the Dark
6) Gumshoe Gone
7) Gumshoe Outlaw
8) Gumshoe on the Run

Visit Leininger's website at www.robleininger.com

Made in the USA
Middletown, DE
13 April 2023